Trey Glass is a man of integrity and good upbringing and subject to the same temptations and challenges we all face. After realizing his dream of becoming a pro basketball player, he could never predict or imagine what lies ahead as he tries to live differently from his peers. In **Intentional***, you will find intrigue, heartwarming scenes, and even some romance as you follow the story of this amazing young man. You will also find a picture of an alternative to "doing church" that should capture the interest of anyone disillusioned with traditional religion.*

Lynn, age 63
High school math teacher

Several years ago, ...a *my contented life when he helped me see real active faith through the countercultural teachings of Jesus. Steve's heart for Jesus and intentional faith community shine throughout* **Intentional***.*

Through Holt's story, we see that our response to Jesus' teachings should include caring deeply for the outcasts of our society, showing grace to others who may not deserve it, and living out the gospel in your community. I found myself drawn to Trey Glass and was eager to complete the journey with him and his family. This book challenges you to move outside your comfort zone and causes you to rethink the religious status quo. **Intentional** *will inspire you to action.*

Kevin, age 38
Insurance adjuster

Steve Holt's book reads like a parable that Jesus himself would tell us today about what His kingdom is like. Like Jesus, Steve understands the power of a great story, and he sends a powerful, inspirational message through the amazing story of God at work in an all-star basketball player and his unlikely neighbors. From the start, **Intentional** *will likely not leave your hands until you've read the final page. It has the potential to change the world as it causes its readers to reexamine the way they follow Jesus. I couldn't put it down. It's an amazing story of what life in Jesus' Kingdom can look like today.*

So thankful for the grace of writing God blessed Steve with so that he could bless and inspire me through it.

Jordan, age 27
Church planter

INTENTIONAL

In Jesus' name we play

STEPHEN M. HOLT, SR.

WESTBOW®
PRESS
A DIVISION OF THOMAS NELSON
& ZONDERVAN

WestBow Press books may be ordered through booksellers or by contacting:

WestBow Press
A Division of Thomas Nelson & Zondervan
1663 Liberty Drive
Bloomington, IN 47403
www.westbowpress.com
1 (866) 928-1240

Because of the dynamic nature of the Internet, any web addresses or links contained in this book may have changed since publication and may no longer be valid. The views expressed in this work are solely those of the author and do not necessarily reflect the views of the publisher, and the publisher hereby disclaims any responsibility for them.

Scriptures taken from the Holy Bible, New International Version®, NIV®. Copyright © 1973, 1978, 1984, 2011 by Biblica, Inc.™ Used by permission of Zondervan. All rights reserved worldwide. www.zondervan.com The "NIV" and "New International Version" are trademarks registered in the United States Patent and Trademark Office by Biblica, Inc.™ All rights reserved.

Any people depicted in stock imagery provided by Thinkstock are models, and such images are being used for illustrative purposes only. Certain stock imagery © Thinkstock.

ISBN: 978-1-4908-2029-3 (sc)
ISBN: 978-1-4908-2030-9 (e)

Library of Congress Control Number: 2013923128

Printed in the United States of America.

WestBow Press rev. date: 01/27/2014

*This project is dedicated to the most important people in my life:
Jesus, merciful friend.*

*Lynn, wife and partner, whose patience and
encouragement make all the difference.*

*Sons, Steve Jr. and Mitch, who have authored their
own spiritual expressions and have, since their births,
greatly added to my understanding of the Father.*

*Steve Jr.'s family, Chrissy, Christian and Sage
Marie who bring joy and great pride.*

ACKNOWLEDGEMENTS

Of the many things I've learned while writing this book, one stands out as a basic principle: a person does not write a book alone.

Being able to write a book doesn't mean I have the words to adequately thank the following people for their immeasurable assistance in bringing the spark of an idea to its fullness. So I simply say, Thank you! I'm grateful from the depths of my heart.

You take a chance asking good friends to be first readers of a raw first draft. In fact, all kinds of things can happen to turn a good friend into a past acquaintance. But such was not the case with the people who graciously agreed to read the book in its infancy and offer valuable feedback. Thank you Lynn Holt, Don and Vicki Kinder, Kevin Conway, Emogene Moore, Rex Fowler, Jordan Bunch and Brian Scott.

Two very busy and extremely talented professionals agreed to take on an untested author as a client. Much respect and appreciation go to editor Kylie Lyons and cover designer Ryan Feerer.

My mentor is a long-time friend who knows more about intentional faith communities than I ever will. Dr. Kent Smith, professor of missions at Abilene Christian University, was a constant source of encouragement and information throughout the project.

Elaine Huckabee, Dora Weathers and Craig Churchill of the Abilene Christian University library provided invaluable assistance.

For more than a year, Lynn and I have met with a small group of men and women who pray about and study various models for intentional communities. We will always be indebted to these who have been faithful to each other and the mission, week-in and week-out. Thank you Laura, Rosten, Shannon, John, Kent, Karen and Natalia.

And to the many people with whom we have shared "church" in the form of intentional faith communities through the years, I express my undying love and gratitude. The world is better because of you.

INTRODUCTION

In regards to church, younger generations are carving out new paths. The faith communities of eighteen to thirty-year-olds look nothing like the churches of their parents and grandparents. But, then again, the faith of the younger generation is radically different from that of their folks. And if our story's hero is any example, that's not such a bad thing.

Trey Glass is a normal twenty-something, red-blooded American kid who also happens to be very good at basketball—good enough to turn his passion into a multimillion dollar career. With his power and money, he could do anything he wanted and have all the "toys" that many of today's star athletes have. But one difference between Trey Glass and other millennial superstars is that Trey had parents who shaped him to be a follower of Jesus. And when he found attending church to be a problem, he sought an alternative. When most parents and certainly church leaders would push back against such a non-traditional solution to his dilemma, Trey's folks gave their blessings. As a result, the young man found a nurturing community and the spiritual support he needed.

Trey and his girlfriend, Cristina, represent millions of young people who, for whatever reasons, are not following their parents' religious traditions. Their decision brings many wonderful benefits as well as heart wrenching disappointments and trials. But despite our couple's struggles with issues of love, faith, expectations, and crime, they find hope and healing from their faith and their faith community.

Intentional faith communities—alternative forms of church—are springing up all over the world. These are simple, peer-led, inclusive groups, easily reproducible in any culture and among all age groups and don't require the huge machinery and expense of institutional religion. They vary in form from small *distributed* communities (all members living in fairly close proximity to one another, but not under the same roof) to *collected* communities (members sharing a large house or living in separate units on common acreage). For those who have done the research, intentional faith communities look and function very much like house churches of the New Testament.

My hopes and prayers for this book and the ones that follow are threefold: First, I hope the message will encourage people of all ages to realize that there are God-approved alternatives to traditional church.

Second, I hope church leaders will begin to take seriously the writing on the wall and step up to guide rising generations to discover their own spiritual paths.

Third, I hope parents, coaches, teachers, youth leaders and mentors will read this book with their charges and delve deeper into why Trey became the man he did and what exactly a true follower of Jesus looks like today.

Stephen M. Holt Sr.
www.stephenholtsr.com

CHAPTER 1

One couldn't tell from moment to moment, let alone day to day, which path young Trey Glass would walk: the one laid out by godly parents or the one paved by another more sinister. One moment he could be on his knees, fervently asking God to heal Mr. Zucker of his cancer; the next, he'd be in the woods with his slingshot, trying to kill birds and squirrels.

His dad, Travis, often called Trey a contradiction—sweet and sour in the same wrapper. Nonetheless, Travis and Becky lived their lives hoping that what Trey and his brothers witnessed at home would catch on and become a part of their lives.

Cletus Raney was down on his luck. Lack of rain spelled doom for much of his cotton crop. His wife had to be taken to Regional Medical Center with an infected boil, and his hay baler needed a $340 part soon or he'd lose the hay he'd cut two days before. In desperation, Cletus went to the elders of Piney Wood Community Church to borrow a thousand dollars until he could sell his hay. He promised to pay it back, although no timetable had been specified for repayment; he was the kind who always kept his word. In one month, Cletus had paid back half. In another month, the elders called him in and asked for the balance. When he told them he needed more time, the elders told Cletus they couldn't wait; the carpeting in the sanctuary needed replacing before the fall gospel meeting. He would need to repay the other five hundred dollars immediately. Cletus was stuck.

One of the elders leaked the predicament to his friend Travis Glass, who told the elder that churches should not be in the business of loaning money.

"If there is a serious need, the whole church should be informed. Give members the opportunity to respond by helping, no strings attached."

Travis paid off Cletus's "loan" in exchange for anonymity. Cletus never knew, but the three Glass boys were watching.

Acts of generosity were not unusual in the Glass household. Trey's mom and dad often said that they were, first of all, followers of Jesus, and then members of the local church. Travis contended that if one wanted to live a good life, it had to be intentional—planned—that good lives didn't just happen. Travis and Becky were intentional about how they lived their lives and taught their boys to approach life in the same way. So the Glass family prayed together, played together, ate together, and served fellow man together. They regularly welcomed people into their home and often visited, unannounced, folks in the community who needed encouragement, prayer, or something else.

One year, right before the holidays, while Becky was visiting her sister in Jackson, Travis got his three sons together.

"We're going to put together some holiday boxes. There are folks in this town who need a little help, and that's what we are going to do," Travis said.

Each Glass male had a specific task: Dad and Trey's oldest brother, Adam, were responsible for buying the hams and all the food that would go into making a first-rate Christmas dinner. Trey's middle brother, Lee, was to find twelve large, clean cardboard boxes and cover them with holiday paper. And Trey was to make twelve Christmas cards wishing the recipients a very Merry Christmas.

"No signature, Trey," Travis said.

One week before Christmas, Mr. Glass and the boys worked late into the night putting together the boxes of food, and in the wee hours of the morning, they loaded up the station wagon, took the boxes "across the tracks" to twelve families who could never afford such delight, and quietly placed each box on the lucky family's porch. They returned home and made hot chocolate.

It seemed that Trey's older brothers caught these lessons long before Trey did, though there were occasions that surprised those closest to him. Once, while with his mom on the way to the grocery, Trey noticed a man asking for money at one of the busy street corners. Tired and frail, the man wore a stocking hat pulled over dingy, shoulder-length hair. His meager frame was covered in a beat-up army jacket, the type that could be purchased at any thrift store for a few bucks. While they were stopped at the light, Trey quickly unzipped his belly bag and pulled out the five-dollar bill he was saving for a treat at the store.

"Give this to him, please," Trey asked.

Becky rolled down the window and handed the crisp bill to the downtrodden man. He smiled, his eyes lighting up briefly before the glimmer was snuffed out as quickly as it had come.

"That was a nice thing to do, Trey," she said, a single tear slipping down her cheek.

Trey's two older brothers were standouts in debate and the arts. Adam won many forensic awards, and Lee had accumulated a roomful of ribbons for his pen-and-ink drawings. They also excelled academically, something that came with more difficulty for Trey. Perhaps the youngest son felt inadequate living in the shadow of his older brothers. Whatever the reason, he struggled to be the "good" boy everyone thought he should be. He was a riddle, for sure. And from childhood through adulthood, Trey Glass was always viewed as a mystery by the adults who witnessed both his good and bad sides. Trey Glass was a contradiction.

A few blocks up the street from Trey's house was Campbell's Grocery, a small mom-and-pop store frequented mostly by folks from the neighborhood. The Glass family had a charge account there so that one of the boys could run up when Becky ran out of something she needed right away. When such occasions arose, Trey was quickest to volunteer for the grocery run.

The elderly couple who ran the store knew Trey and his brothers, so they didn't bother watching them as closely as they did other kids who came in after school or on weekends. Trey took these opportunities to help himself to bubble gum or candy or anything else he could stash in his pockets while the owners were looking the other way. But he never kept all of the stolen goods for himself; he always found someone in the neighborhood to share it with, fifty-fifty.

Despite his orneriness, the youngest Glass continued to surprise people with his apparent deep concern for others, a concern he had learned watching his mom and dad. He didn't know it then, but those lessons would bring troubles he could never have anticipated. For the time being, he was all boy, and boy, did he play that role to the fullest.

CHAPTER 2

Trey was a big kid. Even at age fourteen, his ample six-foot frame served him well during pick-up basketball games in the local park. If an opponent was stupid enough to stand in the way of his vicious drives to the basket, they paid dearly. And he had no remorse. But afterward, Trey was his buddy again, often treating the opponent to a soda. When another player got the best of him—which seldom happened—he never tried to retaliate; he was quick to forgive and readily complemented the player for his skills.

Throughout high school, his good looks and charm attracted lots of young ladies. Although a bit shy, Trey managed to display his affection—often in inappropriate ways—to the many girls who sought his attention.

Trey's family lived in a modest house nearer to the "other side of the tracks" than the country club set. Trey's heart went out to the young black men who walked by his house on their way to caddy at the local golf course. He was moved by their shabby clothing, particularly their shoes. One young man had nothing but two pieces of cardboard duct taped together to form inadequate footwear. Trey decided to help the young men. Borrowing a pair of shoes from each of his brothers and his dad, plus some ties, hats, and belts, Trey handed out the merchandise to the guys when they walked by.

At supper two days later, Travis mentioned that he was missing a pair of shoes and a hat.

"Me too," Adam said. "It's the weirdest thing."

"I can't find my belt anywhere," Lee said.

"Know anything about this, Trey?" his dad asked.

"No, sir," he said.

"Hmm. Anything of yours missing, son?"

"No, sir, not that I've noticed," Trey said sheepishly, ending the conversation.

A few weeks later, Adam noticed a young black man wearing a familiar baseball hat, a New England Patriots cap Adam had traded for last year. Over the next several weeks, the Glass men took notice; more and more familiar items of clothing showed up on various young men around town.

"Trey, got any idea how these guys got our shoes and stuff?" Travis asked again.

"Well, it could be that they really needed some clothes. I don't remember giving that stuff away, but I...I guess I could have," Trey said, looking down at his plate.

"Hmm, well, we're all going to run out of socks if this keeps up," Travis said, chuckling. He could not allow Trey to see the pride swelling deep inside, and so he cleared his throat and picked up his fork, returning to the chicken pot pie without another word.

During the summer before his sophomore year at Wayne County High School, Trey asked his dad if he could try out for the basketball team. He had excelled in neighborhood pick-up games, and although he was rather tentative about it all, his peers convinced him to come out for the junior varsity team. Travis agreed, and that was the beginning of a journey Trey could never have imagined.

To say that Trey Glass was good at basketball would be the understatement of the century. His deadly aim and tenacious defense made him an all-around ballplayer. His only weakness, one might say, was that he was overly aggressive. He often used his size to his advantage.

"Glass, for heaven's sake, this is basketball, not hockey!" Coach Samuels yelled. "Yeah, it's sometimes a contact sport, but there are times to go around another player rather than through him. Play smart, buddy, play smart. We're looking for points, not fouls."

And score, he did. Trey was a scoring machine who helped his JV team go 15-1 his first season. It wasn't until the middle of his junior year that Trey began to understand and accept the tactical power of finesse and began to play smarter rather than rougher. When he did—when he began to focus on the nuances of the sport and deliberately took time to refine his own skills—Trey Glass's game improved dramatically.

At the end of his junior year, he was named All-Conference and All-State, leading the Wayne County Warriors to State, where the team lost to a perennial Knoxville powerhouse in the final game. Beginning in the summer between his junior and senior years, letters of interest from nearly every top Division-1 college began to fill his mailbox.

His senior year was more of the same. Trey averaged twenty-six points a game as point guard and led the Warriors to a 36-2 season and a State Championship, despite a minor run-in with the law.

Alcohol was the drug of choice among the adults in Wayne County, but marijuana ruled among the youth. And although alcohol abuse wreaked far more havoc on citizens and their property than did weed, laws prohibiting the drug were rigidly enforced. Trey, two of his friends and two girls he didn't know as well discovered this when they "found" a joint and decided to try it out in the barn that belonged to one of the boy's dad. They would have gotten away with their little experiment had they not accidently set fire to a pile of hay. The fire spread quickly to two horse stalls and a tack room. Once the flames began to spread, everyone scattered, except Trey Glass, who stayed behind and fought valiantly to put out the flames. Fortunately, two farm hands working nearby rushed to help the lone teen douse the fire before it took down the entire barn, horses and all. When asked to explain the fire to the sheriff, Trey told the truth—almost. He admitted that the fire had begun from a lit marijuana cigarette he was smoking; he failed to say, however, that there were others with him.

That he was quick to admit guilt, that he stayed around to put the fire out, and that everyone knew and liked Trey, officials concluded that this was a typical teenaged screw-up and recommended lenient punishment. He was placed on one-year probation and ordered to pay the barn's owner back the thousand-dollar deductible on the fire insurance. He paid dearly on the court, staying after practice to run laps for Coach Samuels.

The other teens were so moved by Trey's gesture—and mild sentence, no doubt—that they all came forward to admit they were with Trey in the barn, hoping to put the incident behind them as painlessly as possible. Unfortunately, the judge's kindness was apparently depleted, and he handed down a much harsher judgment against the youth.

After the incident, some parents of Trey's peers prohibited their children from associating with the "druggie," as they called him. People at church whispered that certain failure was assured for someone who was into drugs at such a young age. No one stepped forward to ask Trey what he needed or to affirm their love for him during the difficult time in the young man's life.

Trey's parents took the event in stride. Trey's dad offered a semi-stern warning about the implications of getting crossways with the law and required Trey to come up with a written plan for raising the thousand dollars. Mr. Glass never said anything about the evils of marijuana. Over a period of a week, the whole event had come and gone, at least in the Glass household.

Travis and Becky encouraged their son's basketball fascination while coaching him on the more important aspects of life—humility, faith, love for others—and holding him to the family values of work, devotion to family, and honesty. The Glasses hoped the lessons were getting through, though there were times they had their doubts.

Make no mistake, Trey was already a legend in the area, and the girls around those parts loved legends. The young star needed all the help he could get to resist the temptations, even solicitations, from ladies sixteen to sixty who had no shame and went out of their way to get his attention. For the most part, he was able to handle the temptations, but not always. Love for the ladies, it seemed, was his greatest weakness.

By the time Trey graduated from high school, he was a 6'6", 205-pound hunk of chiseled basketball talent with an eighty-inch wingspan. His grades had improved somewhat, and nearly every college in America wanted him to play basketball for their school. He was heavily courted by Tennessee, Kentucky, and Georgia of the Southeastern Conference, as well as other powerhouses like Indiana, Texas, and North Carolina. In the end, Trey chose smaller, less-notable

Murfreesboro State College, about 140 miles from his hometown of Waynesboro. He was excited that he would be playing close enough to home for his family and other hometown folks to come watch him.

Trey did for MSC basketball what he had done for Wayne County High School basketball; he transformed it. His first year the team went 29-4 overall and 14-0 against Sun Belt Conference teams. It was widely assumed Trey would be "one and done"—that he would leave for the pros after his first year—but Trey returned the next year, leading the Colonels to a school record 37 wins and 1 loss. That loss came against Ball State in the NCAA tournament play-in game, the first time MSC had ever qualified for the Big Dance. Trey averaged 29.6 points and five assists per game his second year, and people were again surprised that he returned for his junior year. He explained his team loyalty by noting that he played basketball for the sheer joy of the game; money and fame were not issues for him, and he wanted to play college ball for as long as he was allowed.

Trey began to struggle with the celebrity status he was gaining on campus and beyond. People knew him everywhere he went, and it bothered him that he could not eat a meal out or shop without attracting a large following. He especially disliked signing autographs, except for kids.

Again in college, as in high school, the ladies proved to be constant enticements. He knew if he didn't get a grip, he would make decisions not in his best interest—or theirs. He knew he needed help.

Trey received spiritual support and encouragement from a small group of Christians who met off campus. Colonels for Christ hosted weekly Tuesday-night meals and Bible studies, as well as a larger Sunday gathering in an old sorority house the group had bought and renovated. Although students came and went at each semester change, a core group of about fifteen students remained consistent during his four years of college.

At the beginning of his junior year, during a game against Nashville College, people of the Mid-South had a scare when Trey landed hard on his back after an intentional foul on a steal and breakaway layup. He was slow getting up, and after a while he shuffled to the sideline while the home crowd loudly expressed their disdain to the "wretched" student who fouled their superstar. Trey was out for three weeks undergoing treatment to get him back in playing shape. The team lost all three games during that time, and the college basketball world held its breath during the weeks of uncertainty.

Would Trey Glass ever play basketball again?

That question was answered when he came back stronger than ever with even more savvy of the game of basketball. The MSC Colonels finished the season 33-5 but lost by one point in the conference championship and failed to make the NCAA tournament.

It seemed the entire world knew what was best for Trey's future. Sports commentators and bloggers insisted that good sense dictated that Trey should skip his senior year and enter the pros.

What if he receives a career-ending injury? Look what almost happened. What if his numbers his senior year don't match previous years? That could cost him millions of dollars.

Trey continued to insist that his life wasn't about the money; he played basketball for the fun of it, and college ball was great fun.

His senior year was all and more than he and others hoped it would be. He averaged thirty-one points and ten assists per game on his way to leading his team to a 38-1 record and a place among the NCAA's "Sweet Sixteen" before losing to Baylor in a squeaker.

Now, the April 23 NBA draft deadline loomed; he would have to indicate his desire to enter the pros...or not. While all the sports authorities were certain he would join the pro ranks—some even thought he would be the number-one pick—Trey wasn't so sure. His first commitment was to his family.

What do they need? If the family thinks I should enter the pros, I'll consider it, but this is a family decision, he thought.

In the month between the end of basketball season and the draft deadline, Trey discussed his options with his family and consulted with close friends and others who had had strong influences on him throughout his life.

One of those to whom Trey had grown close during his four years at Murfreesboro State was Calvin Portis, director of Colonels for Christ. After praying with Trey about his decision, Cal offered helpful advice.

"You know, Trey, playing in the pros is not like playing in college. You have thirty-five or so games in college; in the pros, you'll have eighty-plus, played from one end of the country to the other. Sometimes you'll play five, maybe six games in a week. It's rigorous and tiring and won't be as much fun as college. In the pros, if you play well, you'll be adored; if you don't, you'll be hated and mocked, especially by your own fans. Most of the guys you'll play with in the pros won't hold the same values you do. You will come face-to-face with drug and alcohol abuse and swear words you may have never heard before," Cal said, laughing. "And the girls…man. Women will throw themselves at you, Trey. Get ready for a world that you've never experienced. Get ready for temptations you've never faced."

Trey listened intently. He knew he hadn't handled the lure of the ladies well up to now, and he hated to think what might happen if temptations got even stronger.

"Having said all that," Cal said, "the pros will offer you a wonderful opportunity to let your little light shine. If you choose to live like the man of God you are, you can show the world how a real man lives, and there aren't many people willing to do that, even among those who call themselves followers of Jesus. You will have the attention of the world as the premier basketball player I predict you'll become. People will listen to you, and you can influence young men and boys for a generation or longer.

"The money you'll earn will allow you to do things you never imagined possible, things like making life for your family easier and more secure, supporting mission works around the world, helping those who need a hand up, and so much more. The pros can be a tremendous opportunity for you, brother, if you can maintain your balance and live out your convictions. Otherwise, the pros will be an excruciating experience that could eventually wear you down and overcome you. I know this, God needs 'inside' men in the NBA, and I'm not talking about seven-foot centers or power forwards. I'm talking about 6'6" point guards with a heart for God and others."

When Cal left, Trey's head was spinning. Decision time was near.

CHAPTER 3

To everyone's utter astonishment, Trey Glass let the draft deadline come and go. He was more intent on finishing the semester well and not being pushed into making a commitment before he was ready. He knew once he committed, he would forever be in the limelight and life would never be the same. This was too big a decision for a quick decision.

At the beginning of the summer, his college coach called to offer Trey a position as an assistant coach and recruiter with his old team. Accepting the position would mean staying out of the pros a year, which, for most average players, could mean a serious setback. But Trey figured if David Robinson could do it, he could too. And Robinson's two-year delay in entering the NBA because of his commitment to military service didn't seem to have hurt him any. Trey figured it was a matter of priorities—what's really important in life. Evidently, professional basketball, lots of money, and fame were not priorities of the twenty-one-year-old.

What Trey did value was playing the sport for the sheer joy of the game. And if he opted for the assistant coach position, he could spend a few months at home before his coaching duties began in late summer.

After graduation, Trey took Cal's words and his newly acquired bachelor's degree home to Wayne County, Tennessee. Over the summer, he worked at the local drugstore where he had worked every summer from age fifteen until he'd entered college. Local folks were amused and delighted at having an NBA-quality player and college all-star working the cash register, ringing up their toothpaste and Tampax. Trey enjoyed being home, helping people out and signing autographs for every kid who came into Barton's Drugs just to see the local celebrity.

After work, Trey would often head over to the local high school gym for an hour of pick-up basketball with friends he'd played with as a youngster. These days, the gym could hardly accommodate the many spectators who dropped by to catch a glimpse of greatness. Then there were the guys who wanted to challenge that greatness, to show him who's boss, to take him to school. Trey could take whatever they dished out and actually enjoyed the occasional ego-boosting sessions. He could be gentle with those who simply wanted to have fun and hard on those who wanted to hurt. He was quick to encourage and advise the younger players and was willing to coach when asked. It was clear Trey loved the game of basketball and enjoyed the sense of community it engendered among the citizens of Wayne County.

Trey accepted the assistant coaching position, figuring it would keep him in the game until he decided whether to enter the NBA draft the next year. His decision to sit out a year after college, however, didn't sit well with basketball pundits. Everyone from sports commentators to NBA players offered their opinions on why the most promising player since MJ would choose to sit out a year.

"I think he's afraid he can't hack it among the big boys," one player said.

"He wasn't that good in college anyway," one coach said. "He was a big fish in a small pond in, where was it? Murfreesboro, Tennessee? Of course he was going to do well at that rinky-dink school. Once he gets to the NBA, he'll be just another fish in a giant pond."

Trey refused to listen to the critics, preferring to focus on his coaching duties. For some reason—most likely his folks' influence— he was drawn to the more disadvantaged people in the small college town. On Saturdays during the off season, he and a couple of young teammates fixed lunches and took them to men and women who lived under highway bridges around Murfreesboro.

Of course, he was also drawn to the young ladies who swarmed around him like bees. His attraction caused him a bit of guilt; his thoughts about the coeds weren't always the purest. It was as though he was drawn to their attention against his will. He could have his pick of anyone but chose to play the field, dating a different girl every weekend.

Basketball was his passion, and he looked forward to every opportunity to be on the court. He believed his basketball abilities were a gift from God, and not to utilize the gift was an insult to his Lord. He dreamed of a day when he could play at the highest level and use the funds he earned to help others. Every nonprofit agency he'd volunteered for or knew about seemed to be in a financial crisis, and the millions of dollars he would make each year could go a long way toward helping such agencies help others.

The Indiana Pacers, who drafted Trey in the first round, turned around and traded him to the Memphis Rockers for a power forward and a future draft pick. On the advice of friends who knew such things, Trey hired an agent with orders to take the initial offer from whatever team he ended up with. Trey was not interested in long discussions concerning money; he wanted to play basketball and was delighted that he would play in his home state. Because of his year away from basketball and questions surrounding his college injury, the Rockers offered the collegiate all-star a modest four-year, $18 million contract. A clothing endorsement brought his total salary to just under $7 million a year, less than other touted rookies would make but more money than Trey felt he deserved and certainly more money than he ever imagined he would make.

With contracts signed, Trey prepared to move to Memphis, 208 miles west of where he grew up. From the beginning of rumors that Memphis might be his new home, Trey received full attention from local real estate companies. He settled on Homestead Realty—the Rockers' front office recommendation—and was matched with Angel Burgdorf, who specialized in high-end properties.

Memphis in August was hot, and the air conditioner in Ms. Burgdorf's jet-black Lexus was cranked to the max. Angel was the agent of preference for many of the city's pro athletes, not because she was all that knowledgeable about the real estate market, but because she was who the guys liked. Early thirties, slim, tan, beautiful, and well-proportioned, Angel enjoyed the attention her provocative clothing and heavily applied perfume drew from her rich and talented male clients.

And she was known for offering more than just real estate services. Trey was glad he'd brought his mom and dad along to look at houses, much to Angel's chagrin; otherwise, who knows where the house-hunting would end up.

The first day, Angel hauled the Glasses from one posh neighborhood to the next. They started in old and prestigious Central Gardens, worked their way over to older and even more prominent Callaway Gardens, and ended in trendy Harbor Town, where many of the Rockers lived. The prices in these neighborhoods ranged from a mere $1.2 million and upwards into the double-digit millions.

The Glasses were obviously impressed with what they saw. They didn't even know that world was out there. The luxury of the shiny, new homes impressed them. The quaint comfort of the older homes impressed them. Each shared their ideas on how certain rooms in the huge estates could be used: a sewing room for Becky; a workshop for Travis; and a small, quiet study with whirlpool for Trey to relax in before games. Any one of the mansions would serve Glass family reunions well, providing ample room for his brothers and their families.

During one of the breaks in house-hunting, as Angel checked in with her office, Trey broke the spell.

"Look, all of these places are fantastic. I mean, who wouldn't want to live in them? But I'm just not sure it's for me. Can you imagine me bringing a homeless person over here for a meal? And the lots are so large, how would you ever get to know your neighbors? Mom and Dad, I think I'm going to ask Angel to show us some places that are more my style."

Travis and Becky smiled at one another, proud of their son and happy that the young man—who had always seemed to be the last of the sons to get it—was, indeed, getting it.

"Whatever you say, son. We're right behind you," Travis said.

"What are you thinking?" Angel asked when she finally finished her phone call.

"Uh, sorry, but these are all too rich for my blood," Trey said. "I'm looking for a neighborhood that's really a neighborhood, one where you can actually see the people who live around you."

"You serious?" she asked quizzically. "You actually want to hobnob with the people you live around? Give me a price range; maybe we should start with that."

Trey looked at his mom and dad in the backseat of the Lexus and said, "I'd say fifty to a hundred."

"Fifty to a hundred million?" Ms. Burgdorf said, sputtering as her eyes lit up.

"No, thousand. Fifty to a hundred thousand," Trey said. "We'd like to see some homes in real neighborhoods where the houses cost somewhere around seventy or eighty thousand dollars. I might spring for up to $150,000 for the right house in the right neighborhood. Actually, that's probably a better idea, to go a bit higher for a little larger home since my family will be visiting quite a bit. Is that what you're thinking, Mom and Dad?"

I don't believe this guy, Angel thought to herself. "Let me see if I understand you; you're looking for a large home up to $150,000 where you can talk to your neighbors? All white, of course," she said wryly.

"All what?" Trey's dad asked from the backseat.

"All *white*. You, of course, want your neighbors to be white," Angel said seriously.

"Ms. Burgdorf, I think this tour of homes is over," Trey said bluntly. "If you would take us back to my car, we'd appreciate it."

"Ms. Burgdorf, are you even allowed to bring up race in your line of work? I wouldn't think so," Becky said curtly. "We could get you in lots of trouble for that, but we won't. I'll just pray that you have a change of attitude toward people not like yourself. Okay?"

Once back at Trey's car, the Glasses thanked Angel for her time and expressed their disappointment that things didn't work out. Mrs. Glass reached out to hug Angel and whispered in her ear, "I know you're a very nice young lady, but I think a safety pin about there—" She pointed down at Angel's ample cleavage. "—on your blouse would help men keep their eyes to themselves. We ladies have to stick together." She winked. "Goodbye, now."

Angel stood on the curb, mouth open, as the Glasses drove out of sight.

Over the next week, Trey and his folks looked at twenty-two homes in a variety of neighborhoods before deciding on one in south Memphis, not far from the FedEx Forum where the Rockers practiced and played. The culturally diverse neighborhood was comprised of large homes and small—some well kept, some not—but all tied together with a network of sidewalks in various stages of disrepair. Trey bought a large, six-bedroom, three-and-a-half bath home—one that had been a showplace in its glory days—for $179,900.

Even though Trey's parents were three hours away, they planned to visit often. His dream was that eventually Travis and Becky would come to live with him. The acre-and-a-half lot would afford his mom enough room to grow the flowers and vegetables she loved, and Travis could fix up the large, dilapidated workshop to putter around in.

Most appealing of all were the large common living areas: an oversized dining room and eat-in kitchen and two large living rooms, one with a walkout to a sizeable concrete deck overlooking the backyard.

Perfect, Trey thought as he stood in the comfortable foyer, holding the keys to his very first house.

For the next two months, Trey spent most of his time at the FedEx Forum practicing for the upcoming season opener set for late October against the Spurs. He spent the little time off he had overseeing renovations to his house and selecting furniture to fill up the place. He paid careful attention to adapting and furnishing the dining room and den because he knew from his childhood that those rooms were the center of hospitality, a gift of substantial value to those who claimed to follow Jesus.

There was seldom a Sunday when the Glass household didn't have a bunch of people over for dinner. His mom always made pot roast, carrots, and potatoes for the folks from their neighborhood whom they had invited during the week. Mixed in occasionally were people from their little church, usually the ones no one else would have over. Trey recalled hearing his dad quote Jesus about the blessings of showing hospitality to people who could not repay the favor.

Finding a church proved to be a more difficult task than he thought, even though there seemed to be a church on every corner—big ones, small ones, conservative, liberal, independent, every denomination and those claiming to be nondenominational. He had picked up from his own family's practice that the name on the door didn't matter all that much. Trey could still hear his father say, "The question is not what does a church believe? The question is what does a church do? You can tell what they believe by what they do." His parents encouraged him to connect with fellow believers who were committed to doing what Jesus did, especially for people who others ignored or took for granted.

"Every human being is precious to God, and every human being deserves a voice," his dad would say.

When Trey was very young, the family belonged to a fairly conservative community Bible church. When it became obvious that the group was more interested in protecting its doctrine and its property, often at the expense of people, the Glasses found another church that was heavily involved in local missions and benevolence. It wasn't perfect, but, then, neither were the Glasses.

More influential than the local church to young Trey and his brothers were the examples his parents set. Often the family would meet at home with people from the community who were down on their luck. They would sing while Mr. Glass strummed his guitar. They would discuss life and pray. Mrs. Glass would read scripture and then serve one of her pot roast meals. Trey especially liked those gatherings.

He visited around before finally settling on a small congregation near the zoo. He liked New Hope Church's cultural diversity and really enjoyed getting to know Tony Bradford, the young black pastor who also happened to be a huge Rockers fan. Tony was savvy about all things Memphis: her music, celebrities, history, and social ills. Trey often picked his brain about some of the less-famous local blues and gospel artists. Soon the young man's iPod hummed with the local sounds, which impressed Tony.

"You have good taste for a white boy," Pastor Tony said with a laugh and slap on the back.

One necessary luxury Trey allowed himself was a personal chef and nutritionist to make sure he was eating right and to have a hearty meal ready in case he ran across someone who needed one. And that was often.

After practice, his favorite evening activity was walking his neighborhood, getting to know the people he lived around. He had little use for TV, movies, and computer games, unlike many of his teammates; he'd rather be with people. Some of his neighbors paid enough attention to basketball to know that the new kid on the block was former Murfreesboro State superstar Trey Glass, now a rookie point guard for the Memphis Rockers. But most had no idea who he was and thought it strange that a young white man would choose to purchase a home in the nearly all-black neighborhood. Some loved the idea and welcomed Trey with open arms; others were not so sure. A few others were hostile toward the idea and wondered when this white boy's real agenda would be unveiled.

People in neighborhoods like Trey's feared gentrification, the practice of wealthy business people buying up depressed property and creating more upscale residential and commercial ventures, driving up property values, increasing taxes, and, eventually, driving long-time residents out. Because of this, an air of suspicion arose, fostered and fueled by people who didn't want to give Trey a chance. A large wooden fence that bordered Trey's property on three sides was spray painted one night with slurs and threats against the new resident. He didn't like fences in the first place and promptly had it torn down, leaving his property open to anyone who cared to enjoy it. Trey remembered a time when, growing up, his family's home had been broken into, ransacked and robbed. The thieves got a TV, some silver service that had belonged to Becky's mother, and a few other odds and ends.

"That just goes to show, boys, don't own anything you don't want to lose to moths, rust, or thieves," his dad had said philosophically.

From then on, the Glasses were careful about what they owned, forgoing what some would call necessities and others would deem luxuries. Trey grew up in a family that had all they needed but lived very simply, choosing to use their money to the benefit of people who really needed it.

Trey Glass would discover that there were ample opportunities to share his newly gained wealth.

CHAPTER 4

Trey soon found out that the world of professional basketball was worlds apart from college basketball. Emphasis on conditioning alone meant hours in the gym with a personal trainer. Two-a-day practices six days a week and a half-day on Sundays viewing game films took up most of Trey's time, including time he'd normally spend with the church. There was not the congenial camaraderie among his teammates as there had been in college, although, generally, everyone got along. A couple of his teammates on the preseason roster were out to prove that they were better than the new guy, and their overaggressive style pushed Trey's patience and good nature to the limit. But the rookie point guard held his own, and it soon became clear that Trey Glass was the real thing. By the start of exhibition games, he had earned the number-two guard spot and had his eye on a starting position.

Trey's parents visited often in the weeks leading up to the season opener; they knew they wouldn't get to see much of their son after October 28. Even time off for holidays wasn't guaranteed, so the Glass family braced itself for short, infrequent visits once the season began.

The long Labor Day weekend in early September provided a rare opportunity for all the Glasses to gather at Trey's new Memphis digs. His mom and dad, two older brothers, their families, and Trey spent Sunday afternoon hosting a barbecue for a fellow teammate and a neighborhood couple on the deck behind the house. Adam set up a badminton net in the side yard while Lee and Mr. Glass marked off a horseshoe pit. Mrs. Glass made potato salad and baked beans. Trey handled the grill, carefully watching over the chicken tenders and burgers cooking over charcoal in an old barbecue pit left by previous owners.

Their guests seemed happy to have been invited. Gilbert Warner, a single guy, was one of only three rookies on the team and didn't have time to go to his home in California for the holiday. Neighbor Lem Davis, who had helped Trey clear some brush from behind the old workshop, and his wife, Carla, were invited. They were a middle-aged African-American couple who grew up in Memphis's south end with no children but lots of stories about how Memphis had changed since the early days—and how much more it needed to change. It was a memorable afternoon and evening of games, small talk, and relaxation, interrupted briefly by a photographer from a national sports magazine who dropped by, uninvited, to capture the Rockers' new "phenom hunk" at play. He was offered a bottle of water and a hamburger and sent on his way.

Once the magazine hit the newsstands, word was out about where the Rockers' new seven-million-dollar-man was living. The local newspaper picked up the story and wanted to interview Trey about his decision to live in that part of town. He refused the interview but invited the reporter to his house for lemonade and chitchat, off the record. He wanted to show he had nothing to hide and where he lived was nobody's business but his own.

The Rockers' front office didn't see it that way. Brett Bing, the team's director of basketball operations, called Trey into his office.

"We not paying you enough?"

"You're paying me plenty," Trey said modestly. "Why?"

"What's the deal with buying a house in such a bad part of town?"

"Bad? How much time have you spent in my neighborhood, Brett?"

"None. And that's the point. Most white folks wouldn't be caught dead down there…unless they wanted to be *found* dead," Bing said, trying to be funny. "Seriously, Trey, what's this all about?"

"It's not about anything except that I didn't want to spend lots of money on a place to live when I could get the kind of house I wanted in a neighborhood I preferred for the price I liked. Isn't that what picking a house is all about? I grew up with very little, Brett, and I feel blessed beyond words getting paid an obscene amount of money for doing what I love to do. I can use that money for more important things than spending it all on me. And why did you call my neighborhood bad?" Trey always bristled when someone from outside a neighborhood felt qualified to deem it good or bad. "Ask the folks who live there if it's a bad neighborhood. It's their home; for some, it's been their home all their lives. Those are some of the sweetest people I've met since I moved here. Come by sometime and I'll introduce you to some."

"I'll pass. It's just that the front office doesn't think it's a safe place for one of our players to be living. Crime is exceptionally high in that area, and we're afraid something will happen to you," Brett said.

Trey thought for a moment, mulling over the warning and wanting to give Brett a fair hearing.

"I dunno, Brett. Maybe you're right. Maybe I shouldn't be living there. I guess I've always believed that ultimately God's got the last call on things like life and death. It's like…well, like if I'm *meant* to live longer, then God's gonna have my back."

"And the Rockers organization, while wanting you to live long and prosper, most immediately wants you to live healthy. You won't be too much value to the club if someone breaks your legs."

"Where would I go, Brett?" Trey asked sincerely. "Is there any place in this town—in any town—where safety is guaranteed? I'm probably as safe here as you are in your neighborhood."

"My neighborhood's gated," Brett said, as if that would close the discussion. It didn't, and after a few more gives and takes, the compromise agreed upon was that Trey would build a secure garage with remote control doors and a covered and shielded walkway from the garage to his back door, thereby lessening the chance that a sniper would take out the superstar. The Rockers would pay for half the cost. By the time exhibition games started, the project was completed, along with an attached shop and storage room that Trey decided to add at the last minute, at his expense.

During the team's first players' press conference, attention was focused on the Rockers' new point guard. Representatives from local and national sports media outlets were there to ask questions of the players. And they were none too friendly toward Trey Glass.

"Trey, word is that you are pretty squeaky clean. Do you think you're going to have trouble getting along with some of your teammates whose reputations are…well, let's just say, not like yours?" A nervous laugh flooded the room full of sports writers and reporters.

"I don't think so. We've gotten along well so far. Hey, look, I'm not here to judge anyone or preach to anyone or demand that people act the way I think they should. I'm here to play basketball and lend to the team what I might have so that we can make the playoffs."

"Trey, I notice you don't have any tattoos. Do tattoos bother you?"

"Are you saying you've seen my entire body?" he said, eliciting laughs from the crowd.

"Do you have a girlfriend?"

"Not right now. Do you know someone I need to meet?" Trey said, to the delight of the crowd.

"Trey, why did you buy a house in the slums?"

"The *slums?*" Trey retorted, his patience stretched. "I didn't know it was the slums. Still don't. I've made some pretty good friends in my neighborhood. If you knew them, I think you'd like them too. Anybody got any questions about basketball?"

The Rockers won four of eight pre-season games and opened the season dropping four of the first seven games. Off the bench, Trey was averaging thirteen points and two assists per game over twenty-two minutes of playing time—not bad for a rookie, but more would be needed if the Rockers wanted to stay competitive.

The team was on the road in Los Angeles when Thanksgiving rolled around. Gilbert Warner, Trey's on-the-road roommate, invited Trey and Paul Sykes, the assistant trainer, to his mom's house for Thanksgiving dinner. She'd prepared a traditional holiday dinner enjoyed by fifteen various family members and guests. Trey wished he could be at home with his folks, but if he couldn't be, he was grateful to be in such a warm and friendly house. The next day, the Rockers would play the Clippers before heading up to Seattle.

The week before Christmas, the Rockers enjoyed their longest winning streak of the season—five games in a row. Trey's long-range shooting spelled the difference. He was twelve of twenty-seven from behind the three-point line and accounted for two of the team's last-second victories. He felt good about his offense but knew he needed to improve his floor leadership before he could secure a starting position.

As it turned out, the team had Christmas Eve and Christmas Day off before hosting Oklahoma City the day after. Trey spent the holiday with his family in Wayne County. Once in his own bed, he realized how tired he was. The heavy travel and game schedule was taking a toll on the young player. For the two days he was home, he mainly hung around the house, not venturing out where gawkers and autograph hounds lurked. His mom noticed an increase in drive-by traffic now that the county knew their star was home. More than half the cars, she noticed, were driven by young women who gawked, hoping to get a glimpse of the star. Trey realized that folks in his quiet Memphis neighborhood allowed him more freedom than his hometown folks. He could be walking in Memphis and not be bothered other than by the admiring kids who themselves aspired to NBA greatness. And he didn't mind them.

By mid-January, the holidays were long since forgotten as the march toward the playoffs intensified. The first substantial breather came in late February as the teams curtailed play to honor the annual all-star ritual. Except for the two veteran players selected to represent the team in Miami, the all-star break provided Trey and his teammates six days to rest and recuperate. The team offered to ferry any player not needing time to heal or extra coaching down to Miami and cover all expenses if they wanted to support their all-star teammates. Trey decided to stay in Memphis to rest and work on setting and using picks with one of the assistant coaches. He felt he needed both the sleep and the extra coaching.

The first of his days off he slept until 11:30. After he arose and showered, he went downstairs, where Tyler, his chef, had prepared his favorite omelet, which he served with a fruit cup, juice, and 1 percent milk. Trey ate it all, plus an extra slice of toast with cherry preserves, sat in his favorite recliner to listen to music given him at Christmas, and dozed for another two hours. For the rest of the afternoon, Trey puttered around the house, did laundry, ordered his mom flowers "just because," and read for an hour from a new book. At dusk, he decided it was time to get out of the house for a while.

Three blocks down, four blocks over, and across the railroad tracks from Trey's house was a large, abandoned dry goods storage warehouse. Trey had noticed the ominous structure on previous walks but hadn't paid it much attention.

"Hey, buddy, can you give me a hand over here?" In the semi-darkness, Trey could make out nothing more than a form among the overgrown bushes.

"Yeah, what can I do for you? Where are you?" Trey asked as he left the familiar path and walked toward a dark corner of the property. When he got beyond the loading docks, he felt a crushing blow to the head, and then the lights went out.

Trey woke up six hours later in the emergency room of the Med. Memphis police, making their usual rounds, found Trey lying motionless in a pool of blood and broken glass. The police called EMTs and administered first aid until more help arrived. Since the victim had no ID, the cops surmised as to why a white boy was out here alone at night.

"Probably buying drugs. Maybe sex. Maybe both. This should teach him," a male EMT said.

"Sir, can you tell us who you are?" a female voice asked in the ER.

Boy, my head hurts, Trey thought as he awakened. "Where am I?"

"You're at the Med. Can you tell us who you are? Do you know what happened to you?"

"Trey Glass," he said through the fog. "No, I have no idea what happened. What is this place again?"

"The Med. The Regional Medical Trauma Center. The police brought you in last night and you've been sleeping pretty soundly since. Did you say Trey Glass? The basketball player?"

"I guess so," he said, his head spinning.

"The doctor will be in shortly. Just lie still. Do you need anything?"

"Water, please. Can I have a drink of water?"

"I'll get it for him, Angie." Another voice came from behind him. Soon, a soft hand lifted his head slightly and offered a straw. The cold water tasted good.

"Whoa, babe." The woman holding the cup pulled the straw away and lowered his head. "Can't give you too much until we find out what's going on. Mr. Glass, I'm Dr. Garza. What do you remember?"

"Nothing," he said, straining to see who was asking the questions. The bright light over the examination table kept him from making out more than a human figure. "I was just walking along and someone asked me for help. That's about all I remember."

The doctor shined a penlight into both of his eyes and applied pressure to various points near his temple.

"No concussion. Looks like you have a pretty good gash on the top of your head though. You were hit by a glass bottle, and the bottle won. We'll get that sewn up shortly. The police will have some questions for you after we get you taken care of."

Trey could feel the head of the table being elevated, and he was able to get his first view of Dr. Garza.

You're beautiful! he almost said out loud. And she was. If there was one thing Trey knew—and liked—nearly as well as basketball, it was beautiful women. The young intern, in her late twenties, had dark skin, glossy brown hair, and chocolate-colored eyes. Only thing he couldn't see, though he tried with all his might, was her body. He wouldn't have been disappointed if he had died and this was his first glimpse of heaven.

"Angie will be in to shave your head, clean you up, and then I'll come back to put you back together. Dr. Mabry may come in to make sure I did it right; I'm still a rookie, just like you. Okay?" Dr. Garza asked with a smile that could light up a room.

Okay by me, he thought.

When the nurse finished cleaning the wound and shaving Trey's head, Dr. Garza reentered and said those dreaded words, "Just a little stick," as she administered the painkiller.

"Yeow!" Trey yelped. "A little stick?!" He really hated to be such a wimp in front of such a lovely woman.

"Oh, come on now, that wasn't nearly as painful as the beating you guys took against Westbrook and the Thunder the other night, was it?" the doctor said, trying to divert his attention. He couldn't tell if she was smiling.

"Ouch. Now that was a low blow," he said, trying to act relaxed. For the next fifteen minutes, as Dr. Garza inserted eight sutures, the two engaged in casual conversation about basketball—she knew her stuff—, Memphis, and the best places to buy groceries.

When his wound was expertly repaired, checked, and bandaged, Dr. Garza reached out her hand and said, "Nice meeting you, Trey Glass. See you at the Forum."

"Wait a minute," he said with unusual boldness, "you know my name, but I don't know yours."

"I told you...Dr. Garza," she said, smiling. She looked around to make sure no other staff was listening, then said, "Cristina."

"Thank you, Dr. Cristina Garza. Good job."

She hesitated, as though she would say something more, but then turned and walked out the door, stopping once to look back and smile.

Man, that was worth it all right there! Trey thought as he watched her walk out.

After a few minutes, Angie returned with Trey's bloody shirt and was followed by the two Memphis police officers who had brought him in.

"You may have this back, Mr. Glass, though I don't know why you'd want it. Take aspirin or Tylenol for the pain as needed, and I recommend you take it easy for a few days. After these two gentlemen finish with you, you may go home."

"Actually, we don't have much we want to ask, now that we know who you are," one of the officers said. "We assume you were out walking?"

"Yeah," Trey said, rubbing his eyes.

"Why are you living in that neighborhood? Didn't you know its reputation before you bought?"

Oh, here we go, he said to himself. "Because that's where I wanted to live," Trey answered as nicely as he could.

"Do you remember if you had your wallet with you?"

"I never take my wallet with me when I walk in the evenings. But I did have my keys. Have you seen those?" he asked.

"Yeah, almost forgot." The officer dug in his pockets. "We took these when they loaded you in the ambulance. Did you have anything else on you of value that they might have taken? Watch? Necklace? Anything?"

"No. Wait, just a little pinky ring my niece gave me at Christmas. I never wear it; just put it on this afternoon. Not worth much. No big deal."

"Is there anything else you can remember? Did you see who did this?" the officer said, probing.

"I'm sorry, sir. I really couldn't see anything. It was dark, and whoever hit me blindsided me. We'll probably never see him again."

"Do you think it was more than one?" the other cop asked.

"I think so. It seems one person, a guy, called me over, and another hit me, but I'm really not certain."

"Well, you were lucky, Mr. Glass. Lucky you didn't have your wallet, lucky they didn't take your keys to your house and car, and lucky they didn't take your life. You might want to think about moving."

Trey sat up, swung his legs off the table, and put on his bloody shirt.

"No offense, sir, but I don't believe in luck," he said, feeling the back of his head. "Hey, could you guys give me a ride home?"

"Sure. You'll have to sit in the back of the car, and we'll have to cuff you," one of the cops said, smiling while elbowing his partner. "Just kidding."

Trey felt a little woozy as he stood but dared not say anything for fear they would keep him longer. It had been quite a day. He had met an angel, although he was dreading another encounter with Brett Bing over his choice of neighborhoods. But he had met an angel.

On the ride home, sitting in the back of the police car, he wondered how he could get to know Dr. Cristina Garza better.

CHAPTER 5

Trey woke around noon and decided he would initiate what he knew was coming: a discussion with the team about his injury. They didn't like it when one of their players got hurt, especially when it was away from the court. He braced himself for the full ire of the front office.

But first, he knew he needed to tell his parents. He couldn't help but think of a story his dad had once told him about his grandfather.

"Your Grandfather Gaither Glass was in Seattle on business when he was confronted by a man wielding an ice pick.

"'Give me all your money or you die,' the frightened young man threatened. Your grandfather felt the pick against his ribs and carefully moved his hand toward his wallet.

"Your grandfather could tell the kid was young and scared. He thought maybe this was his first crime. Once he had his wallet in his hand, Grandfather looked the young man in the eye and said, 'Look, you don't need to do this, to be a thief. You're about to do something that could send you to jail for years for a measly few bucks. Let me give you all my money, as a gift, and then you won't have to go to jail. What do you say?' The young man stood speechless for a few moments, then pushed the ice pick a little harder up against Gaither's ribs.

"'Say, what are you trying to pull?' he asked.

"'Nothing,' Gaither said. 'I'm just trying to do you a favor. You need money; I have money. You need to stay out of jail. I think you can become something great someday, but jail will make that more difficult. Here, take this money as a gift.'

"With that, the young man stuffed the ice pick in his pocket and ran away empty-handed."

The beep of the voicemail prompted Trey to begin his message.

"Hey, Mom, it's Trey." *Wonder where they are?* he thought. "Just wanted you guys to know I was hit in the head the other night while I was out walking, but I'm okay…just a few stitches, no concussion. I'll be fine. Got your note the other day, Mom. Thanks. Love you guys. Talk to you later."

In early afternoon, Trey strode into the Forum and headed to the Rockers' front office. Everyone was in Miami at the all-star game except a few assistant coaches. Derek Tims was the first to see him.

"What the…?" Tims exclaimed when he saw Trey's bandaged head. "Glass, what happened to you?" At that point other coaches and secretaries filed out of their offices to find out what was going on.

"Lost a battle with a beer bottle," Trey said calmly.

"You poor thing," Carly, a barely-twenty-year-old office assistant, said as she approached for a closer look. She took his head in her hands and pulled it down toward her low-cut top. "How many stitches?" she asked as she gently kissed the top of his head, then let go, meeting his eyes with a coy wink.

"Oh boy, Coach Rollins isn't going to like this," another assistant said.

"What happened?" asked another.

"I was out walking last night and got jumped…by two guys, I think. I'm really okay."

"Yeah, well, we have a game in four days. Doesn't look like you'll be ready," Coach Tims said. "I'll call Coach tonight. We'd better not take a chance on re-injury; we'll skip the extra practices. Go home and rest, and I'll let you know what Coach says."

Trey gathered a few things from his locker and headed out the back door. He pulled his car out of the parking garage and headed toward the Midtown Walgreens to pick up a few items. On his way past the store's magazine section he saw his photo on the front of *Sports Enquirer*, a sleazy rag that featured photographs of the rich and famous in the world of sports. The caption on the front in bold yellow letters next to a photo taken Labor Day screamed, "Is Trey Gay?"

My goodness, what's going on? he asked himself. Trey was sensitive to any issues dealing with his sexuality. He knew he had not been faithful to his teachings and faith when it came to his exploits with young women. Despite not having much success in controlling his urges, this bothered him greatly. He had prayed about it and had even come up with a strategy to avoid situations when he might cross the line. Still, the temptations were strong, and occasional lapses added to his guilt and sense of defeat. Now, these questions about his attractions?

If they only knew, he thought as he placed the magazine back where he found it, paid for his merchandise, and left the store.

Trey arrived back home just in time to encounter two Mormon "elders" waiting at his front door. He parked in the driveway and walked to the porch to greet his guests.

"Hey, guys, I'm Trey," he said, extending his hand.

"Good afternoon, Trey," the older of the two said. "I'm Elder Morgan, and this is Elder Kelvin."

"Good to meet you both. Come on in and I'll get you some water," Trey said as he unlocked the front door. "But there's one thing," he said, turning back around, "we won't discuss religion. If we can't agree on that, you may as well move on. Because we won't agree, and I don't want that to be a sore spot between us. What do you say?"

The two young men looked at each other.

"Can we leave you some literature?" Elder Morgan asked.

"No," Trey said. "I simply want to offer you a cold drink and a comfortable seat while you get your breath. I know it must be hard, doing what you're doing. I'd like to get to know you, find out something about your families and hear some stories about your mission so far. I bet not a lot of people want to get to know you, am I right?"

"Yes, sir. You are right, and we really thank you, but we'd better just move on. Thank you for your hospitality."

"Well, would you take a couple of bottles of water with you?" Trey asked.

"Sure," the elders said simultaneously.

"Wait here." Trey disappeared inside and brought back two cold plastic bottles of spring water and two bags of Skittles he'd found. "I hope you guys have a good day. If you ever need a place to crash, come on back. I have lots of room and some good food. Take care."

"Thank you," Elder Kelvin said, and the pair mounted their bicycles and rode out of the driveway.

The rest of the afternoon, Trey read and dozed and dozed and read. Mid-afternoon, his dad called, wanting the full scoop on Trey's injury. Mr. Glass promised to tell his mom what he knew and to assure her Trey was okay. Before he hung up, Mr. Glass said, "Trey, you know, the guys who jumped you are looking for something. Keep your eyes and ears open, and you might have the opportunity to minister to them. Sounds like they need some direction." Trey had already been thinking the same thing.

At 9:30 that night, Trey's cell phone buzzed. *Uh oh*, he thought. *Coach Rollins.*

"Hey, Coach," he said, trying to sound upbeat.

"Trey, hope I'm not disturbing you," Horace Rollins said.

"Not at all, Coach. I knew I'd be hearing from you soon. How's it going down there?" Trey asked, stalling.

"Going well. Big game's tomorrow. Been in meetings all day today and ready to hit the hay. Coach Tims tells me you were injured in a fight. That right?"

Trey couldn't tell if the coach was kidding or not; he thought he'd better play it straight.

"No, sir. Got a little bump on the head from a bottle a guy hit me with. If it was a fight, it was one-sided."

"How bad?"

"Not bad. A few stitches. No concussion. I should be ready to play next game," Trey said, offering his own unprofessional prognosis.

"Well, we'll be the judge of that. Where did this happen?"

"Uh…down the road from my house. I was out walking and these guys—"

"You know we're not happy with where you've chosen to live, don't you, Trey? For this very reason. Chances are this won't be the last, and we can't afford to have our players not at 100 percent when they're needed. Who did you see? What doctor?"

"One of the doctors in the ER at the Med."

"What's his name?"

"Dr. Garza," Trey said hesitantly.

"Garza," the coach repeated. "Never heard of him. Tomorrow I want you to go see our neuro guy. I've asked Coach Tims to make the arrangements. Call the office early tomorrow morning and get the details. We'll see what the experts say about your little injury. Okay?"

"Yes, sir."

"Don't worry about it, Trey. These things happen. Just be careful; we don't want our rising star incapacitated before he reaches top status. We'll see you in a few days." Coach Rollins hung up, and Trey breathed much easier.

"Thank you, Jesus," he said, fully meaning it.

By 11:00 the next morning, Trey was sitting in Dr. Barry Wharton's private office, waiting to go over the results from a series of tests begun an hour earlier by various members of his staff. The doctor entered carrying a file folder, apparently in a hurry.

"Trey, I'm Barry Wharton. Nice to meet you."

"Dr. Wharton," Trey said, rising to shake hands.

"Just Barry. Please have a seat." The doctor walked around his desk and sat down. "Everything looks good. The people at the Med did a great job. No internal issues that we can see. I'd say play when you feel like it, but you might want to wait till after the weekend as a precaution. I'll pass this on to the team, and they can decide. If you experience any dizziness, that could mean trouble. Get it checked out. Anything else?"

"No, sir. Thank you."

As quickly as he came in, the doctor was gone.

For the next few days, Trey hung around the house, reading, listening to music, watching an occasional movie, and going over the team offense notebook. On the day before their first team meeting after the all-star break, the front office called with a list of names and phone numbers of people who called the Rockers' office looking for Trey Glass—five calls from two sports magazines, two calls from the local newspaper, one call from the pastor of his new church, and one call from the Med.

The Med, he thought. *Cristina?* He decided to return that call first.

The first voice was a recorded message asking the caller for the extension of the party they sought. He punched in the number given by the front office and heard, "Angie."

"Angie?" he repeated. "This is Trey Glass."

"Oh, hi, Trey Glass. I'm the nurse who was on duty the night the police brought you in. Remember?"

"Of course. How are you?" He tried not to sound too disappointed.

"I'm good. Thanks. The question is, how are you? I'm just making a follow-up call. We're wondering how you're doing. Any questions? Need anything?"

I can't believe they call every patient who's been through the ER, he thought.

"No, no, I'm fine. Just chillin' until we start back. How's everyone there?" he asked, fishing.

"Oh, we're busy, as always. We're glad you're doing well. Just let us know if you need anything, okay?"

"Yeah, sure, will do," he said. "Thanks for calling. Tell everyone down there hello." He cringed.

"Yeah, I will. I know your team doctors will want to take a look at your injury. But let us know if we can help in any way. We'll be watching for you the rest of the season. Hope you win a lot of games. Goodbye, Mr. Glass."

"Bye," he said, hanging up. *We? Wonder who we is?* he thought, hoping Cristina Garza was one of them.

Next, he called Tony Bradford, the pastor of New Hope Community Church.

"Tony, this is Trey Glass."

"Hey, man, thanks for calling me back. I saw your name in the paper yesterday, something about getting mugged? You okay?"

"I didn't know it made the papers. Yeah, I'm fine. Bump on the head, a few stitches, that's all. What's up?"

"That's good. I was sorry to read about your mishap but am glad you're okay. I was wondering if you'd help me with something. I have this idea about helping some of our teenagers stay out of trouble this summer. Thought maybe you'd be available to help."

"Maybe. But I don't do public speaking. What do you have in mind?" Trey asked.

"Oh, don't worry. Kids these days don't want to hear preaching. I was wondering if you might let us start a garden somewhere in your yard. We would supervise, transport the kids back and forth, stuff like that. All I ask is that you'd help pay for some tools, seeds, and things, about a thousand dollars or so, and let us use your water. Then occasionally you can show up to encourage the kids. What do you think?"

"I think that's a great idea. I've got the room, that's for sure. You probably want to get started soon, right?"

"Pretty soon. The kids get out of school the second week of May, but we might start earlier with some of them, maybe on Saturdays beginning in March. We need to get some seeds in the ground."

"Yeah, sure. I'll send you a check today for two thousand, and you can begin whenever you want. I'm going to be pretty tied up until the playoffs are over—hopefully in June—but you never know. After that, I should be around most of the summer. And there's a new storage room off my garage where you can keep your tools and stuff. I'll give you a key and you can come and go as you please."

"Hey, that's great, Trey. Thank you so much. The kids will really enjoy getting to know you. They need to see a man of God who is also a superstar. We'll be in touch as things move along. Blessings, brother."

"See ya."

The next call Trey made was to a plumbing company he chose out of the phone book to get a price on putting water lines out to where he thought the garden might go.

Cool, he thought. *This is something Mom would like to be involved in.*

He decided not to call the sports magazines back but instead dialed the number of the reporter from the local newspaper, Tom Byron.

"Byron here."

"Mr. Byron, Trey Glass."

"Trey! Thanks for calling me back. Was just wondering how you're doing after your little neighborhood tangle the other night."

"Doing fine. A few stitches, that's all," he said for what seemed to be the hundredth time.

"When will you get back to playing?" the reporter inquired.

"You'll have to ask the coach. It's not up to me, but I feel good enough to play tonight," Trey said.

"Are you happy with your playing time so far?"

"Yeah, you know, a player always wants more playing time than he's getting. But I know that will come, so no complaints."

"Guess you saw the spread about you in the *Enquirer*. Any comment?"

"Oh, about me being gay? Yeah, I saw that, and no, I don't have any comment."

"Not even to confirm or deny?" the reporter asked persistently.

"No comment," he said. "That's a stupid issue. What difference does it make?" Trey was nearing his tolerance level.

"Well, you claim to be a Christian, and we all know what Christians think about homosexuality. I just thought you might want to put this matter to rest once and for all."

"I can't speak for all followers of Jesus, but I know plenty of godly men and women who have a same-sex attraction. And I know plenty of Christians who love all people, no matter their sexual preference. So, again, no, I don't want to comment. Is there anything else, Tom?"

"That'll do it, Trey," Tom Byron said, taking the hint. "Talk to you soon, buddy."

CHAPTER 6

It didn't take long for Trey to discover how reporters turned chitchat into a full-blown issue—two issues!

Laid out on the breakfast bar was the *Memphis Appeal*, folded neatly to reveal Tom Byron's gossip column about the comings and goings of sports celebrities. Trey knew to take note when Tyler, his chef, arranged the paper in such a way.

"'Overheard…Memphis Rockers' sixth man says he's not getting enough playing time. The rookie point guard also refuses to confirm or deny *Sports Enquirer's* suspicion that he is gay. Stay tuned…'"

"You ought to sue that sucker," Tyler said as he poured Trey's coffee.

"Well, that wouldn't end it. I suppose I should be thankful he didn't use my name. I just need to be more careful about what I say and to whom I say it," Trey said.

"Yeah, that too. But you should still sue that sucker."

"Hey, Tyler, you're gay, right?" Trey asked.

"I am and proud of it," Tyler said. "Why?"

"I was just wondering what you think about stuff like this? I mean, how does it feel for your personal preferences to be made an issue?"

"Oh Lord, Trey, I'm so used to it. It used to really bother me, but now I don't even think about it. I suppose it will always be an issue as long as it sells papers."

"And what do you think about what supposed Christians say about being LGBT? Does that make you just want to jump up and be baptized?"

"I had an uncle who helped me see the difference between God and so-called religious folks," Tyler said, chuckling. "He said, 'Pay very careful attention to God, but close your ears to God's people.' That's pretty much what I've tried to do. And it's been straight people like you, Trey—you are straight, aren't you?" Tyler asked, grinning. "It's good people like you who give me hope that maybe someday all God's children can accept all others just as we are. After all, doesn't the good book say, 'There is no one righteous, not even one'?"

"Romans 3," Trey said. "You know, I don't care what anyone says about me—I hope my life speaks for who I am—but it really bothers me when others are questioned or put down just because of prejudice or fear."

After breakfast, Trey went back to his room and prayed. He had learned that when he let God in on matters of concern, things always got better. After thirty minutes of prayer and meditation, Trey grabbed his gym bag and headed to the Rockers' practice facilities in the Forum. He spent an easy hour shooting around and working on foul shots. He spent another hour in the weight room and finished the session with a massage and shower before returning home. Tomorrow morning at 9:00, the team would gather once again to prepare for their upcoming game against the Dallas Mavericks Friday night at the Forum. Trey didn't expect to play but wanted to be ready, just in case.

He had heard other players say that the hardest things to deal with in the pros were boredom and loneliness. He was beginning to understand. Lots of time off and few close acquaintances aside from teammates made the down times tedious and long. He really missed his family, and although he never dated one girl very long, he missed the company of a female, *any* female. But he was learning to fill his time with things that nurtured his soul and strengthened his relationship with God. His iPod was full of his favorite music—Lecrae, Israel Houghton, and others—and podcasts of inspirational speakers he admired who built up his faith. He started and ended his days with prayer and often found himself talking to God at other times throughout the day. And while basketball season afforded little time to volunteer, he knew that commitment to helping others drew him to God as effectively as anything else he practiced. Trey had been taught that human beings were on this earth to help other human beings. He looked forward to the time when he could again become a regular volunteer with an agency that improved the lives of others.

As important as minding the things he put into his mind and life, Trey was constantly on the watch for those things he didn't want in his life. He knew his susceptibilities, his weaknesses, so he took care to avoid anything that fueled them. He subscribed to basic cable TV that showed primarily news and sports, and he programmed his computer to repel pornography, solicited or unsolicited. Porn had never been a big problem for Trey, but he knew it could worm its slimy way into his mind if he gave it even the slimmest of opportunities. He knew guys from college and in the pros who were as addicted to porn as others might be to drugs or alcohol. Trey's dad used to say that pornography explains the apparent uptick in rape and other violent acts against women, relegating women to mere objects, not people. He knew he didn't want to get started down that path.

Trey spent twenty minutes on the phone with his mom and five more talking with his dad before hanging up, taking a shower, and turning in. He wasn't really excited about explaining the comments in the paper to his coach and teammates.

Maybe they don't read the newspaper, he thought, chuckling to himself as he reached over and turned out the light.

CHAPTER 7

The next morning, after a light breakfast of Frosted Mini Wheats and dry toast, Trey packed his gym bag and drove toward the Forum. He could walk the few miles from his house, but usually after a hard practice, he was too tired to walk back.

Today should be a light day, discussing strategy and running plays half speed, Trey hoped, though he never knew until practice was over. *Things should wrap up by noon.*

Coach Rollins caught Trey in the hallway as he entered the building from the parking garage.

"Dr. Wharton says you're fit to play. I think we'll watch you at practice today before we decide if we'll use you tomorrow night. Sound good?"

"Sure, Coach, whatever. I'll be ready when you are."

"And we'll try to get you more playing time, okay?" Rollins said with a wink before walking away.

"Yes, sir," Trey said, the heat of embarrassment crawling up his neck and into his cheeks.

Trey was happy to see his teammates after nearly a week of everyone being scattered. The only repercussion from the newspaper's remark about Trey's sexuality came from the veteran center, who whispered, "Trey, I know this guy I want you to meet," before giving the young rookie a bear hug and hearty laugh. "Don't worry about it, man. We're used to such trash talking. I say, who cares if Trey Glass is gay; the dude can sink a three from beyond downtown."

The team meeting lasted an hour, and then they all walked down to the practice facility to run through some of the Mavericks' offense. Trey was assigned to play the Mavs' hot point guard, Levon Williams, in a walk-through scrimmage. The Rockers had played Dallas twice this year—winning once—and were already familiar with the perennial division rivals' style of play, their strengths, and weaknesses.

After practice, Coach Rollins pulled Trey aside.

"We're going to let you sit tomorrow night. First of all, that patch on your head is a target—might as well be a big red X. Some of the guys on the other team will be aiming to hurt you in your most vulnerable spot. Maybe by Sunday night's game we can make that patch a little more invisible. But mainly, the bench will give you the best perspective on their point guard. I want you to focus on Williams the whole game, watch everything about him, particularly how he runs the floor. That's what we want from you eventually. I think what we're missing is a point guard who can spread the defense like they do, giving you more options. With your shooting eye and the inside threat that Jacobs and Bernie offer, we can win some games. How does that sound?"

"I like it. Should I dress out?" Trey asked.

"Yeah, why not?" Coach answered. "Go through the pre-game and everything. The Mavs will think you're an option, and who knows, we may need you."

"See you tomorrow, Coach. And thanks," Trey said.

On his way out the door, he stopped by the trainer's office to have his injury checked. The assistant trainer removed the small bandages, dabbed on some antibiotic ointment, and applied a new bandage.

"It's looking good," he said. "These stitches will dissolve on their own before too long, but keep it clean for now."

Just before he left the building, Carly, the assistant who had kissed his newly bandaged head right after his assault, caught up with him in the hallway.

"I sure would like to see more of you," she said in a near coo, running her eyes up and down his body. "If you know what I mean."

He knew exactly what she meant and was tempted to know more. She represented one temptation he fought hard to keep in check. In the brief moment he stood there, he wondered what the harm would be.

It wouldn't mean anything. She is cute and probably needs some company. No one has to know.

"Uh, thanks, Carly," he said, coming to his senses. "I'd really like to be your friend, but nothing more. I hope you understand."

Carlene made a little pout, then winked and walked away, exaggerating her strut for Trey's benefit. He never saw it because he was out the door in an instant.

Trey Glass felt pretty good as he drove back home in his ten-year-old Camry.

Sounds like the team has a plan for me, he thought. *Lord, help me do my best and not worry about the rest,* he prayed, repeating what he'd heard his dad say many times.

Trey decided at the last minute to go to a movie. He looked up the times on his phone and stopped by the house to check his mail, drop off his gym bag, and wash up. He picked a movie that began mid-afternoon at a mega-screen theater in east Memphis. On the way, he drove through Arby's and ordered a Hawaiian Chicken Sandwich and a small vanilla shake. He parked on the side of the theater twenty minutes before the movie started and enjoyed his lunch while listing to *Sports Talk* on a local radio station. The show's hosts were discussing the Rockers' upcoming game with the Dallas Mavericks.

"…actually, they're going to have to get more playing time for Glass if they hope to make the playoffs," one caller said.

"I disagree. I don't think Glass has what it takes. He's young, way too passive, and can't drive."

"…they need someone who can get things going; just not sure Trey Glass can do it in the stretch. Give him a couple more years maybe…" said yet another.

"…but he sure is cute," added a giggling female caller.

Trey flicked the radio off and started inside. Halfway to the door, an old, shabbily dressed man approached from in front of a fire exit door where he'd been standing.

"Got any spare change?"

"I do," Trey said, reaching for his wallet and producing a twenty-dollar bill. "Hey, I bet you haven't been to a movie lately, have you?

Would you like to go with me to see 'Fearless'? I'll even buy you a hot dog and—"

"Uh, no thanks," the old man said, seemingly stunned before stumbling away.

"Hey, if you're here when the movie's over, I'll buy you a cup of coffee!" Trey yelled as the man disappeared around the corner.

He bought his ticket, a bucket of popcorn and a Diet Sprite, and then found his theater. In the ten minutes before the movie, Trey made a note in his phone to put together a list of helping agencies in the Memphis area for the next time he encountered a beggar. He knew from his volunteer work that the down-and-out who prowl Memphis city streets needed people who care more than they needed money, and he assumed that Memphis had an abundance of agencies that he could direct such people to when he met them. He also committed to being more attentive to the people in his own neighborhood who needed food, even the basic commodities most people take for granted.

Wouldn't it be great to host a house full of folks for a feast once a month or so? His dreaming was interrupted by movie previews. For the next two hours, Trey Glass escaped the real world.

After the movie, he looked for the old man but didn't see him.

On his way home, Trey drove past the abandoned warehouse where he had been jumped a few nights before. He was tempted to stop, to get out and see if he could find someone who might know the guys who assaulted him. Better judgment won out, and Trey decided to drive by and nothing else. Maybe he would come back with his neighbor Lem or someone else to do a little investigating.

Game day arrived, and Trey began his usual home-game ritual by sleeping till 11:00. Lunch at 1:00 consisted of a small, lean rib-eye steak, expertly prepared by Tyler; a baked potato; and a salad, no dressing. He had one glass of sweet tea and finished off his meal with a small bowl of rainbow sherbet. The team was required to be at the Forum at least two hours before game time at 7:05, although most players arrived much earlier to shoot around, well before fans began arriving. The rest of the afternoon, Trey lounged around listening to music and reading.

He spent some time searching the Internet to find out all he could on the Mavs' point guard, Levon Williams, and made notes in a small notebook.

Things were hopping in downtown Memphis when he drove into the parking garage at the FedEx Forum. Beale Street was already packed with revelers, some engaging in pre-game drinking before walking over to the arena; most were just there for the music, food, and fun.

There was a twenty-minute team meeting followed by taping, conditioning, individual coaching, and relaxing. No matter how many games these guys played in the course of their playing careers, pre-game jitters still reigned. There was a muffled quietness in the locker room, guys sitting in front of their lockers reading, nearly every one with wires dangling from their ears.

The official shootaround began ninety minutes before game time. Trey donned his uniform and joined his teammates on the court. The tension eased once the guys felt the leather orbs in their hands, and relaxed conversation and good-natured ribbing accompanied the pre-game tune-up. The second and final shootaround began thirty minutes before game time when the starting five were given their space to work on moves and shooting. The FedEx Forum was near capacity; there were more fans than usual, no doubt in attendance to watch their home team battle the reigning NBA Champions.

With the National Anthem and player introductions out of the way, Trey and the other subs settled on the bench. Coach Rollins went over final instructions with his starters, and the mayhem began.

Trey kept this attention trained on the Mavs' number 5, Levon Williams, making mental notes of every significant move that differed from his own style. He knew he would have to give an account of what he saw to the coaches at Saturday afternoon's team meeting. Trey was not accustomed to spending such extended time on the bench. He worked hard to maintain his concentration, telling himself that his visual observations from the sidelines would be vital contributions to the team's success in the future. Yet, despite his important job, his mind began to wander halfway through the second period. Usually he was so into the game that he blocked everything else—cheers, jeers, and beers—from his mind. Now, his eyes wandered to the fans within his line of sight seated in the bottom tier of seats across the court.

Third row up, center section, he thought he spotted her—Dr. Cristina Garza. He squinted to make sure it was her; sure enough it was, sitting next to a muscular Latino in a Rockers jersey. He was certain she was staring at him. She sat quietly when others cheered, occasionally sipping on her Coke, her eyes fixed on Trey Glass.

Can it be? he wondered. *Cristina, here?*

An out-of-bounds ball caught Trey by surprise, nearly knocking him out of his chair, snapping him back to reality. For the rest of the half, Trey's eyes moved from the game to the stands. At half-time the Mavericks had a slim four-point lead, which meant a more subdued locker room. Trey took his seat in front of his locker to listen to the coach's first half analysis and what adjustments the team would have to make to guarantee a win.

"We've got to get more production from our back court," Coach emphasized. "Glass, do you think you're ready to play?"

"Yes, sir. Just say the word." Trey felt his heart rate increase as the adrenalin began pumping.

"I'm not ready to use you right now, but if we don't get some points from you, Derek, and you, Paul, we'll have to try something else. Playoffs are coming, guys, and we don't have the luxury of losing games. We got that?"

"Yes, sir!"

During warm-up for the second half, Trey moved over to the far side of the court to see if, indeed, Cristina Garza was in the stands. He looked, but her seat was empty. He felt a twinge of disappointment.

"Darn," he muttered to himself.

Just before the second half began, he looked again; Cristina and her date had returned.

Who's the muscleman? he wondered.

Since there was a renewed chance of playing, Trey redirected his full attention back to the game. The third quarter ended with Dallas holding on to a five-point lead. Two Rockers were in foul trouble with four each, and Coach Rollins was clearly not happy with his team's play up to now.

"Glass, I want you starting this last quarter," Coach said. "We need some production. Show me what you've learned."

Several of Trey's teammates smacked his backside as he moved down the line of chairs to the scorer's table.

"Go get 'em, Trey," his friend Gilbert said. "Pretend those guys are the thugs that whacked your head the other night."

Trey smiled and was encouraged by his team's confidence in him, but his extended time off the court proved costly to his timing. On the Rockers' first possession, Trey threw the ball out of bounds on an errant pass to his small forward breaking for the basket. Second Rockers' possession, Trey missed badly on a three-point attempt.

Settle down, guy, he admonished himself.

With seven minutes left in the game, Trey had a measly three points and one foul. He decided to try some of what he had learned from Levon Williams. It was risky but a chance he was willing to take. Coming down the court, he waved his small forward and center off the key toward the baseline, freeing up the middle. He drove and was met by the Mavs' 7'3" center. At the last minute, Glass kicked the ball out to Bernie Kearns, who nailed a three-pointer. Good defense at the other end got the ball back for the Rockers. The same play resulted in a hard foul to Trey on his way to the basket. The opposing power forward aimed for Trey's head injury and landed a solid blow, just missing the wound and knocking the smaller point guard to the hardwood. The Forum got quiet as Trey Glass lay still on the floor longer than usual. All four of his teammates rushed to help him up and make sure he was okay. He wobbled to his feet and made his way to the foul line, where he drained both shots.

On the next play, Williams, the point guard Trey had been assigned to watch, made a quick move around Trey for an easy layup. For the last few minutes, the score was back and forth. With twenty-three seconds left, Mavs up by two, Rollins called a time-out and drew up a play that would free Trey for a three-point shot.

"You don't have to take it if you're not open," he coached. "You've got Bernie or Paul if you need to dump it. We don't have to have a three. We just need two to tie. Okay?"

With the Forum crowd on its feet and roaring, Trey brought the ball down the court and ran the play; three passes later, the ball came back around to the rookie point guard, who was hounded by Williams. He faked a pass inside, which gave him all the breathing room he needed. With five seconds left, Trey Glass took a dribble, stepped back behind the arc, and launched the game-winner.

Memphis Rockers win, 97-96.

The first thing he did before his teammates mobbed him was turn toward where Cristina was sitting. He made eye contact with the doctor and pumped his fist in victory. She was watching, and, with a broad smile, she repeated the fist pump.

On the way off the court, Levon Williams came over to hug his counterpart.

"Great game," Williams said. "You had some of my moves out there, bro."

"Guess you could say you took me to school tonight," Trey said, knowing that was truer than anyone could imagine. "Good game."

The locker room was electric with the team's first victory after the all-star break. Coach Rollins took a few minutes to review.

"Good game tonight, guys. We still have to work on our defense down low. You guys in the middle aren't moving your feet; you're trying to body block and you're drawing too many fouls. You know what you have to do. Good effort by the back court. Looks like we might have a new offense emerging. Good job by Glass spreading the defense and giving us some more scoring options. I want us to work on that tomorrow afternoon for a little while. Come in at two and be prepared to sweat a little. We'll be out of here by four if everyone works hard. Overall, great game, guys. Now, go home and get some rest."

As Coach passed Trey, he asked, "How's the head?"

"Pretty good, Coach. Almost got it banged, but I'm okay. Thanks."

"Good job tonight. Depending on how practice goes tomorrow, you may have earned a starting position. We'll see. Keep up the good work."

During the post-game interview, Trey noticed that the questions turned a bit more serious than previous press conferences. The reporters wanted to know how his injury was healing, what brought on the sudden change in offense tonight, and how the Rockers might handle the Pistons Sunday night. He answered like a pro. The final question, however, caught him off guard.

"Trey, reports are that you have a strong Christian faith. If that's so, how come we don't see you doing all the things other guys in the league who also have strong faith do?"

"Like what?" he asked.

"You know, kneeling, genuflecting, pointing to heaven, crossing yourself, praying—the usual."

"I don't know, haven't really thought about it. I am very conscious of God on and off the court, but I guess I feel I don't have to do any of those things to prove my love or my faith. I want the way I live my life to reflect my faith. If I truly live the way God wants me to live, I figure people will know."

Chef Tyler had prepared a roast beef sandwich and left it in the refrigerator for Trey, along with a note: "Great job tonight. Go Rockers!"

As he slowly ate his sandwich, he watched a local station's game recap on the small set in his kitchen. The reporter was very complementary of Trey's play, even though he only scored nine points. Soon his cell phone buzzed.

"Hey, bud," Travis said. "We watched the game tonight."

"Yeah? What'd you think?" Trey asked.

"You done good," his dad said in a joking tone. "Mom says hi."

"Thanks, Dad. Coach said I might start Sunday night."

"That would be good. How's your head?"

"Healing. Kind of got it roughed up tonight, but it held together. Hey, when are you and Mom coming over for a game?"

"We'll talk about it. We want to see you play. I'll check the schedule and pick out one soon. Well, I know you're tired. I'll let you go. We're proud of you, son. Keep thanking the Lord for your talents, hear?"

"I do every day, Dad. Thanks for the call. Tell Mom I love her."

"Night, son."

"G'night, Dad." Trey had no idea at the time how significant the short phone call was.

After another hour of winding down, Trey crawled into bed, tired and content. He was asleep in minutes.

CHAPTER 8

Trey could smell the omelet cooking downstairs when he awoke at 10:00. Tyler had heard his alarm go off and had Trey's favorite breakfast ready when his boss walked into the kitchen a few minutes later wearing a bathrobe and slippers.

"Good morning, game winner," Tyler said in his usual jovial way.

"Mornin'," Trey said, rubbing the sleep from his eyes.

"You got some pretty good press this morning. The paper's on the table over there," Tyler said as he dished the omelet onto a plate. "Oh, and that was in the bag with the paper."

Trey sat down and noticed the square envelope with his name handwritten on the outside.

"What's this?" he asked.

"Well, open it," Tyler said.

He opened the card and read, "'Great game last night. You look like you've played this sport before. How's the head? Cristina (Dr. Garza), 901 555-3277.' How'd this get in the paper?" Trey asked, showing the note to Tyler.

"Hmm." Tyler read the note. "Who's Cristina? Your paper girl?"

"She's the doctor who sewed my head up. I saw her at the game last night."

"Bet she came by early this morning and stuffed it in the paper. She must be after you, boy," Tyler said with a wink. "Surprised she didn't stuff her underwear in there too." He laughed, embarrassing Trey.

"She's not that kind of girl, Tyler," he said in mock displeasure.

"Yeah, that wasn't very kind of me. Sorry," Tyler said, still smiling. "Still, I'm just sayin'… So, what are you going to do about it?"

"About what?"

"About the note. About Cristina."

"I don't know. I've got more important things to worry about right now…like basketball," Trey said.

"Uh huh."

"Well, I can't rush right in to call her back. She may think I'm interested," Trey said, defensively.

"And you aren't? *Right!*" Tyler countered.

"I may be, but I can't show that I am."

"When are you going to quit playing these kid games?" Tyler asked, chastising. "It's not like you've beaten down her door. Other than last night, it's been a week since you've seen her—"

"Six days," Trey corrected.

"Six days since you've seen her. She probably thinks you don't care. If this woman is someone you might be interested in, then quit acting like a school boy and give the girl a call. It might not be too bad to be married to a doctor—you know, in case your career tanks."

Trey picked up a dish towel hanging on the back of a kitchen chair and threw it at his cook.

"If I need advice about dating a chick, I sure won't get it from a gay guy," he said with a wide grin.

"*Touché*," Tyler parried.

Trey was mid-bite when his cell phone buzzed.

"There she is now," Tyler said, laughing.

"It's Mom. Hey, Mom," Trey said.

There was gasping on the line that soon gave way to full sobs. Finally, his mother said, "Trey, it's your dad, he's been in a wreck. They've got him stabilized, but he's pretty banged up."

"Mom, where is he?" Trey asked in a panic.

Tyler look at Trey, concern evident in his face, one eyebrow raised.

"At the local medical center, but they're about to bring him to Memphis. He's going to need surgery."

"Have you told Adam and Lee?"

"Yes, they are on their way over here."

"Should I come home?" Trey asked.

"No, honey. As soon as your brothers get here, we're leaving to come there. Just pray for your dad, Trey. He's hurt pretty bad."

"I will, Mom. Let me know when you get to town and where you'll be, okay?" Trey said.

"I will, honey."

Trey hung up and started back upstairs.

"Is everything okay?" Tyler asked.

"Don't know yet. Dad was in a wreck. I don't know any details, but they are on their way over here."

"Oh my, Trey," Tyler said. "I will be praying for him."

"Thanks. And thanks for breakfast…great meal," Trey said, trying to act upbeat.

Trey climbed the stairs back to his room and shut the door. Tears ran down his cheeks as he sat in his reading chair and prayed.

"God, I need my dad to stay alive. Please spare his life, Father. Thank you for this good man and for all the good things he's done for me and our family and so many others. I kind of believe you need him here more than you need him in heaven. Be with the doctors and give them wisdom. And be with Mom right now and comfort her. Thank you, God. Amen."

Trey walked into Coach Rollins' office at 1:30, catching him diagraming plays on a large whiteboard hung on one wall.

"Hey, Trey, come on in. Here a little early, aren't you?"

"Yeah, Coach, but it's my dad. He was in a wreck back home, and they're bringing him to Memphis this afternoon for surgery."

"Well, that's not good. I am so sorry. Are they thinking he'll be all right?" the coach asked.

"Too early to tell. He's a pretty strong guy, never been sick a day in his life, as they say," Trey said, smiling. "Coach, I've never been through this before; got any advice on what I need to do about practice and the game?"

"What do you think you need to do?"

"I don't see my dad getting here until later today, so I'm good to practice. Just not sure about the game tomorrow night."

"Let's take one thing at a time. If you think you'd do better at practice than sitting around thinking the worst, then let's go ahead with our plan for this afternoon. We'll think about the game later. How does that sound?"

Trey was thankful for such an understanding coach. He'd heard horror stories about some coaches in the league and their hard-nosed team policies.

"I think I'd rather be on the court, if that's okay with you."

"Good. See you in a few," Coach Rollins said.

The team spent nearly two hours working on the new offense with Trey running the floor. Although it was clear Trey's mind wasn't completely on the practice, he did well enough for Coach Rollins to give the team a "good job" before turning them loose.

"Mind your curfews tonight, guys. We want everyone safe and rested for our game tomorrow afternoon—2:05 tip. Don't be late," he said, warning the team. "Oh, and let's all remember Trey's dad, Travis Glass, in our prayers. He was hurt in an accident, and he is pretty bad off. Let us know what you need from us, Trey. See you guys tomorrow."

Trey left the gym immediately for home. He showered and tried to call his mom. When she didn't answer, he left a short message and settled in to wait for her call.

They must be on the way, he thought. While he waited he called his pastor.

"Tony, Trey here."

"Trey, my man!" the ever-exuberant young minister replied. "What's happening?"

"My dad was hurt in a car wreck, Tony," Trey said. "Might need surgery. I'm waiting for a call from my mom now. They're supposed to be bringing him to Memphis sometime today. Just wanted you and the church to pray for him. Not sure I'll get to see you tomorrow morning."

"Aw, man. That's terrible!" Tony said. "I want to pray right now. Father, I ask that you hold this brother and his dad in your hands. Make this thing go away, as I know you have the power to do. I just ask that you be with all those attending to Mr. Glass. And may he be completely well soon. And keep the devil away, Lord God. Through *Jesus*," he prayed, "amen."

"Thank you, Tony. Tell everyone I'm sorry I'll miss them tomorrow. Probably won't see them next week either. We start a six-game road trip Wednesday. But y'all will be in my prayers."

"Will do. I'll come see you sometime tomorrow. Where will he be?"

"Methodist University Hospital."

"All right, that's a good place. Just know we'll be in prayer for your dad and your family. In the meantime, you call me if you need anything at all, okay? You playing tomorrow?"

"Not sure. Coach said we'll take it day to day."

"Okay, buddy. You take it easy. And don't forget, the Lord can make it all right, no matter what happens. God is good…"

"All the time," Trey said, completing his sentence. "See you, Tony."

At 7:05 the phone rang.

"Hi, honey, we're at Methodist now. We got a late start because his blood pressure dropped, and they didn't want to move him. Lee's here with me. Can you come up?"

"I'll be right there." Trey left immediately, praying the whole way.

When he walked into the ER waiting area and saw his mom and brother, Trey almost cried but knew that might further upset his mom. He gave her and Lee big hugs.

"How is he?" Trey asked, resting his hands on his mother's shoulders, looking down into sad brown eyes.

"He's in surgery right now," she said, fighting tears. "I'm so worried; he's never had anything like this happen to him before."

"What happened, Mom?" Trey asked.

"The state trooper said he was hit by a drunk driver near that old mill on Route 12."

"Do they know who it was?" he asked.

"Lonnie Long," Lee said.

"Oh, poor Lonnie," Trey said. "I bet he feels so bad about this. Has anyone talked to him?"

"You know Lonnie," Lee said. "He won't be in any condition to talk until he sobers up. It's a miracle he wasn't killed on impact."

"Any idea how bad Dad's hurt?" Trey asked, although he really didn't want to know.

"Trey, honey, I think we need to hope for the best and be prepared for the worst," his mother said, grasping his hand. "Doctor said one lung was pierced, and he has multiple head injuries. They couldn't tell us much more than that."

A little before midnight, as Trey and Lee were beginning to doze off, a surgeon entered the waiting room, knocking lightly on the door frame.

"Mrs. Glass, surgery is wrapping up. We'll be taking your husband to ICU for observation. We've yet to be able to determine his prognosis, probably be a few more hours. He's hurt pretty bad. We are most concerned about one of his head injuries and trauma around his heart. Thank goodness he's in good health, but we can't be real encouraging right now. I'll be back as soon as we know more."

"Thank you, Doctor. Please let us know as soon as you can," Trey said, his mother fighting tears again.

"You're in our prayers, Doc. Take care of our dad," Lee said.

"Mom, why don't you two go over to the house tonight and get some rest? I'll sit up here and wait for more information. I'll call you when I find out something," Trey said.

"There is no way I can leave him," she said passionately. "You have a game tomorrow, son; you need to get your rest. You and Lee go on home."

"I'm not leaving you here alone, Mom," Lee said.

"Me either," Trey said.

Trey had always considered his mom an extremely strong person, and he was surprised to see her so vulnerable. She held tightly to her sons' hands and shed more tears in those hours than he'd ever seen before. The three prayed often through the night, pleading with God to spare this good man, taking great care not to dishonor God with selfish demands.

"Your will be done..." his mother said repeatedly.

In their mid-fifties, Rebecca and Travis Glass were enjoying their first two grandchildren, both girls. Their three sons would agree that their mom and dad were the strongest Christians they had ever seen, a couple who lived out their faith with courage and love. They were not swayed by public opinion, political positions, or church doctrine; rather, they based their lives on the story of God they learned from the Bible that they studied often and from observing God at work in nature and in other people.

"Sometimes you have to look beyond scripture to find God's will for your life," Travis told his boys often. "God is at work now as he has been from the beginning. Sometimes what he says might seem a contradiction to what you've read in the Bible. So, let the Bible guide you, but listen for the voice of God."

Although Travis's teaching sometimes brought puzzled looks to his boys' faces, Adam, Lee, and Trey Glass had seen their parents' faith in action hundreds of times in the ways they cared for the people in Wayne County who needed help. The sons might forget the words, but they would never forget what they saw.

"You boys need to know that God is at work right under your noses every moment of every day," their dad would say. "Pay attention. There are no insignificant people, and there are no insignificant events. Everyone and everything has a purpose."

The sons sat wide-eyed as their father spelled it out.

"God is at work in storms and fires and illnesses. He is at work during good times; he is at work in difficult times. He is at work in churches and bars and fields and alleys. He is at work in beggars and sultans and kings. He is at work in good economic times and depressions. He is at work in wars and in peace. He is at work then and now and later. He is always at work, and he is always present. Nothing happens that escapes his notice. Nothing dies—bird, mammal, fish, plant, or planet—that doesn't get his attention."

Especially impressive to the three young men was what Travis said about the value of human beings.

"No one person or position has more importance in God's eyes than any other. He is not more impressed with famous preachers and basketball superstars than he is with gardeners or bookkeepers or panhandlers or dentists. He is not more in love with good people than he is with bad people. He is not less in love with bad people than he is with good people. He doesn't care if gays or kings or criminals or saints are born or created out of their circumstances; he loves all people the same. He can't love anyone more or less than he does right now. He doesn't love the unborn more or less than he loves the unborn's mother and father or the terminator of unborns," Travis would say.

Trey was particularly stirred when his dad talked about things that seemed to contradict what he heard at school or church.

"God is not a respecter of cultures or nations. There is no nation under the sun that deserves to carry his son's name; there are no nations or persons beyond the reach of his loving, outstretched arms," Travis would preach.

And perhaps what impacted Trey most was what his dad said about the worth of disenfranchised people. These lessons would become his major motivation later in life.

"Boys, scriptures seem to imply if God's heart is more tender for one group, that group would be the ones that society has forgotten. If his patience is stretched by one group, that group might be those who take advantage of others through a gang, government, or church. Just remember that the true spirit of Christianity is found in the life and words of Jesus Christ, specifically how he related to those who were shunned or rejected."

Trey sincerely believed that his dad was still needed on this earth, and he could not imagine what life would be like without his best friend and teacher.

The Glasses's long night stretched on.

CHAPTER 9

Word came to the family at 4:07 a.m. that Travis Glass died on the operating table.

Becky, Lee, and Trey were in the surgical waiting room when the same doctor they'd met earlier came to deliver the news, along with the hospital chaplain.

"I'm so sorry, Mrs. Glass," Reverend Cole said.

"Your husband's injuries were just too extensive to repair," Dr. Grant said. "Dr. Shah and Dr. Lawson did their best; they are some of the most gifted surgeons in the Mid-South. Again, I'm so sorry."

"We will be nearby when you want to talk about next steps," Reverend Cole said softly.

For the next hour, the family was too shocked to move. The sons surrounded their mom and held her while she sobbed. Trey prayed and occasionally wiped tears from his eyes. His emotions spun from disbelief to shock to anger to deep sorrow. He wondered how he could go on without his dad.

When they were able, the three gathered Travis's personal items, signed the necessary papers, and moved to Trey's house, where they called Adam and, later that morning, close family friends. Then they set about to make funeral plans. Travis had always said he wanted to be cremated, and the family decided to have that done in Memphis.

"Trey, you don't know how sorry I am for your loss," Coach Rollins said. "I know Travis must have been a good man, judging from the good man he raised in you. Look, you take things one day at a time. The team is leaving for Phoenix on Wednesday. You can catch up with us when you're ready. Just keep me informed. Okay?"

"I'm really hoping I can leave with the team on Wednesday, Coach. I'll let you know. Thanks."

For the rest of the afternoon, the Glass family consoled one another, received calls from well-wishers, talked about the future, reminisced, and caught naps when they could. Long-time hometown friend and pastor, Charles Brandon, called Becky to express his sorrow and get her ideas for a memorial service.

Around noon, Tony Bradford arrived with a tray of Lenny's Deli sandwiches and two gallons of sweet tea.

"I went up to the hospital this morning early and was hit with the bad news," Tony said. "I met with the church and then rushed over here as soon as I could. We prayed long and loud for you all. How you doing, buddy?"

"Not good, man," Trey said. "I've always had this awareness of Dad in the back of my mind, that if I ever needed anything—advice or whatever—he would be there. Now, I just have this big hole. I really feel sorry for Mom; she's lost her friend and mate of thirty-three years. If there's been any time in our lives that we needed my dad, it's now."

"Yeah, that's tough," Pastor Tony said. "Just remember all that you've learned about God the Father, Trey. He's as close as your skin, and he has very big shoulders. Lean on him; he can take all your weight. You can even get mad at him if you need to. Sometimes it helps to have a close friend you can yell at and know that friend won't ever leave you."

Tony stayed about an hour and left, promising to check in with the family periodically.

The Rockers game was already into the second quarter when Trey first thought about turning it on and checking on his team. His mom was resting, and Lee had just awakened from a three-hour nap. The two brothers sat and watched as the Rockers took a twelve-point lead into halftime.

"Looks like they don't need me today," Trey said.

"I was just thinking the same thing," Lee said jokingly. It was the first time the brothers had laughed that day.

"Hey, that sounded like something Dad would say," Trey said, smiling as a tear escaped from his left eye.

With eight minutes left in the game and the Rockers up by thirteen, Trey's mom came into the large den where her sons were watching the game. Trey reached for the remote to turn it off, but his mom wouldn't hear of it.

"You boys just sit there and enjoy the game. I'm going to bring some sandwiches in here. You must be hungry; I sure am." She returned with a tray of food and drinks just as the buzzer sounded, marking another "W" for the home team. Rockers 87, Pistons 77. The three munched sub sandwiches and watched the post-game show. Several references were made about Trey Glass losing his dad overnight, and the Rockers' broadcast team expressed their sympathy to Trey and the family. During the post-game interview, Coach Rollins repeated the sad news to explain the absence of his new star player.

"Fans can expect more wins as the team gears up for the playoffs," Coach Rollins said, completing the post-game interview with confidence.

"Well, every Rockers fan knows about Dad now," Lee said.

"I just wish every Rockers fan could have known him," Trey said, his voice cracking.

"They will know him well enough just by knowing you," his mother said. "All my sons reflect both fathers in wonderful ways. Dad was certainly proud of you boys, and I'm sure that goes for the Heavenly Father as well."

In the quiet, Becky let the ready tears come easy. Trey couldn't contain his sorrow any longer, and soon the three sat crying and comforting each other over their loss.

On Monday afternoon, after receiving Travis's ashes in a bronze urn, Trey drove his mom and brother back home to Wayne County. Travis Glass's funeral was originally scheduled for Wednesday morning, but Becky decided to wait for Travis's brother to arrive from Arizona. Trey would not meet up with the team until later in the week. The funeral would be on Thursday.

Trey and Adam decided to handle their grief as they believed their father might have. On Tuesday morning, the two Glass brothers attended the arraignment of Lonnie Long at the Wayne County Courthouse, where he was charged with public drunkenness and one count of vehicular homicide. Lonnie entered the courtroom dressed in a white prison jumpsuit, accompanied by his court-appointed attorney. For a brief moment, Trey caught the eye of his dad's killer and offered a smile before Lonnie looked away. After the charges were read, the judge asked Lonnie how he pleaded.

"Guilty, Your Honor," Lonnie responded in a near whisper.

"Can you imagine carrying the guilt of being responsible for someone's death?" Adam asked, leaning over to his brother. "That man needs a friend."

The judge set the date for sentencing Lonnie for May 13.

"Man, that's right in the middle of playoffs," Trey whispered. "I might not be able to make it."

"Could you visit him sooner?" Adam asked.

"I'll try."

Several hundred friends and family gathered in the small Belle Street Church on a partly cloudy Thursday morning to remember their friend, father, husband, and grandpa, Travis Glass. The bronze urn holding Travis's remains stood on a pedestal amid dozens of floral arrangements. Next to the pedestal was a small table that displayed photos of the Glass family. The Rockers were represented by Brett Bing, who expressed the team's deepest sorrow over Mr. Glass's passing. Among the flowers was an elaborate spray from the Memphis Rockers.

Reverend Charles Brandon gave his tender eulogy of a man most people in the county knew and respected. A small choir offered a few traditional hymns, and one of the members led the congregation in singing Travis's favorite hymn, "Amazing Grace."

Each of the sons gave short tributes to their father. Trey was last and encouraged everyone to remember Lonnie Long, the driver responsible for Travis's death, and his family.

"This is a very difficult time for Lonnie, as you could imagine. Please pray for Lonnie, and when you can, offer an encouraging word to Mrs. Long. My dad would've been over there this morning with groceries and flowers to make sure that family knows they are loved. He would've said something like, 'Mrs. Long, Jesus knows we are bigger than our biggest mistake,' or, 'There's no mistake that God can't forgive.' And he'd probably find a way to worm his way into the county jail to see Lonnie and tell him the same thing."

The congregation laughed, and hearty "amens" rang throughout the crowded room.

"I think the best way we can honor my dad is to try to live like he lived. That's my aim. And if any of you ever see me doing something that my dad wouldn't do, you jump on my case."

By then, tears were streaming down Trey's cheeks.

"I love you, Dad, and I'll see you soon."

After the funeral and a sumptuous lunch provided by the ladies of the church, Trey said goodbye to his family and drove back to Memphis. Ordinarily, he would take more time off to comfort his family, but his mom made it clear that Travis would want him on the court, doing what he did best. He planned to catch the first flight out to Denver the next morning, so he did laundry, started packing, and called Tyler.

"How did things go today?" Tyler asked.

"Pretty good, I guess," Trey said. "I really hated to leave Mom."

"Good thing she has two other sons nearby," Tyler said. "Have you ever thought about moving her over here?"

"I have. One reason I bought this big old house was to have room for her and Dad to visit, maybe even live here when they thought the time was right. Right now, she needs her friends there. But we'll see. Hey, I'm leaving tomorrow morning for about a week," he said, changing the subject. "Can you check on things around here while I'm gone?"

"You bet," Tyler said. "Hope you guys win all your games. And why not give your doctor friend a shout before you leave? She would probably love to hear from you and offer her condolences."

"I don't know how to get in touch with her."

"Yes you do, you big turkey," Tyler said laughingly. "She left her number on the card she wrote. It's on the kitchen counter."

"If I didn't know better, I'd say you're promoting this relationship."

"Ya think?" Tyler said, still chuckling. "I'll see you when you get back. Don't worry about a thing."

Trey hung up, knowing that things would be well taken care of while he was on the road.

On the basketball court, Trey Glass wasn't afraid of anything. He could charge seven-foot giants knowing there would be pain and not flinch. He was cool as ice at the foul line in front of thirty-thousand screaming fans when the game was on the line. But picking up his cell phone to call a woman who obviously wanted to hear from him was almost more than he could handle. On his third attempt, he heard her phone ringing.

Oh man, he sighed, *what if she answers?*

"Hello?"

"Uh, hello," he stammered. "Dr. Garza? I mean, Cristina?"

"Yes, it is. Who is this, please?"

Long silence. Trey couldn't think or speak or even breathe.

"Hello?" she repeated.

"Cristina, this is Trey Glass, the guy you patched up in the hospital?" he said. "I'm sorry if I'm bothering you. Maybe I should call back—"

"Oh, Trey, no, this is fine. Great to hear from you." She sounded friendlier than when she had first answered. "I just wasn't sure who this was, that's all."

"Yeah, well, it's me, Trey Glass," he said, repeating himself nervously. "I just wanted to thank you for the note you left me and to say I saw you at the Mavericks game."

"Oh, you're welcome. The note was Angie's idea. Not that I didn't want to send it, but she put me up to it. Kind of brazen, wasn't it?"

"My chef and I thought it was nice," Trey said, feeling more at ease.

"Your chef saw it? Oh dear," she said, sighing. "Hey, I was so sorry to hear about your dad. That's awful. How are you doing?"

"I'm doing okay. I'm not sure it's really hit me yet, but I think getting back in a routine will help."

"He must have been a wonderful man," she said softly. "Is there anything I can do?"

"Thanks, but I think time will be the best healer. By the way, speaking of healing, my head is doing really well."

"I'm glad," she said. "And how is the rest of your family getting along?"

"Pretty good. It's going to be really hard on my mom for a while. She and Dad were very close. We're going to miss him a lot. We just talked last week about him and Mom coming over for a game. Guess he'll have to watch me from the skybox on high."

"Aww, guess so," Cristina said, her voice warm and kind.

After an awkward silence, Trey said, "Well, I guess I'll be seeing you at some games, huh?"

"Sure," she said. "I try to get to every one my schedule allows."

"Hey, I don't want to pry or anything, but did I see you with a guy at the Mavs game?"

"That was Antonio. We have known each other for years. I love him a lot."

Trey sat in silence, mustering up a soft, "Oh," in response.

"Yeah, Antonio is my little brother," she said, giggling, "although he's not so little."

"Oh!" Trey said, a little more upbeat. "Your brother. Well, good. Yeah, he looked like he could play football."

"He played three years at U of M before he got hurt. Now he's working on his MBA and volunteering at the Boys and Girls Club. I'd like for you to meet him sometime. He thinks you're a great player."

"I'd like to meet him. Maybe we could all go out to dinner," Trey said, his confidence building.

"Just say the word, I'll work out the arrangements with Tonio. Looks like you're going to be out of town for the next few days."

"Yeah, I'm meeting the team in Denver tomorrow, and then we have five games away before coming home. We have two days off when we get back, so maybe we could get together then?"

"I'd like that a lot, Trey," she said.

"Why don't I call you when we get back, and we'll pick a time to go out? Sound good?"

"Okay," she said. "I'll be praying that God blesses you with peace and comfort while you're away from your family. I'll be thinking about you."

"Thanks, Cristina," he said, his heart racing. "I look forward to seeing you when I get back. Try to watch the games."

"You can bet I will," she said.

"See ya."

"Bye, Trey. And thanks for calling."

Trey finished packing, showered, and went to bed earlier than usual. He had trouble falling asleep, and it wasn't because of basketball.

CHAPTER 10

Despite the distractions in Trey's life, his outstanding performances helped the Rockers to a 5-1 road record. The only game the team lost was the first one, the one that he missed while traveling to catch up with his teammates.

The new offense was working, and it was obvious to all that the one who made it work was Trey Glass. As a result, Trey enjoyed greater respect from his coaches, his teammates, and even opposing players. He was quickly becoming a celebrity around Memphis, but success had its disadvantages, and Trey found it more difficult to move about the city—eating out, going to movies, shopping—without attracting autograph hounds and adoring women, some of whom offered more than he was willing to take. He felt most at ease among the folks in his humble neighborhood who let him come and go in peace. He still enjoyed undisturbed evening walks up and down the streets near his house and often stopped to talk to familiar neighbors or meet new ones.

Charlie and Precious Smit lived three streets over and often sat in rocking chairs on the front porch of their small, well-kept house. Trey had seen them when he passed by and waved, but he had never stopped because Charlie was most often asleep in his chair. This evening was different. Trey left the sidewalk and made his way up a gravel path toward the Smits' porch.

"Hey," he said.

"Hey, yourself," the elderly black man responded with a chuckle.

"I'm Trey Glass, and I live over on Handy. Just thought I'd say hello."

"And I'm Charlie. Precious is somewhere 'round here," the old man said. "You kind of stick out in this area, don't you, boy?" Charlie's dark eyes twinkled, as though a thousand stars were nestled in the brown pools of his irises.

"You mean 'cause I'm so tall?" Trey asked in jest.

"Yeah. What are you, seven foot?" Charlie said, playing along.

"Six foot seven in my socks. I'm hoping people won't look down on me because of my height," Trey said, amused at his own pun.

"We seen people your size around here before, nothing but trouble," Charlie said with a loud laugh, slapping his knee at his own joke. "Come on up here and take a sit," he said, patting the rocker where Precious usually sat.

Trey opened the small wooden gate and walked up three steps and onto the porch, where he took a seat next to his new friend.

"How long you been in this neighborhood, Charlie, if you don't mind me asking?" Trey asked.

"Let's see, Precious would probably correct me, so I'll take a guess before she gets out here. I'm seventy-nine years old, so that would make...let's see...carry the one...," he said, looking up as if he were doing math in his head. "About seventy-nine years," he said.

"Wow, you've probably seen a lot of changes over the years."

"You wouldn't believe, son. Some good, some not so good. You see that vacant lot over there?" Charlie asked, pointing across the street. "I was sitting right here when some misguided young folks set fire to the house that sat there the very night Dr. King was shot back in '68. I didn't sleep all night; sat right here, fearin' someone might try to burn my house down too. That was quite a time," he said, staring into the distance.

Trey heard shuffling behind him and turned to see Charlie's wife, Precious, coming out the door with a tray of lemonade.

"Thought you was out here talking to yourself...again. Imagined I'd better come out and check on you, and I brought some refreshments," Precious said, speaking to no one in particular as she sat the tray on a small table at one end of the porch.

Trey jumped up to offer the elderly lady her rightful seat.

"You jus' sit right back down there, young man. I has me a seat over here I'll take." He helped her move a rusty, old lawn chair closer to where the men were sitting.

"This here's my precious wife, Precious," Charlie said with a smile.

"He'd better say that," she said, faking a scowl.

"I'm Trey Glass, ma'am," he said, wondering if she were as angry as she sounded.

"I know who you are. We was sorry to hear about your daddy," she said as she patted his hand.

"Thank you, ma'am. I'm really going to miss him."

"The Lord gives and the Lord takes away," Precious said. "Blessed be the name of the Lord because everything the Lord does is blessed."

"Now, Precious, don't you go to preachin'," Charlie warned, half kidding. "From what I hear, it wasn't the good Lord what's took this young man's daddy away. Sounds to me more like the devil got into someone who thought they could drink too much alcohol and drive an automobile at the same time."

A brief silence hung over the elderly couple and the young basketball star. As they sipped their lemonade, watching the sun sink into the horizon, tree frogs called from their perches in the surrounding trees.

"You know, we was talking about changes we've seen over the years. Tell you what, Trey, there's nothing like neighbors to help you through whatever comes your way. And when folks know that you're with them for the long haul, they's nothing they wouldn't do for you—nor you for them. There was several times we couldn't have made it if we didn't have the good folks around us, right, Precious?"

"Sure is true," she said, nodding her head. "And it don't hurt to have a good wife, right, Charlie?"

Trey chuckled at the couple's banter; he recognized instantly how comfortable they were with each other, just as his own mom and dad had been—the type of relationship he wished for himself someday.

"There's something to be said about moving to a neighborhood and staying put. Neighbors can be more valuable than church folks, I've found," Charlie said.

"How's that, Charlie?" Trey asked; he knew he felt the same way but had never considered why.

"Well, in most cases, you sees church folks just once a week, all dressed up and looking their finest. When you're with 'em, you most likely be staring at the back of their head most of the time. You says hello when you sees 'em, you says goodbye when you leaves 'em, and you don't see 'em again till the next week. What kind of commitment is that? But neighbors, you see 'em all the time. You see 'em when they's looking good, and you see 'em when they's looking bad. They're the ones who comes to see you when you're sick or to help you when your tool shed catches fire. They help you deliver your babies, and they're here when you bury your aunties. Makes sense, don't it, to pour more attention on your neighbors than the folks you work with or go to church with? I don't—"

"Now who's preachin'?" Precious said, chuckling.

"I'm just saying…" Charlie concluded.

"I think you're right, Charlie," Trey said. "I've been kind of concerned about my church being so far away that I have to drive some distance to see everyone. Makes more sense for my church to be the folks right here in our little community. I'd like to talk to you more about that sometime. Right now I need to be getting on. I have practice tomorrow morning early. So glad to meet you both. Thanks for the lemonade, Ms. Precious." Trey stood and placed his empty glass back on the tray.

"I think God has you here for a reason, young man," Precious said, a serious tone in her words.

"You know where we live, Trey. Don't make yourself a stranger, you hear?" Charlie said, rising to his feet. He reached out to the young man and shook his hand boisterously. Precious had made her way down to the sidewalk, leading Trey down the path.

"I'll come to see you again real soon. You two have a good evening."

As she reached for the latch on the gate, Trey standing behind her, she paused, then turned around, eyes locking with Trey's.

"You take care of yourself, honey boy, you hear?" she said as a single tear dropped onto her cheek. She turned and let him out the gate, and Trey began his walk home.

"Wonder what that was about?" he muttered under his breath, recounting the evening's conversation and missing his parents more than ever.

Trey slipped the key in the lock, let himself inside, and shut the door tightly behind him, dropping his keys and cell phone on the kitchen table. His home was quiet—more quiet than it had seemed in a while. As he looked around the room, his eyes fell on the phone; in that moment, he decided to make a phone call.

"Trey, hello!" Cristina said, her voice cheerful.

"Hey, what's up?" he said after she answered.

"You had quite a road trip, didn't you?"

"Guess so," he said modestly.

"Guess so?" she said. "You averaged twenty-seven points and three assists over five games, including a three at the buzzer to beat Utah. I'd say that was a pretty good series...not that I was interested or anything."

"Not interested, huh?" Trey asked laughingly, glad Cristina could not see the blush overcoming his cheeks. "Enough about me, Cristina; how are you?"

"Good. Been working a lot lately. Just finished seven days in a row, and I'm ready for a break. When are you free for dinner?"

"How about tomorrow night? You think Antonio would like to join us?" Trey asked.

"I'm sure he would. He's asked me about it nearly every day." She laughed. "I'd like for everyone to come over to my condo. I'll cook, that way we won't be heckled by your zillion fans."

"*Zillion fans?*" he said. "Ha! I don't think so. Sounds good to me. What can I bring?"

"Nothing this time. Just come and relax. Do you drink wine?"

"Not during the season, but I'll gladly pick up a bottle or two for everyone else."

"Don't worry about it. I'll let Antonio take care of that. Tex-Mex?"

"My favorite. When and where?"

"Forty-three North Carter Street, near Le Bonheur Hospital's new wing, say around 6:00?

"That sounds good. You sure you want to do this?" Trey asked.

"Well, of course I do. Don't you?"

Trey, caught off guard, hesitated ever so slightly, the warmth in his cheeks rising again.

"Never wanted anything more. Good night, Cristina."

Trey leaned back in his chair, his thoughts racing. The beautiful doctor was never far from his mind. Before his thoughts could take him into dangerous territory, Trey stood and walked out the back door. The moon had risen overhead, its gentle glow illuminating the vast sky.

"Father, you are so good to me. You have blessed me far beyond what I deserve. You allow me to honor you with the special gifts you've given me. I am so thankful for all I have and the people you've put in my life. Please keep me humble. Please keep my mind focused on the important things, not the urgent things that push into my life every day.

"I pray for wisdom in my relationship with Cristina. She seems like a great person, and I don't want to mess things up. Take hold of my thoughts about her and help me focus on her inner beauty. And God, please help me resist the many temptations that come at me each day. Most of all, God, please forgive me of my sins, my idle thoughts and my careless actions. I stand completely in need of your mercy every moment. Thank you for your unbelievable grace. You are wonderful. Thank you, Jesus. Amen."

CHAPTER 11

"Well, I called her," Trey said.

Tyler, standing over the kitchen stove, was stirring vigorously.

"You didn't! What'd she say?" Tyler asked, whipping around, skillet in hand.

"None of your business," Trey said, grinning broadly. "Except that she invited me to dinner tonight."

"Boy, you are gaining ground by the day."

"We shouldn't get our hopes up," Trey said. "It may turn out neither one of us is interested, you know, once we get to know each other. Besides, as soon as she finishes her internship, she's probably out of here."

"You know, you have a real way of sucking the joy out of potentially wonderful things," Tyler said, feigning annoyance. "No supper tonight?"

"We're having Tex-Mex," Trey said. "And I think I'll drive over and see Mom tomorrow. Short visit, but I need to see her, so no meals needed tomorrow."

"You should go, and be sure and tell her about your doctor friend. Maybe it will cheer her up," Tyler said. "Good luck, champ."

At a quarter to nine, Trey headed for the gym. Practice wasn't as strenuous as Trey had expected. Coach Rollins was feeling good about how the team was playing these days. The Rockers would need to win six of the remaining ten games to make the playoffs, and most of the teams left to play were struggling. Still, he warned his guys to maintain their season regimen of enough sleep, healthy diet, and wise personal habits.

When he got home, he found the lunch that Tyler had prepared. He ate while searching the Internet on his laptop for helping agencies in Memphis. Over the next hour, Trey put together a list of agencies that provided free meals, housing, medical care, addiction counseling, and clothing—with addresses, phone numbers, and contact persons—and printed out twenty copies for the next time he encountered a beggar.

Next, he called and instructed his accountant to send a thousand dollars a month to six different nonprofits he had chosen that were dedicated to helping homeless or indigent men and women. He promised himself he would increase those amounts after he had a chance to better understand each agency's mission and effectiveness.

At 5:58 that evening, Trey stood in front of 43 North Carter, gripping a bouquet of spring flowers as sweat dripped down his back.

Cristina opened the door, and Trey nearly gasped.

Jesus, she is beautiful, he thought, a sincere expression of wonder and gratitude.

"Come in, Trey," she said, hugging her much taller guest.

She smelled good too.

"For me?" she asked, gesturing at the flowers.

"Actually, they're for Antonio," he said, smiling.

"So maybe the tabloids *are* true," she said.

"Don't start," he said laughingly.

"Antonio's going to be a little late, as usual," she said, accepting the bouquet. "Thanks so much. These are beautiful. Make yourself at home while I get a vase."

Trey walked around the small but neat living room, looking at the many framed photos that sat on tables and hung on walls. He could easily distinguish her family members from her friends and was impressed by their apparent closeness.

"Is this your entire family?" he asked as Cristina returned with the vase of fresh flowers.

"Yeah. That was taken at my med school graduation reception down by the river last year. That's my mom, that's my dad. This is Maria and Sara and Daniela and Ana. This is Alex and Ricardo and Antonio. And that's me," she said, pointing to each one as she moved closer to Trey. He was trying hard to concentrate but was distracted by her nearness. "Most of my family lives in Texas."

"Nice," he said, at a loss for words.

"Here, have a seat," she said, walking over to the sofa. "How's the head doing? Mind if I look?"

"No, help yourself," he said, sitting down.

Cristina traced the faint scar with her finger, which created stirrings deep within him. Every other time he fell for a girl, sex soon became the center of their relationship. He knew there was something special about this one, and he vowed to keep the physical in check...if he could.

"Yeah, looks great. Can hardly see a scar. Must've been a great doctor."

"Must have been," he said with a laugh. "So, tell me about yourself," he said, grimacing as the question escaped his mouth. *Geez, a pickup line?* he thought to himself.

"What do you want to know?"

"Everything," he said. "What's your family like? What are your hobbies? Why Memphis? Everything."

"Well, let's see, where do I start? I love my family. We've always been close. My dad's a contractor; my mom's a nurse, although she's taken lots of time off from time to time to raise us kids. I went to Texas A&M because it was close to home. I came to Memphis to med school because Antonio was here. I like hiking, eating out, photography, writing, sports, and eating out," she said with a girlish giggle.

Trey was enraptured by her story, perhaps because it was so much like his own, especially the part about her close family.

She's beautiful, he thought again as he mentally traced the lines of her body through her soft yellow top and short navy skirt.

"What are your long-term plans?" he asked, trying to keep his mind off less noble things.

"I eventually want to go back to Texas. There are so many poor Latinos down there who don't have adequate healthcare. A large Catholic charity in Houston is begging doctors to come help them help the poor."

Just as his mind was about to drift again, the doorbell rang.

"It's open!" she yelled from the sofa. Antonio entered wearing a Rockers jersey—number 32, *Glass* printed on the back—and carrying two bottles of wine.

"Dude!" he exclaimed and gave Trey a bear hug as though they had known each other their entire lives.

"Tonio, this is Trey," his sister said.

"I know, man," he said. "This is so cool!"

"Hey, Antonio. What's happening?" Trey said.

"I've been waiting for this chance to meet you for weeks."

"Me too," Trey said.

"He brought you these flowers," Cristina said, pointing to the vase on the coffee table.

"Aw, man, you didn't have to do that." They laughed as Cristina took the two wine bottles from her brother's arms.

"You two get to know each other. I'm going to get things ready for supper," Cristina said, walking into the kitchen.

"So, Cristina said you are working on an MBA?" Trey asked.

"It's working on me," Antonio said, shaking his head. "Toughest thing I've ever done. Got one more year, if I can handle it."

For the next few minutes, the guys discussed Antonio's college football career, Trey's basketball career, and the upcoming playoffs. It was clear that Antonio idolized Trey Glass and made frequent references to great plays he had seen the Rockers' starting point guard make this year. Trey was a bit embarrassed and tried several times to redirect the conversation, but to no avail. They laughed about Trey confusing Antonio for Cristina's boyfriend, then even more as Trey described his plan to win her over, worried—but not much—over repercussions from an angry, jilted boyfriend.

"Dinner's ready," Cristina said, emerging from the kitchen, a dish towel in her hands. Antonio and Trey made their way to the small dining table in the corner of the kitchen as Cristina pulled steaming enchiladas from the oven.

"Trey, please sit here," she said, indicating a seat at the table.

Antonio reached for a bottle of wine and began to open it deftly.

"Water's good for me," Trey said as Antonio reached over to fill his glass. "Season's still going."

"Right," Antonio said, understanding Trey immediately. "Gotta stay in tip-top shape to get to the playoffs."

The three dug into their meals and enjoyed both good food and good conversation, dominated by exuberant Antonio. Every once in a while, Trey snuck a quick glance at his hostess, and once or twice he caught her looking back at him. She smiled each time their eyes met. If she hadn't swept him off his feet by now, she was well into the process.

An hour later, Antonio was still talking.

"So then I told him that we need to focus on the receiver—"

"Antonio, don't you have some studying to do?" Cristina asked, smiling slyly.

"No, I'm fine…all caught up," he said but soon realized that was the wrong answer; he abruptly stood up from the table. "But I do have a busy day tomorrow, so I'd better be going. Great to meet you, Trey. I'll see you at the Forum. And another great meal, sis," he said, kissing Cristina on the cheek.

Cristina and Trey followed Antonio into the living room.

"Nice to meet you, Antonio," Trey said.

After the door shut, Trey and Cristina were left alone.

"How about some coffee?" Cristina asked. "I have decaf."

"I could eat some more cobbler and ice cream too," Trey said. He had never had peach cobbler that could compare with his mother's, but Cristina's recipe was a very good contender.

Bowls and coffee mugs in hand, Cristina and Trey sat close on the couch in the living room, laughing about childhood mishaps, crazed basketball fans, and unbelievable experiences in the ER.

In the middle of their conversation, Cristina's cell phone rang. She glanced at the Caller ID and said, "I'll be just a second," as she stood and retreated to the hallway.

Trey's ears perked as he heard snippets of her hushed conversation.

"No, he's still here… Yeah… I don't know, probably… Angie, I'll tell you later… Gotta go."

"Nosey coworker?" he asked, as she reentered the living room.

"Oh brother, you wouldn't believe," she said. "You may as well know, you are the talk of the ER at the Med. And please know that I don't kiss and tell." She giggled nervously, realizing what she had said.

"I believe you. But let me ask you something, if I weren't a basketball player, would I be sitting here tonight?"

Cristina thought for a moment, looking intently into his eyes.

"Can't say. Maybe. When you came into the ER, I did not see a basketball star; I sensed a warm, friendly man who was humble and kind and grateful, even though he had reason to be angry and scared and belligerent. Okay," she said with a wry smile, "I also saw a very cute guy."

Trey smiled, embarrassed.

"And I want you to know that it was Angie's idea to make the follow-up call. And send you the note. And—"

"So you didn't really want to pursue this?" he wondered aloud.

"I didn't say that. Actually, I was kind of glad Angie pushed me, or else we would never have gotten to know each other. Right?"

"Maybe, although I was trying to figure out a way to meet you without seeming too forward. And my friend Tyler, well, let's just say he's as crazy as Angie," Trey said, laughing. "I'm glad it worked out this way."

"Me too," she said softly.

Trey could feel the sexual tension increasing. For an instant, he imagined his lips on hers and thought he detected a slight willingness on her part. She laid her hand on the couch near his. As he adjusted his position, he wondered if he was hoping for something that wasn't yet there.

"How long you been a basketball fan?" Trey said, moving to a more familiar subject.

"Since I can remember. My dad was a big Spurs fan when I was growing up, and he used to take my brothers and me to games while my sisters and mom went shopping."

"So you're close to your family, who, for the most part, are in Texas, and you're here. How much longer will you be in Memphis?" Trey asked warily.

"Depends on what I decide about a residency. I'm thinking about staying here and doing a residency in internal medicine. I've even thought about a master's in hospital administration. I could be here another few years."

"That's good," he said.

"And what about you? How long do you plan to be here?" she asked.

"I hope to retire here."

"Can't they trade you at any time?"

"Yeah, but that doesn't mean I have to go. I've already earned enough money to keep me fed for life," he said with a chuckle. "Besides, I don't think I want to leave Mom any time soon. I'm hoping she will come live with me when she's able. But I trust God to put me where he wants me, so, in a sense, it's not up to me."

"Your faith is pretty important to you, isn't it?" Cristina asked.

"My faith—rather, my *God* is my life," he said. "What about you, Cristina? Where are you and God?"

"Born and raised Catholic. Mass was very important growing up. I'm still a believer, but I don't practice my faith as I should," she said.

"Who does? I'm just thankful for a Father who wants to be my friend and is there no matter what happens. He's really helped me through Dad's death. I can't imagine being a professional ballplayer and not having God by my side."

"Maybe that's what's different about you. I'd like to know more about your relationship with him. You talk about God like he's a real person, a real friend."

"Well, he is," Trey said. "I grew up hearing these great stories about Jesus and thinking, *Man, I want to be like him.* I'd like to treat everyone I meet just like he did. I'm especially impressed with how much he cared for people without a voice. See, I could see Jesus moving to Texas to take care of poor people who don't have healthcare."

"I never thought of him like that," Cristina admitted. "Mass was more of a ritual than something that really worked in a person's life. I think my models for how a person is supposed to live are my parents. Thank God they're good people. I'd like to know more about your faith, Trey. It seems to work pretty well for you."

"I'm thankful for good models too," he said. "I owe them everything for what I am and what I become. I'd love to tell you more, but hey, I really have to go. I told Mom I'd visit tomorrow, and I'll need to leave early in the morning if I'm going to make the trip in one day."

"Oh, no worry. I'm so glad you came over."

"Yeah, it was nice. Thanks for the food. It was great. And I really liked meeting your brother and talking to you," he said.

"We'll have to do it again," she said.

"Of course. Maybe next time it can be at my house. Tyler's a great cook too. You could even bring Antonio."

"Or not," she said with a smile.

"Or not," he said. "Goodbye, Cristina. And thanks."

Trey reached out and grasped Cristina's hand. She squeezed and patted it. It was all he could do not to pull her close and kiss her.

"My pleasure," she whispered, waiting for him to do more. "Hope your mom's okay," she finally said.

"Thanks. Mind if I call you when I get back?"

"I'd be sad if you didn't," she said, smiling coyly.

"Good night," he said as he walked out the door.

The Memphis air felt warm against his face as he walked toward his car.

"God, thank you for Cristina," he muttered. He never remembered feeling this way about a girl. He liked the feeling.

CHAPTER 12

After the three-hour drive back to his hometown, the first place Trey stopped was the Wayne County Justice Center. Jail officials told Trey he had to have the prisoner's consent to visit, and, as of yet, Trey Glass was not on Lonnie Long's visitors list. Trey sat in his car and dialed Averill Jenkins, Lonnie's attorney.

"Is Mr. Jenkins in?"

"Yes, sir. May I say who's calling?"

"This is Trey Glass."

"Hold, please."

"You guys gonna make the playoffs?" The booming voice of Attorney Averill Jenkins soon came through the phone.

"Gonna give it our best shot," Trey said.

"Well, I got my money on you through the first round. Not sure you can go much farther. You boys need a more aggressive middle," Jenkins said. "But I bet you didn't call to talk basketball, did you?"

"No, sir, I didn't. I was calling to see if you would ask Lonnie if I can come see him."

"If it were anybody else, I'd say, 'No, sir, you can't see my client.' If it were anybody else, I'd think you were up to something. It's not every day that a family member wants to see the man who will stand trial for allegedly killing that person's loved one," the bristly lawyer said. "But just so I have this straight, what you want to see Lonnie about?"

"Nothing special. I just figure he needs a friend right now. I want to tell him our family forgives him and offer to help in any way I can."

"That's what I thought. I'll see him tomorrow, and I'll ask him. By the way, Trey," the attorney said, changing his tone, "I thought your daddy was one of the real class acts in these parts. I always liked Travis and was sad to learn of his passing. How's your momma and them?"

"She's doing okay. She's the reason I'm here now, checking on her. It was a real blow when she lost Dad," Trey said, his emotions rising.

"Well, you tell her I asked about her, will ya? I'd say the next time you're up here, your name will be on the visitors list. Lonnie is feeling real bad about all of this. I'll tell him he needs to see you. Anything else, Trey?"

"No, sir. Thanks."

"You bet. I'll be talking to ya, hear?"

"Yes, sir."

Trey sat at the kitchen table as Becky Glass made chicken salad for lunch. They talked about Travis, his will, how Adam and Lee were doing, and how his mom was coping without her soul mate.

"Mom, would you consider coming to live with me in Memphis?" he asked between bites. "I mean, at the right time."

"Oh, I don't know, Trey-boy. This place is all I've known. All my friends are here, my grandkids, my memories…" She stopped and looked out the back door, thinking. "They all need me," she said seriously.

Trey chuckled to himself, knowing she needed them far more than they needed her. He decided to let it go for now.

"Momma, I think I have a girlfriend," he said, finally having summoned the nerve.

"Well, that's wonderful!" Becky said with delight. "Who is she?"

"She's a doctor at the hospital where I had my head sewn up. In fact, she's the one who sewed me up. Her name is Cristina, and she's really nice. She had me over for dinner last night."

"I think that's great, Trey. I've been telling you and Lee for a long time that you both need to find good women. Life's too short not to have someone to share it with."

Tears began to well up in her eyes as thoughts of Travis overwhelmed her.

"Yeah, and she's from a real big family in Texas. Her brother is in school in Memphis and used to play college football before he got hurt. He really likes me. They come to nearly all the Rockers' games—Cristina and him. And she's a great cook; not as good as you, but she can cook. We had homemade enchiladas last night. I told her she and you would hit it off."

"How is your head anyway, Trey-boy? Lord, I don't know why I didn't ask about that sooner."

"It's fine, Mom. Haven't had a bandage on it for a while now."

"Any word on the guys who jumped you?" she asked.

"Nothing. And I don't expect any. I've gone by the warehouse a couple of times, but I haven't seen anyone I could ask. Good thing Cloe didn't spend a lot on that pinkie ring. We'll never see that again. I'd like to find the guys, so I could see if they needed some help.

"I met this older couple who live a few streets away. Been in the neighborhood almost eighty years. I think they're people of peace because they talk about how important neighbors are and how they couldn't have gotten through some tough times without their friends and God. And they seem to be a little burnt out on church—kind of unusual for a couple their age. I think you'd like them too," he said. "Oh and Mom, my friend Pastor Tony is bringing over some kids from the neighborhood tomorrow morning to start a garden in my yard. I thought this would be something you'd like to help with since you're so good at gardening and all, you know, if you move to Memphis."

He wondered if it might be time to put the move issue to rest for a while.

"How long can you stay?" Becky asked.

"I've got to get back tonight," he said. "We start a three-game series at home tomorrow night then hit the road for a few games. We've got to win six of our next ten games to make the playoffs. And if we do that, I'll be very busy until we get knocked out or win it all. Might not get back over here until June, but you can visit me any time," he said intently. "Get Lee to bring you over for a game. You could stay for a while, and he could pick you up later."

"That might work out," she said, much to his surprise. "I'll talk about it with the boys. You want more tea?"

"No, I'm fine," he said, pushing himself away from the table. "Want to go with me over to Adam's? I think Cloe and Madison need a good tickle before I head home. Oh, and if I give you the money, would you mind picking up some hams and taking them to Reverend Kimbrough? I guess he still has a mission church down in the Pinker district, doesn't he?"

"Oh, honey, that'd be so nice. I'd love to. He and Kathryn do such good work down there. They could sure use those hams."

"And Mom, think about what I said about moving to Memphis. There's no hurry, but I could sure use you there, when you're ready to make the move."

He could tell she was pondering the option, but he knew the choice was hers alone. And he knew it was a big step for someone who had lived their entire life in Waynesboro.

"Hey," Trey said, calling from a rest area ten miles from Memphis.

"Hey yourself. What are you doing?" Cristina's voice was warm on the other end of the phone.

"Just getting into town from visiting Mom and wondered if you wanted to grab something to eat." He grimaced, waiting for her excuse.

"Yeah, I'd love to."

"I'm about thirty minutes away. Mind if I pick you up then?"

"Sure. I'll be waiting," she said.

Not since high school when blonde-haired, blue-eyed Sarah Balch first stole his heart had he felt this way. He couldn't stop thinking about Cristina and wanted to be with her every moment he could. Something about his newest love aroused the best and worst in him, yet he was determined not to let the worst take over. He offered little prayers throughout the day that God would help him navigate the dangerous tides swirling between young love and lust. He knew he was vulnerable, and he knew one mistake would spell the end of their relationship.

Cristina was sitting on the steps of her condo when Trey pulled up out front.

"You like barbecue?" he asked as she buckled her seatbelt.

"Love it."

"There's this little place outside of town that has great barbecue, and chances are no one will interrupt us," Trey said as modestly as he could.

"We'll see," she said.

Sure enough, when the two walked in, nearly every eye in Bardeaux's Barbecue turned to look at the Rockers' point guard and his date, most of which were trained on Trey.

"Guess I was wrong," he whispered. "Want to go somewhere else?"

"No. This should be fun," she said with a wide grin.

The folks who had chosen Bardeaux's for dinner and the staff who served them were happy to have a celebrity in their midst. Only a few people, mostly young boys, had the gall to ask for Trey's autograph. Still, they all stared, which made conversation between the two difficult. After gobbling down their pork plates, Trey suggested they leave and find a quieter environment.

"Wow, that was exciting!" Cristina exclaimed once they were back in his car and headed for a park nearby. "You know that's just going to get worse, don't you?"

"I'm afraid so," he said. "You kind of wish God received the same attention. After all, whatever talents or skills a person has come from him. We don't do anything on our own except mess up."

Cristina reached over and took Trey's hand.

"I like you," she said and held his hand as they drove through the quiet park, looking for a place to stop. They found a place to pull over, got out, and walked to a picnic table that overlooked a small pond.

A young family fed ducks down below them, and the squeals of delight from the children prompted Trey to ask, "You have nieces and nephews?"

"Not a one," she answered, seemingly disappointed. "None of my siblings are married."

"I have two nieces," Trey said. "I can't wait to have my own children." He blushed at his words, fumbling to explain himself. "I just mean, I love kids, and, well, it will be nice to have some around all the time… you know, when the time is right…and I find the right person. I mean, you know, kids are fun and—"

"I know, I know," Cristina interrupted, laughing at his dilemma. "I know what you mean; you don't have to be embarrassed by that. In fact, you don't have to be embarrassed about anything with me." She reached for his hand and looked up into his eyes.

He squeezed her hand and returned her gaze.

"Look," he said, breathing in heavily, "you might as well know that this stuff is new to me. The kinds of girls I dated in high school were… well, let's just say they weren't like you. With sports and all, I just didn't take the time to date one girl steadily. So I'm just not sure what to do. It was all I could do to call you up tonight. I really like being with you, and—"

She leaned over and kissed his cheek.

"And I really like being with you, Trey. Don't worry about all of that. Let's just enjoy our time together and see where it goes. If you think I'm coming on too strong, please tell me. Let's just keep the lines of communication open and be honest with one another."

"Yeah, I think that's a good idea. What about you? Did you date a lot?" he asked.

"Yes," she said with reluctance, "but I can count on two fingers the guys I was really interested in. Guess I was too busy getting ready for med school. I think the boys thought I was too nerdy. And I've never felt as comfortable with anyone as I do with you. I know this: I don't want to be a distraction to your career. And if I don't hear from you for a while, I'll understand. You have some important weeks ahead. Just know I'll be thinking about you and pulling for you. Okay?"

Trey was entranced by Cristina's beautiful brown eyes.

Is this where I'm supposed to kiss her? He leaned in and found her responsive as she met him more than halfway, her eyes closed. The kiss lingered longer than he'd imagined.

"Mmm," he uttered, unaware.

"Yeah," she said.

The combination of her nearness, the night air, and Trey's passions increased the moment's tension.

God, are you hearing me? This is difficult, he thought as she pressed closer.

"Cristina," he gasped as he broke away and stood up. "Let's walk."

"Something wrong?" she asked.

"We want to be honest with each other, right?" he said, turning to face her. "Well, the truth is, I'm very attracted to you in *all* ways. And I don't want anything to spoil what's happening between us. I'm weak, Cristina. I need help with this."

She stood, took his hand, and they walked toward the lake.

"I told my parents about you," she finally said. "My little sisters are jealous that I'm dating a celebrity. My dad asked if I'm a Rockers fan. He's a big Spurs fan. I told him it was moving that way."

The two walked around the lake as the sun began to set. Trey wondered how Cristina was processing his inner turmoil.

Is she feeling it too? Does it matter to her? Do men and women deal with these things differently? Does she think I'm weird?

It was nearly dark when they arrived at Cristina's house. Trey walked her to the door and leaned down to kiss her cheek.

"I had a great time tonight," he said.

"Not as good as I had," she teased and stroked his cheek. "I'll look forward to the next time."

"Not as much as I will," he replied and turned toward his car. She waited until he was out of sight before she went inside.

God, how long can this continue?

CHAPTER 13

At nine the next morning, Tyler lightly tapped on Trey's bedroom door.

"Trey, Pastor Tony is here with several young men. He said you'd be expecting him."

"Tell him I'll be right down." Trey jumped out of bed, quickly put on a pair of blue jeans, a t-shirt, and sandals and then headed downstairs. When the boys saw Trey, they got quiet and gawked at him, awestruck.

"Hey, guys," Trey said.

"Gentlemen, this is Trey Glass, starting point guard for your next NBA Champions, Memphis Rockers!" Tony announced in his best faux radio voice and gave Trey a bear hug.

The five young men—ranging in age from fifteen to seventeen, Trey estimated—offered muffled greetings.

"Ready to do some gardening?" Trey asked, only to receive underwhelming responses. "Aw, come on, guys; this will be fun. But first, I need to know who you are."

Trey went boy by boy asking each one his name and age and shaking hands.

"I'm proud to know each of you and look forward to getting to know you better over the summer. As you know, we are working hard to make the playoffs, so I won't be around much for a while. But Tony here will keep me informed of how you're doing, and I'll check in here and there as time permits."

Trey showed Tony and the guys his ideas on the best spots for a garden, unlocked the storage room, and gave Tony a key. For the next hour, Trey helped the gardeners mark out and drive stakes at the corners of the plot. As he left to go inside, the boys were wrestling pitch forks to turn over the soil. Suddenly, he was back in time, recalling his own early farming experience.

"Trey. Trey...Trey," came the firm, familiar voice of Travis Glass. It was 4:00 a.m. "Hop up, son. Time to go."

For a month each spring, Travis dragged his three boys out of bed early in the morning to pick strawberries at a plot he rented two miles out in the county. By the time they dressed, ate breakfast, and arrived at the field, it was 5:30, which left two-and-a-half hours to pick, grade, and package fruit before school began at 8:00. On mornings when picking ran over and the boys were late for school, Travis would send two quarts of the largest, reddest berries with each son, hoping to appease their upset teachers.

"Mr. Glass, we can't have your sons late for school every day for a month. What in the world are you doing raising strawberries anyway?" Principal Harris said, unimpressed.

"I'm not raising strawberries," Travis said. "I'm raising boys."

Trey could smell the omelet before he walked through the back door. Tyler had been watching from the kitchen window and had breakfast ready just as his boss walked in.

"Paper's on the table," his chef said, nodding toward the front page. "Looks like your friend is being traded to the Jazz."

"What?" Trey exclaimed as he opened to the sports page.

"Warner to Jazz in three-way deal. Oh man, Gilbert is leaving."

Gilbert Warner was Trey's closest friend on the team. Both were rookies, about the same age, and had spent time in each other's homes during holidays. They had joked that each would be the other's best man at their weddings. And now, Trey was losing his best friend and away-games roommate.

As things worked, the deed was already done by the time it hit the newspaper. The two days off meant that Gilbert was probably already heading for his new team in Utah, leaving lots of unexpressed goodbyes.

The latest trade reminded Trey of the vicissitudes of life in the NBA; no one was guaranteed that life tomorrow would be as it is today. He took little comfort in knowing he would see Gilbert again when the Rockers played the Jazz. He would greatly miss his friend, and he wondered if a trade would ever happen to him.

The Rockers were gelling at the right time. They won all three home games then went north, where they lost to Chicago before easily beating Milwaukee. The game against the Indiana Pacers proved more of a challenge; the Rockers won after two overtimes. The rematch with the Oklahoma City Thunder—the last regular-season away game—was a disaster as the Rockers were trounced 106-83, and Trey scored only twelve points. Returning home bruised and battered, the Memphis team was buoyed by knowing they had to win only one of the three remaining games to make the playoffs.

Trey slept till noon after the late-night flight from OKC. Today was a day off, so after lunch he sat in his favorite chair and called Cristina.

"Hello, this is Cristina. Leave me a message."

"Hey, Cristina, this is Trey. Just wanted to say hi. Call me when you can."

He was reading back issues of the paper's sports section when his phone buzzed.

"Did I wake you?" he asked jokingly.

"No, smarty pants. I bet I was up hours before you."

"You would win that bet, for sure. What are you doing?"

"Updating charts. What are you doing?"

"Updating reading. What time do you get off?" he asked.

"Um, about four. Got something in mind?"

"You," he said, a bit embarrassed by his own boldness.

"That's sweet. I'd sure like to see you. Want to come over for dinner?"

"You sure? I'd like that. We need to catch up. What time?"

"How about 6:00? We'll grill burgers, if that's okay."

"Yeah, that sounds great," he said. "Can I bring anything?"

"No, I think I have everything. It won't be fancy, but at least we'll be together."

"That will be nice. See you at 6:00."

"Bye, Trey."

Early afternoon, Trey walked toward Charlie and Precious Smit's house. Charlie was sitting in his usual seat and smiled broadly when he saw his tall friend coming his way.

"You boys afraid of the Thunder?" Charlie chided even before Trey made it to the porch.

"And hello to you too, Charlie," Trey said with a smile, offering his hand.

Charlie shook it with gusto.

"I'm just joshin' you, Trey. You guys looked pretty good overall 'cept for a game here and there. You should be able to make the post-season with a win, right?"

"That's what we're hoping," Trey said. "How you been? And where's Precious?"

"She's over at her niece's house. Been doing okay for a man my age." Charlie laughed.

The two sat chatting about the weather, basketball, getting older, and the like. Finally, Trey asked what had been on his mind since their last conversation.

"Charlie, tell me more about your neighbors."

"Whachu mean?" Charlie asked.

"You know, last time I was here you said you couldn't have made it without your neighbors. And that one should invest more in neighbors than fellow church people. What did you mean by that?"

"Just what I said. Who do you spend most of your time nearest? Who are the folks that are closest to you and most likely to come to your aid when you's needing something? Who are the folks you for sure want on your side when bad times come? Who are the people who have the most interest in how you keep up your property? And vice versa? Who are the folks you want next to you in eternity, your kinfolks, your church folks, or your neighbors?" Charlie laughed heartily.

"And how do you do that? I mean, most of the people who live right around me keep pretty much to themselves. A few sit on their porches, but most stay inside."

"Well, it takes time. You just been in there a few months, boy; give it time. You'll see folks outside from time to time. When you do, make the most of each opportunity. You'll begin to get the rhythm of your street. You'll hear of Mrs. Smith's operation or a new child over at the Joneses', and you'll take flowers or food, and people will begin to learn that Trey Glass cares. Yes, sir, it jus' takes time."

After a period of contemplation, Trey asked, "You go to church, Charlie?"

"Don't need to," Charlie said with a wry grin.

"Don't need to? You that perfect?"

"Far from that, young man," Charlie said. "Don't need to *go* nowhere. Guess another way of saying it is, we *are* the church. Everywhere we goes is church. Me and Precious have hosted the church here in our house in many forms through the years. Other times, it's jus' been a church of two, me and the wife. You know what I mean?"

"Yeah I do, and I was thinking the same thing, Charlie. I was thinking about finding folks right around here who want to form a community of faith, a community that takes care of one another and helps the people around us. That's what my dad said the real church was anyway."

"Well, you had a smart daddy," Charlie said, squeezing Trey's shoulder with his broad hand.

"I was thinking about some of the people I see on the street. They seem to have lots of needs, maybe the folks I could invite in for a meal or to pray or just read scripture a couple of times a week. I know that's taking a chance, but that's what it's all about, isn't it?"

"Yes, sir," Charlie agreed. "You know, Precious and me always thought of this neighborhood as our congregation anyway. We have felt sort of responsible for its welfare. When we was younger, we'd go house to house seeing if everything was okay with folks. Back in '88 we had this huge snow that covered the whole town. People was snowed in for days. We went up and down our street every day checking on folks. Even had Lisa Lindsey and her three youngins over here for a week, living with us. Whew, that was a time! But we made it, and them children ain't never forgot that. They's still talking about it."

"It's all about caring, isn't it, Charlie?" Trey said observantly.

"It's all about caring. And you're a mighty young fellow to be caring like you do. Guess your momma and daddy done brought you up right."

"Speaking of my mom, I'm trying to get her to move here and stay with me. I told her about you and Precious. Told her she would like you...well, told her that she would like Precious. I'm not sure she'd like you too much," Trey said, chuckling.

"You's a funny man too," he said, laughing out loud.

"When's Ms. Precious getting home?" Trey asked.

"Not till tomorrow. She's staying over to care for the younger children while her niece deals with some things. That family sure got some problems. Her older boy, Douglas, is about to drive her crazy. He's in to all sorts of stuff."

"That's too bad. Anything I can do?"

"Probably not right now, but who knows? Young Douglas does love the Rockers, so maybe one day he can meet you and get an idea of how a real man lives. We'll wait and see."

"I'd be glad to do what I can, Charlie," Trey said reassuringly.

After a while, Trey said goodbye to Charlie and walked toward home, stopping briefly to say hello to Lem and Carla Davis. When he reached his house, five young men and Pastor Tony Bradford were hard at work in the garden.

"Wow, this looks great!" Trey exclaimed when he saw what they had done. The boys were noticeably proud of themselves, and Trey could see they were more relaxed than the first time he'd met them.

"Mr. Trey, we planted these carrots, radishes, and onions. Later we gonna plant some beans and tomatoes," said one of the boys, excited.

"Yeah, and we're going to put up a little fence to keep the raccoons and cats out," said another.

"Man, these guys have been working hard," Pastor Tony said. "And we've been learning a little scripture along the way, right, men? Say it with me…"

"'This is what the kingdom of God is like. A man scatters seed on the ground. Night and day, whether he sleeps or gets up, the seed sprouts and grows, though he does not know how. All by itself the soil produces grain—first the stalk, then the head, then the full kernel in the head. As soon as the grain is ripe, he puts the sickle to it, because the harvest has come.'"

"And where is that found in scripture?" Tony asked.

"Mark chapter 4, verses 26 through 29," the boys said in unison.

"Awesome! I had an idea, Pastor Tony. Do you think these guys would like to see the Rockers play the Hawks tomorrow night?" Trey asked; he noticed excitement building in the teens before him.

"Well, I'm not sure, Mr. Trey," Tony said with a wink as the boys' excitement turned to silence. "They'll probably be too tired to go to a basketball game after working in the garden so hard."

"Oh no, we won't be too tired!" cried one of the teens; a chorus of protests rose in unison from the young gardeners.

"In that case," Trey said, "I'll make the arrangements. You guys will be my guests and sit five rows behind the Rockers bench. If you come early, you can watch the shootaround. Wait here; I'll be right back."

Trey ran inside and pulled seven tickets from a drawer in the hallway. At the beginning of each season, Rockers team members were given ten tickets to each home game and encouraged to distribute them among the rich and influential, with hopes that they would, at some point, purchase season tickets. Trey believed the tickets could not be used any better than on kids who ordinarily would have no hope of affording the steep price of seeing an NBA game, especially courtside.

"I'm going to give these tickets to Pastor Tony, and he'll give you yours as you walk in the Forum, okay?"

The young men stood still, amazed at their good fortune and Trey's generosity.

"And Tony, there's an extra one in there for Rosalee. You guys enjoy. See you tomorrow night. Be sure and let me know how I did when I see you next time. Go Rockers!" he shouted as he ran back toward the house.

"Go Rockers!" the boys echoed.

Trey spent the rest of the afternoon resting, reading, and waiting for six o'clock to roll around.

When Cristina opened the front door, her beauty nearly took his breath.

"Come in," she said.

Once inside, the two enjoyed an extended embrace, obviously glad to see each other after a few days apart.

"Smells good in here," he said.

"I decided to make a hash brown casserole at the last minute. Sit down and relax while I finish up."

Trey began leafing through a coffee table book of Memphis before putting it down and joining Cristina in the kitchen. "I'd rather talk to you. Anything I can do?"

"Yeah, if you want you can slice those tomatoes." She handed him a knife and put ice in two tall glasses. "Tea or water?"

"Water for me," he said. As he watched her, he offered a quick and silent prayer of thanks for his life right now—a life that included making a living at his favorite pastime and Cristina Garza.

After dinner, the two sat close to each other on a sofa in the living room.

"Would you come to church with me?" he asked.

"I think I'd go just about anywhere with you," she said, squeezing his hand.

"I'm thinking about asking some folks from my neighborhood to gather at my house on Sundays when the season is over to pray and talk. What do you think?"

"Well, in all honesty, I think it's a stretch to call that church, but whatever," Cristina said honestly.

"We don't have to call it anything. I just think there are some people around my neighborhood who would like some type of spiritual family. After the playoffs, I'll have the time to get something going and hope it will continue once the season starts again in the fall."

"You can count me in," she said, nestling closer.

The two sat in silence for a while, his arms around her, listening to Nora Jones from Cristina's iPod. James Taylor's "You Can Close Your Eyes" got the better of her; she looked up and pulled his face toward hers. He complied and found her lips warm and eager. The days of separation and the normal sexual tension of two twenty-somethings merged to create an inviting but dangerous mixture. By the time he realized what was happening, he found himself on top of her. Trey pulled himself away and stood up, then paced around the room.

"I'm sorry," he said, picking up his car keys from a small table by the door and walking out the front door.

She didn't try to call him back.

The short drive home gave him time to think about his dad's many warnings that such a time would come; he needed a plan to avoid a regrettable mistake in the future. He knew he didn't want to lose Cristina and decided then and there that he would not allow things to get to a point of no return. When he got home, he dialed her number.

"Cristina, I'm so sorry," he said.

"Trey, I'm the one who's sorry," she said, her voice trembling.

"Look, this doesn't change anything," he said. "I don't want to mess up what we have going, that's all. I care very much for you; in fact, I think I'm in love with…you."

Her sobs continued.

"I may not be the one for you, but I promise that I will never take advantage of you." He paused. "I'm not saying any of this right."

"You are everything I have ever wanted in a man, and I want this to work. Tell me what we have to do, and I'll do it."

"We just have to make sure we don't get into situations we can't control. I don't know if that means not being alone for long periods or what, but we both know where it can lead. Let's talk about it sometime, okay? Thanks for dinner tonight; it was great."

"Okay," she said softly. "It was great seeing you, Trey. I think you're a wonderful man, and I…care very much for you too. Beat the Hawks, hear?"

"We'll do our best. Good night, Cristina."

"Good night."

CHAPTER 14

After a restless night, Trey awoke earlier than usual. He threw on sweats and sneakers and started out the door.

"Will you want breakfast when you get back?" Tyler called from the kitchen.

"Yeah, sure," he mumbled. At the end of his driveway, Trey stopped to stretch then began a brisk run-walk through the neighborhood. He wasn't interested in seeing anyone this morning; he just needed time to think about the events of the previous night and his last conversation with Cristina. He thought about how silly most of his teammates would think this issue was—avoiding sex, especially with someone you love.

On his second trip around the block, Trey walked by the warehouse where he had been accosted a few months before. As he approached, he heard loud cursing and what sounded like glass bottles breaking. He had already decided not to stop, but as he walked by he caught the attention of one of the young men throwing bottles against the vacant building. For an instant, the two stood staring at each other until another young man ran up and grabbed his buddy and both ran away. Trey continued his walk back toward his house.

After breakfast, Trey ran some errands, caught up on mail and the newspaper, and lay down to catch a nap. He awoke mid-afternoon and smelled his pre-game steak cooking. He washed up and went downstairs where Tyler had a lean rib-eye, lightly buttered baked potato, and small salad on the table. For the next hour he hung out, relaxing with music and meditation. At 5:00 he left for the arena.

A small crowd of people, mostly female, had gathered at the players' entrance to the parking garage of the FedEx Forum. Some held signs that read, "Go get 'em, Trey," "Rockers Power," "Trey, Trey, he's our man," and, "Smooth as Glass."

One woman who appeared to be on the far side of middle age held a sign that read, "Trey Baby, you can autograph my bra any time." Trey blushed and pulled into the garage, being careful not to run over anyone.

The Atlanta Hawks were sure they weren't going to make the playoffs, and they played like a team that had nothing to lose, outscoring the Rockers in every quarter and winning the game 98-84.

Throughout the game, Trey faintly heard the familiar voices of Pastor Tony Bradford and the five young men he had treated to the game. From the few quick glances he made in their direction, the group was having a great time, sitting five rows up behind the Rockers bench. Their cheering was not enough to change the course of the game, but it did inspire the team's point guard. Trey led all scorers with thirty-one points and fell one assist shy of a double-double.

Coach Rollins was not happy with the outcome. Two games left to win one.

The final win came the next night against the Denver Nuggets at the Forum. Trey had a season high thirty-five points, eleven assists, and seven rebounds. He played like a man possessed, and everyone who watched his performance knew that Trey Glass carried his team into the playoffs.

To celebrate, Trey asked Charlie and Precious to join him and Cristina the next night at Trey's favorite Midtown restaurant, The Pantry. For two hours, the four enjoyed Southern home-cooking and lively discussion, with only a few interruptions by well-meaning, but pesky Rockers fans.

"After the playoffs, Cristina and I are thinking about getting together with a few people during the week to eat a meal and talk about spiritual things. Wonder if you two would like to join us?" Trey said to his two guests.

"Maybe so," Charlie said. "How you planning to do the food?"

"Is that all that's on that little mind of yours?" Precious said, elbowing her husband.

"Haven't really thought about it," Trey said. "I could ask Tyler to take care of that. I'd like to keep him on during the off-season anyway, and this would be a good excuse."

"You's setting yourself up for freeloaders," Precious said. "If it was me, I'd fix the main dish and ask others to bring stuff."

"Yeah, that's a good idea," Cristina said. "Why don't you let Precious and me handle the food? Could we do that?"

"Why, we sure can. Seems like anyone who comes for a free meal can bring something—cornbread, napkins, ice, *something*," Precious said.

"And if they can't, they can come anyways," Charlie said with a chuckle.

"Good. We'll begin the week after our last playoff game," Trey said. "Is any day better than another?"

"The folks around here count Sundays as a special day," Charlie said. "If you want to push this as church, you'd have better luck if you have it on Sunday."

"That's the thing, Charlie. I'm not sure I want it to be like church. I see it more as a time to get together with friends from the neighborhood to eat and catch up...you know, get to know each other better. Fellowship."

"Well, then I'd say any time is good. Most people around here reserve Sundays for chillin' out. I think it's a fine plan," Charlie said.

Conference playoffs began in three days, so Trey committed himself to daily personal workouts in addition to team practices. He explained to Cristina that he would have to wait until after the playoffs to see her again, but that didn't mean he couldn't talk to her on the phone, which he did every evening before bed. His socializing would be restricted to the people he might run across on his regular neighborhood walks.

Late one afternoon while walking, he happened upon a group of men throwing dice in an alley not far from his house. He heard their raucous conversations before he actually saw them, and when he rounded the corner, he caught the group off guard. The men froze and stared at the tall white boy who stared back. Money, cigarettes, and nearly-empty booze bottles littered the area around the crowd of men of all ages.

"You better get on away from here," a tall man said threateningly.

"Maybe we should teach him to mind his own business," another said as he rose from his spot, a short piece of chain dangling from his right hand.

"Guys, I meant no harm. I'm just out for a walk," Trey said, standing his ground.

"Hey, ain't you Trey Glass?" a younger man said. "Hey, everybody, this here's Trey Glass of the Rockers."

"I don't care if he's Crystal Glass; he ain't got no business 'round here," the man with the chain said.

"Oh no, y'all, he's cool. Come on over here, Trey. We's just playing a little game. We could teach you." All the men laughed at the same time. "Got any money on you?"

"No, that's okay." Trey laughed. "I'm afraid I wouldn't be any good. But you all keep playing. I'll just watch."

Trey stood behind and watched as the men resumed their game. A couple of guys came over and greeted the star, saying they thought Trey had done a great job for the team this year. Others continued to eye him suspiciously. One offered him a draw of an unknown substance wrapped in a paper bag. He declined. After a few minutes, Trey excused himself, assuring the gamblers their secret was safe with him and that he hoped to see them again next time he was in the area. Most of the small crowd had warmed up to the stranger, and several even invited him back.

"We have to keep moving, so if we're not here, we're somewhere close."

Trey shared his adventure with Charlie the next time they spoke.

"You be careful around those guys, Trey," Charlie warned. "A few of them would as soon cut your ears off as look at you. Most of 'em are just good old boys having a good time."

Trey Glass's rookie season came to an abrupt end when the Memphis Rockers lost four straight games to the Oklahoma Thunder in the first round of the playoffs. In an interview with *Sports Magazine*, Rockers owner, Randall Parrent, promised better things next year.

"We'll be taking a hard look at everything; nothing will be exempt from review to discover how we can be better. Our fans deserve better, and we plan on delivering."

When asked specifically about Trey's performance, Parrent said, "Trey Glass was one of the bright spots this year. We watched him mature into a real important part of our team. Still, we're going to assess every element, every player, every coach, everything in terms of how it all fits together. If we find we have to fire a coach, we'll do it. If we have to trade a player or players, we'll do it. If we have to change team colors, we won't hesitate—whatever it takes. Our goal is to become the best basketball team in the world."

In one sense, Trey was glad the season was over. He loved playing basketball, but other interests were calling. First priority was to move his mom to Memphis and get her settled. He wanted to volunteer at a job-training agency located near his house. He was excited about the possibility of starting a neighborhood faith community. He wanted to spend more time learning from Charlie and Precious. And, of course, he wanted to deepen his relationship with Cristina. Throw in regular off-season workouts and a few other odds and ends and the few months between the season's end and fall start-up would seem like just a few days.

Trey knew he'd better get started…right after he got some rest. The hard-fought series with Oklahoma City took its toll on the players. For the first few days after the playoffs, Trey slept until noon, ate lunch, then slept some more. Usually after dinner, he would stroll his neighborhood, talking to anyone he could find outside.

Once he felt rested, Trey attacked his list of off-season tasks.

"Tony, I got a problem," he said to his pastor over chai at a downtown shop.

"I'm here to listen, buddy."

"You know how sporadic I've been in coming to church?"

"Yeah. So what? Your work demands it. No big deal."

"And even when I'm there, I feel disconnected…like I'm a visitor. And when it comes to being involved, I just don't feel a part. I don't think it's supposed to be that way, Tony."

"Well, what can we do about it?" Tony asked.

"I've been thinking. There are some folks who live in my neighborhood or nearby who would make a great faith community. I think I need to provide a family for the people I live around before I travel halfway across town to be with people I hardly know," Trey said, sipping his tea.

"Hmm," Tony uttered. "And how would that family be fed? I mean, who would do the preaching?" Tony asked.

"Same as now. The Holy Spirit would do the teaching. Do you think the Spirit talks only to preachers, Tony?"

"No, I don't suppose he does."

"I agree. I think when one opens his or her heart to the Spirit, the Spirit guides. Many of the people I have in mind forming our little community are pretty tired of hearing sermons, no offense, Pastor," Trey said, smiling.

"Ha. None taken," Tony said.

"See, I just think God would like to see a house of faith within easy access to every human being on Earth. I'm not all that sure he is thrilled with all the churches we have that demand people come to it rather than the church going out to be among the people." Trey stopped and thought before continuing, sipping his tea. "Maybe I'm out of my league here—"

"No, no," Tony said. "I think you're on the right track. During my seminary days, I recall being shocked to learn that the model we have today in Christendom is more like the model of fourth-century Rome than what we have in the Bible. There's probably not enough attention paid to helping folks focus on those they are around most naturally. I say go for it, buddy. And if you need anything, just let me know. I'll support you any way I can."

"That means a lot, Tony. I'll keep you informed as to how it goes."

"One thing, though. You still going to let my kids use your yard for their garden?" Tony asked with a concerned look.

"Of course," Trey said. "I love those kids. And my mom is really going to enjoy being around them."

A week after the season ended, Trey went home to Wayne County, accompanied by Cristina. When Becky met her, she threw her arms around Cristina's neck and gave her a long, warm hug.

"I am so glad to meet you...so glad," she kept saying. "I feel like I know you from all that Trey-boy has said about you."

Trey-boy? Cristina thought.

"I feel the same," she said to Becky. "I feel like I know your whole family."

Over the next two days Cristina got to meet Lee, Adam and his family, plus an assortment of cousins, aunts, and uncles. When she wasn't looking, all who met Cristina gave Trey "thumbs-up" for his selection of a girlfriend. Everyone loved her.

After supper one evening, as the family sat at Adam's dining room table and the kids were playing in their room, Trey surprised everyone when he asked, "What would you say if I told you I've invited Mom to come live with me in Memphis?"

Becky turned red and looked down at her hands, embarrassed she hadn't mentioned it to her other sons before. The room was quiet.

"Really, Mom?" Lee finally asked.

"I was going to tell you all, but I just had to work it out in my head first," Becky said.

"What are you thinking, Mom?" Adam asked.

"Well," she began nervously, "I think I'd like that, only if you think you could get along without me."

"We could never get along without you, Ma," Adam's wife, Evie, said as she patted Becky's arm. "But it's your choice. Maybe the move would be good for you."

"I bought that big house in Memphis with hopes that one day Mom and Dad would move in," Trey said. "I have plenty of room, there's a garden, and she can come and go as she pleases. I will also make sure she has plenty of chances to come back here to see you guys and her friends. Of course, the door is always open for you to visit her."

"Now that Daddy's gone, I think I need…oh, I don't know. I think I need a new…another place to get started. There are too many memories of Travis at the house," she said, overcome with tears.

Each member of the family sat around the table in silence, their thoughts on Travis and the man he was. Soon, there wasn't a dry eye among them.

"Mom, I think all of us would say do what you believe is best," Adam offered. "We love you so much and would love to always have you nearby, but only you know what you need. Dad will always be near to you no matter where you live. Sounds like Trey has the perfect setup to keep you busy and useful. I say go for it."

"We'll even bring Adelia and Fran over to visit occasionally. I know how you three like to laugh," Evie said.

"Oh, I know I'll miss them so much," Becky said, still crying. "Do you think Cloe and Rachel will be able to get along without their grandma?"

"They will be sad they can't see you every day," Evie replied. "But they will do fine, and we'll make sure they get to see you often."

"When do you think this might happen?" Lee asked.

"I have some rooms to clean up and paint; might take me a couple of weeks. Then we'll rent a truck and make the move. How does that sound, Mom?" Trey asked.

"That'll be about right," Becky said. "I've been cleaning stuff out of the house for weeks now. I should be ready in a week or two."

"I say we keep the house for a while, just in case…well, in case Mom wants to come back or something," Adam said. "Or in case you get traded, Trey. Then she can come back here."

"I won't get traded, but I still think it's a good idea to keep the house," Trey said. "It's paid for, and I'll cover the taxes and maintenance until we decide to sell it. Sounds like—"

"And I'll be near my newest daughter-in-law," Becky said. Just as she reached to hug Cristina, she realized how that sounded. "Uh, I didn't mean it that way. I just meant I'll be near my new friend. Oh my, I am so embarrassed."

While everyone laughed, Trey reached under the table for Cristina's hand. He wondered how that sounded to her. He didn't look to find out.

Nearly every day, Trey received phone calls from national and local sports media seeking interviews. Reporters wanted to know his reaction to the possibility of being traded during the off-season. His response to each was the same: "Let's see what happens."

On Wednesdays, Trey stopped in at LoveWorks, a nonprofit agency that helped unemployed men and women develop job skills. He ate lunch with some of the guys, getting to know them and encouraging them to stick with the program. In the afternoon, he also helped sort and stock donated personal hygiene items and other commodities to be handed out to those who couldn't afford to buy them. LoveWorks was one of six local nonprofit agencies he had been supporting with a thousand dollars a month.

The garden continued to grow, and Trey enjoyed the time he was able to spend with the five young gardeners. Once a week, Trey and Tony loaded the crew up in Tony's SUV and drove them to Sonic for lunch. Pretty soon families of the young men would be enjoying the fruits of their hard labors.

Trey's summer was shaping up to be the most memorable and enjoyable that he could remember. His mom was coming to live with him. He loved volunteering at LoveWorks. Five young men were getting a well-rounded education in life and farming. He had met the love of his life. The number of new neighborhood friends was increasing daily.

Then something happened that put a screeching halt on the perfect summer and cracked open the door of doubt on Trey Glass's integrity in the minds of some.

CHAPTER 15

One late afternoon while out walking, he again stumbled across the dice game in a nearby alley. By now, the men were used to Trey walking past and greeting them with a simple hello before continuing on; they seldom gave him a second notice. On this night, he decided to stop and watch, hoping to get to know them a little better. After he had been there just a few minutes, four police cars pulled up—two at one end of the alley and two at the other—their headlights and flashing strobes lighting up the dusky sky. The twelve or so men were trapped. Police officers ordered the men to put their faces up against the wall, feet spread apart, while the officers searched each man before cuffing them for the ride downtown.

"Sir, I wasn't gambling; I just stopped to watch," Trey said in his defense.

"He's right," several of the men said. "He was just passing by. Y'all need to let him go."

"He can tell that to the judge," the officer in charge said as one of the officers led Trey to a waiting patrol car.

Once downtown, the men were placed in one large cell. One by one, they were brought out, fingerprinted, photographed, and then returned to the cell. When it came Trey's turn, he requested his one phone call and dialed the only lawyer he knew in town, Gerald Maizano III, the Rockers' corporate attorney. He left a message with the answering service that Trey Glass was at 201 Poplar Avenue and needed bail money.

The press will have a ball with this! he thought in disbelief.

Within an hour, Maizano arrived with Brett Bing to see what was going on with the franchise's premier player.

"I got caught watching these guys roll dice," he said, an honest defense. Bail was five hundred dollars but was waived when the jail officials received confirmation of who was in the holding cell. Trey was released on his own recognizance, given information about his court date, and quickly shuffled out of the jail by two embarrassed rescuers.

"What were you thinking, Glass?" Bing yelled once they were safely inside the attorney's Mercedes S400 and headed away from downtown. "Don't you know what this could do to the Rockers organization? Who are those people back there anyway, your friends?"

Trey could tell he was being mocked.

"Well, yeah, some of them are. I was hoping we could bail out the whole bunch," Trey replied, knowing it would get Brett going.

"Are you crazy?" Bing shouted, as animated as Trey had ever seen him. "If you post bail for those goons and they don't show up for court, you lose your money. And chances are pretty good they will not show up. I'm sure not going to waste the organization's money on those losers."

"I wasn't planning to use the Rockers' money," Trey said quietly, mostly to himself.

"I don't know if you've noticed, but the neighborhood you've chosen has been nothing but trouble for you. It's time you came to your senses and got out of there," Bing chastised.

"Sorry, Brett, but that's my home, and I'm staying. Mr. Maizano, what would I have to do to bail those guys out of jail tonight?" Trey asked.

"You just go back down there and bail them out. And you'd have to bring cash. But Trey, I'm inclined to side with Brett. Most of those guys will never return for their court date, and you'd be out a lot of money."

Cash, huh? Now where can I get that much cash? he wondered. He did the math and figured he would need six grand or so, and his ATM only allowed five hundred dollars in withdrawals per day.

When the three arrived at Trey's house, there were news teams from the three local networks waiting.

"Oh my God," Brett said. "Now what do we do?"

"I'll be glad to handle the questions," Gerald offered.

"Leave it to me. It's my issue," Trey said as he opened the car door to get out. "Thanks for the help, guys; I truly appreciate it. I'll be in touch."

The moment he stepped out of the car, the crowd of reporters descended on the superstar.

"What can you tell us?"

"Is it true you were caught gambling?"

"When is your court date?"

"Were you using drugs?"

"There's a rumor that you have a drug problem; is that true?"

The questions came from every direction, especially left field.

Trey stood in the middle and raised his hand to quiet the frenzy.

"Here's what I can tell you, I was not gambling, and I do not use drugs. Now, I've got some business to attend to, so I'm going inside. You guys are welcome to stay here as long as you want, but I won't be saying any more about this. Please excuse me," he concluded as he made his way through the throng.

Once inside, he called his accountant, Brad Tual.

"Brad, Trey Glass. Hey, I've got a situation I need your help with. How much cash can you come up with tonight?"

"What? How much cash? How much do you need?" Brad asked.

"Let's say $10,000 to be safe. Some friends of mine are in trouble, and I want to help them out."

"Yeah, I heard. I've got exactly ten grand in my safe at the office for just such emergencies. I can meet you in thirty minutes," Brad said.

"201 Poplar Avenue, Brad. Thanks." Trey hung up and went upstairs to put on a clean shirt, nicer pants, and docksiders, then carefully backed his car out of the garage to avoid hitting the gang of reporters still congregating at the end of his drive.

Bail for each man was five hundred dollars. Trey handed over six thousand dollars to the clerk and signed the appropriate papers, stating, among other things, that if any of the men failed to show up for his court date, Trey would be out the five hundred dollars, and an arrest warrant would be issued for the no-show. Once outside, Trey called the twelve to him and began his sermon.

"Looks like I picked the wrong day to stand around and watch, huh?" he said; some of the men laughed nervously. "Seems like all of us were at the wrong place at the wrong time. But here we are; we're all in the same boat. We got caught, and it's time to pay the piper. They've got us all scheduled for the same court date, so here's the deal. I expect each of you to be there when you're scheduled to be there. Understand?"

A few of the men looked down at their feet, knowing they had no intention of showing up.

"Because if you're not there, I will do everything in my power to have you arrested and prosecuted, not because I want my money back, but because you need to pay for your crime. There's a better way to make a few bucks, and I'm willing to help you find a job, if that's the issue. And one more thing, the gambling in our neighborhood has to stop. Any questions?"

No one spoke up, and slowly the men dispersed.

Guess we'll see what happens, he thought as he watched them go. He didn't know it, but he'd just bought himself some trouble from some of the more decent downtown folks.

There were a few times in his life when Trey was compelled to shake his head in disbelief at the insensitivity of supposedly redeemed people—people who had experienced the mercy of God and who marveled at God's love.

Of all people on earth, the person of God should know better, he would say to himself on those occasions.

The call from the Reverend Leonard Gosnell came around 10:00 the next morning. Tyler fielded the call and told the reverend that Trey was not available at the moment. After his shower and brunch, Trey returned the call.

"Reverend Gosnell? Trey Glass here. You called?"

"Yes, Mr. Glass," the reverend replied in typical manner. "Word has reached us that you were caught gambling. Is that true?"

Trey was sure he didn't want to have this conversation but was curious as to why this was of interest to the caller.

"Caught, yes. Gambling, no. Why do you ask?"

"And it's also come to our attention that you provided bail money to your fellow scofflaws."

"Mr. Gosnell—"

"Reverend, that's *Reverend* Gosnell," he corrected.

"Right. Reverend Gosnell," Trey replied, deciding to go along with the game. "Again, I respectfully ask why this might be of interest to you."

"It's just that the Downtown Clergy Association, of which I am the president,"—the reverend paused for effect—"is trying to get this kind of activity out of the downtown neighborhoods. You being a high-profile figure and all can help us rid the city of this kind of riffraff. But it concerns us that you have apparently joined their ranks. It seems that if you were indeed innocent, as you profess, and if you truly are interested in the welfare of this city, you would have left your friends in jail where they belong."

"Have you spoken to any of the charged? Do you know any of those men personally?" Trey asked, his blood beginning to boil.

"Well, certainly not, Mr. Glass. What kind of impression would that leave for clergy to interact with such people? We surely don't want to encourage that sort of stuff. Those men will be back in the alleys and rat holes corrupting our youth before you know it."

"What would you have me do, sir?" Trey asked sincerely.

"Anything that gets those degenerates off the streets so that our self-respecting citizens don't have to encounter them. We certainly don't want to do anything that impedes their conviction and incarceration for such ungodly activity."

Becky Glass's father farmed 165 acres of land in north Alabama for more than fifty years. He was a model citizen and part-time preacher. His best friend from the army lived in North Dakota, and Bertran "Berty" James occasionally left the farm to go preach a weeklong gospel meeting in the small town of Casper, North Dakota, for his army buddy's church. Such was the reason for Berty's visit in the fall of 1967. When he arrived, the leaders of the church had a special request for their visiting evangelist: to clear the local park of a "gang" of homosexuals that had taken up residence there.

For the first three days, Berty spent his mornings in study and prayer. In the afternoons, he spent a few hours knocking doors and inviting people to his preaching service that night. He always finished up his afternoons in the park, sitting quietly on a bench near the squatters' camp, reading.

By Wednesday, he had met three of the unwelcomed park residents and enjoyed discussing baseball, politics, and movies, although he didn't know anything about movies. By Friday, he had met all the squatters and was invited to join them for dinner of fried Spam, Vienna Sausage, and some kind of drink he was afraid to ask about. By Saturday afternoon, the affectionate mob of park inhabitants was curious about their new friend, whom they had come to like a lot.

"I'm here to present a series of lectures at Casper Community Church," he said. "I'd love for you to come hear my final lecture Sunday morning."

They were shocked to learn they had been infiltrated by a "religious" man, but they seemed open to the idea of visiting the church. They would consider his offer.

Come Sunday morning at 10:15, twenty-seven raggedly dressed young men and women entered the front door of the church building and filed down to fill the first two rows of pews in order to hear the best sermon they had ever heard. The topic was the grace and love of God, and some were moved to tears. After the service, sad farewells were exchanged between the squatters and the aging preacher; shortly after, the church leaders demanded to speak with Berty in the pastor's study.

"We are very disappointed by what you've done," said one of the men. "We asked you to rid the park of the likes of these sinners, and instead you brought them to church. What do you have to say for yourself?"

"I did exactly as you requested. I emptied the park. You didn't say where you wanted them relocated. I thought church was as good a place as any," the wise man said as he put on his hat and walked out.

Trey was jostled back to his senses by a frustrated sigh on the other end of the line.

"Thank you for calling, Reverend Gosnell, and for your concern. I promise I will do everything I can to help these men change their ways. Goodbye." Trey hung up and let off steam by taking a brisk walk in the neighborhood, stopping at Charlie's for doses of comfort and wisdom.

"What too many preachers and pastors forget is that Jesus didn't come to Earth just to get us out of trouble," the old neighbor said. "He came to get into our trouble with us. A rescuer has to go down into the cave to lead the lost out. He can't just sit at the top and yell instructions."

"What should I do, Charlie?" Trey asked.

"You's doing it, boy. You probably have the attention of those men you helped. Now, just live like Jesus around them. Don't preach, just love. But as I told you before, not everyone responds to love like we hope for. You know where loving his enemies got our Lord," Charlie said.

"I know that one of the guys lives right around the corner from me. I'm thinking about inviting him over for supper. Maybe he'd come to our faith gatherings," Trey said. "Which reminds me, do you think we can get together this weekend?"

"Don't see why not. Precious!" he called.

"Who's that yelling?" Precious emerged from inside, wiping her hands on a dish towel.

"Trey's wondering if we can meet this weekend," Charlie said.

"Hello, Trey," Precious said, patting his arm. "Can you ask Miss Cristina to give me a call? We'll pull something together. How many you figuring on?"

"Probably not that many. I'd say six to eight."

"Oh, Charlie, I told Missy that we'd spend time with Douglas this Sunday," Precious said, remembering her pledge to her niece. "You think he might go with us to Trey's?"

"Of course he can," Trey said. "Is he the young man you said was getting into trouble?"

"Yes, he is. I think he'll do fine," Charlie said. "He's a good boy but angry over something we ain't figured out yet."

"Well, bring him along. We'll love the hate out of him," Trey said with a laugh.

Toward the end of the week, Trey figured that Carla, Lem, Precious, Charlie, Douglas, Cristina, and himself would make up the first faith gathering on Sunday.

"Precious is going to make a pork dish, and I will bring veggies and bread. We're thinking we'll do it all this first time. Once we find out who will be regulars, we'll ask them to share in the food next time. Can you take care of drinks?" Cristina asked Trey.

"Sure," he said. "That sounds good—nothing fancy, but something everyone will like."

"Hey, that sounds like you...nothing fancy but someone everyone likes." Cristina laughed.

"You're so funny...and cute," he said. "I'm supposed to pick up Mom next weekend. Want to go with me?"

"Sure. I'm off until that next Tuesday, so I can help her get settled."

"I was thinking about our predicament, you know, about being alone and all?"

"Yes?" she said quietly.

"I was thinking maybe it would be best for us to spend time in public places—movies, parks, restaurants—rather than just by ourselves. And if we're going to be together for a long time, to have other people with us," Trey said.

"I'm for whatever it takes, Trey," she said.

"Cristina, I am hopeful this relationship can be long term," Trey said.

"Me too, Trey."

"Look...how do I say this? I think you are the most wonderful woman I have ever met. You are not like anyone else. And...it's just that... I..."

"What is it, honey?" she said.

"Cristina, I love you."

Trey waited, the silence stirring the depths of his stomach. Soon, he could hear her crying softly.

"I love you too, Trey. And I want what's best for us in the long term. I never dreamed this would be so difficult."

"Neither did I. Thanks for understanding. A lot of girls wouldn't."

CHAPTER 16

"Trey, I have pretty good sources who say you're headed to the Knicks in the fall. Any comment?" asked the caller after identifying himself as a reporter from *Sports Magazine*.

"I'm sure that's all they are…rumors," Trey answered. "I can't imagine my club talking trade until they discuss it with me. Until that happens, it's just rumors, so I have no comment."

The thought upset Trey, the idea that his team might possibly do such a thing behind his back. He'd heard of this happening but couldn't believe the Rockers would pull such a stunt. He put in a call to Coach Rollins, who was vacationing in the Caymans with his family. Later in the day, Rollins returned Trey's call.

"Trey, this is Horace. What's up?"

Trey explained the phone call he'd received and asked if the trade talk was true, even a possibility. The quicker he could resolve the issue in his mind, the better the rest of his summer would go.

"Son, I haven't heard that from anyone upstairs, and, to be honest, I'd be shocked if the team traded you," Rollins said. "I've made myself perfectly clear about where you fit in our long-range plans in Memphis. Just between you and me—if you go, I go. Don't quote me on that; I'll deny it to my grave. But our plans for winning a championship depend heavily on you at point guard and the kind of offense we began refining last season. Does that help?"

"Yes, sir, it does," Trey said. "I'm sorry to have bothered you. I guess I'll continue to make no comments when asked. You all have a great time down there. Tell Marie hello for me."

"Will do, Trey. I'll see you in a few weeks."

"Whew," Trey said under his breath.

Trey spent two hours that afternoon at the gym working on three-point and foul shots and thirty minutes on strength conditioning. He ended his workout with ten minutes in the whirlpool and a semi-hot shower. On the way home, he decided to swing by the Med and surprise Cristina.

He parked three blocks away and walked toward the ER entrance to the hospital. About a block from the door, an elderly, unkempt gentleman appeared from behind a wooden fence that separated hospital property from a vacant field.

"Can you spare some change?" he asked. Trey could smell alcohol on his breath and noticed his wobbly stance.

"I think I can spare a little bit to help you out," he said. "But before I give you money, I'd like to know your name."

"Percy," the old man said.

"Percy, I'm Trey. Nice to meet you. You live around here?"

"Not far," the man said, eyeing Trey suspiciously.

"You have family?"

"No, sir. My family's all gone."

"I'm sorry to hear that. No one deserves to be alone. If you don't mind me asking, what kind of work have you done in the past?"

"Little bit of everything, masonry and landscaping mainly. Did some commercial fishing up on the Tennessee River. I lost my hand a few years back and ain't had no solid work since." He lifted his arm from his coat pocket to reveal a missing right hand.

"Man, that's the pits," Trey said. He fished around in his wallet and found two twenties, which he handed to Percy, along with one of the cards he'd created bearing names and numbers of helping agencies in Memphis.

"When you get a chance, Percy, take a look at this card. It has the names of places that can maybe help you get ahead a little. My address is on the back, so you come by when you need something. I might even have a job for you. My yard is big, and I could use some help keeping it mowed."

"Yes, sir. Thank you, sir," the man said.

"One more thing," Trey said, reaching for the man's only hand, which he held firmly. "Alcohol works for only a short time; there are some people in town who care for you and can help you overcome your dependency, if you'll let them. Maybe we can work on that together if you'll come by the house."

"Yes, sir," the man said, unable to control tears from spilling over his eyelids.

"It's been my pleasure to meet you, Percy. I hope to see you again." Trey watched his new acquaintance turn and amble up the sidewalk toward Union Avenue, where an ample selection of discount liquor stores awaited.

Trey wove his way through the maze of hallways linking various components of the emergency department until he saw his girlfriend at the far end of a hall, looking over a patient's chart. He crept up from behind and whispered, "Ma'am, can you tell me where to find—"

She wheeled around and nearly lost all decorum until she remembered where she was.

"What are you doing here?" Cristina squealed as she grabbed his arm and pulled him into an empty room. She kicked the door shut and threw her arms around his neck. Her kiss was long and warm. She stopped long enough to gaze into his eyes while she stroked his cheek. "I have missed you *so* much," she said and resumed their kiss.

"I've missed you too," he said after they broke their embrace. "Couldn't stay away any longer."

"Get your own room; this one's taken." An aging woman grunted from behind the curtain that surrounded her bed.

Cristina gasped, obviously shaken by her mistake.

"Jeez! I am so sorry. I thought this room was empty," she said.

"Does it look empty?" the old woman snorted before changing her tone. "It's okay, honey. There was a time…" she said, winking. "You two make a cute couple."

"I will make sure you get extra ice cream for dinner," Cristina said, pulling Trey out behind her and pulling the door quietly behind her.

Trey and Cristina made a hasty exit and nearly fell on the floor laughing once they were well down the hall.

"Come on, I want you to meet some people," she said, holding securely to his arm. "Do you mind?"

"No, I guess not. Will you be in trouble for that?" he asked, looking back over his shoulder toward the room they'd just left.

"No, I don't think so. Maybe she'll forget it all by evening."

Cristina enjoyed introducing Trey to her colleagues. The male staff stared in awe. The female staff swooned and gushed. Angie, the nurse who helped Cristina tend to Trey the night of his attack, ran up and gave him a huge hug, as if she'd known him forever.

"I just knew I'd get to meet you someday. You can thank me for where you are right now," she said, boasting about urging Cristina to pursue the NBA star.

"Thank you, Angie," he said, a bit embarrassed by all the attention. "Well, I need to let you all get back to work."

"I'll walk you out," Cristina said. At the entrance to the ER, the two hugged and parted with a quick kiss. "I'll see you tomorrow night."

"Looking forward to it," he said. He hummed as he walked back to his car.

On Sunday afternoon around 4:30, Precious and Charlie knocked on Trey's front door.

"Mind if we let this finish cooking in your oven?" Precious asked as they walked into the large foyer. Trey took the casserole dish from her hands and headed into the kitchen.

"Hey, where's Douglas?" Trey asked.

"Got cold feet when we told him we're coming over here. Guess he feels a bit intimidated meeting a celebrity," Charlie said. "We left him at home."

"You know how to operate this thing?" Trey asked, looking at the front of the large double ovens with more knobs and gauges than a space shuttle. Just at the right time, Cristina knocked and let herself in. "Can you turn the oven on?" he asked Cristina as she set a large grocery bag on the table.

"Yes, if you'll get the box of dishes from my back seat. You probably should learn to operate this thing in case Tyler ever leaves you," she said, giggling.

Soon everyone had arrived. After introductions, the group sat down to the hot meal at Trey's extra-large dining room table. For the next hour, the group talked and ate. During the meal, Trey looked around the table and marveled at the diversity: black, white, Latino, old, young, and in-between, very wealthy and not at all. He envisioned a time when representatives from other cultures and life situations would grace his table.

Toward the end of the meal, Trey picked up a basket of bread and said, "May I officially welcome all of you to my home? You don't know what a blessing each of you has been to my life since I moved in here. Thank you for what you mean to me. I look forward to days ahead when we can fill this table with folks from the neighborhood. I encourage you to keep an eye out for people who need a community, a family. My mom will be joining us next week, so that will be very special for me.

"One of the blessings of my walk with God has always been communion," he said, holding up the basket of bread, "a time to remember the sacrifice of Jesus. I know the custom is to take the Lord's Supper in church with a tiny bit of cracker and some grape juice, but I have always thought that defeats the real purpose—the spirit—of that beautiful act. One of the things my dad taught us early on is that you can share this meal any time and anywhere you happen to be. His theory was that Jesus selected the two most common elements of his day as symbols of his body and blood so that everywhere you went—your kitchen, a neighbor's kitchen, an inn—you would find these common elements, bread and wine, and remember him. And it's no accident that he instituted this ritual during a meal. Can you think of a better time to celebrate the greatest gifts of God than during a meal with your best friends?

"So, I'll thank God in a prayer, and then we'll pass this bread around. Take as much as you want and as long as you need to savor his goodness, then we'll do the same with the wine.

"Father, thank you for this special gathering of special friends. And Jesus, thank you for being here with us. As we eat this bread, may we be renewed with the memory of your goodness and love. Amen."

"Amen," the friends around the table said in unison.

Cristina was overcome with emotion. Warm tears slid down her cheeks, and Precious reached around and hugged her; the two ate bread together. The mood was subdued, but the glances and verbal exchanges were warm and sincere.

After a while, Trey picked up his wine glass and said, "Whatever you have in the glass in front of you can serve as a reminder of Jesus' blood given for each of us." Then, bowing, he said, "Father, again we thank you with sincere hearts for the life we enjoy in your family because of your son's love. We look forward to being with him when he returns. Amen."

After scattered amens, each guest drank from the glass in front of them. Some had water, some tea, and some wine. Lem clicked glasses with his wife, Carla, and Charlie as a toast. Precious and Cristina spoke quietly to each other.

After a few minutes, Trey said, "One of the things our family did at supper every night to help us find out how everyone was doing was to 'cruise.' My dad would usually start, and he would tell us how he was feeling by using letters that make up the word *cruise*. C.R.U.I.S.E. is an acronym for curious—something you've been wondering about; really happy—something that has made your day or week; unsure— something that you're not sure how it will turn out or perhaps a decision that's coming up and you don't know which way to go; insecure— something that made you afraid; sad—self-explanatory; and excited— something that you're, well, excited about. So, I'll start. I'm really happy about this group of people and excited about what can happen through us. Up until this afternoon, I was unsure about my future in Memphis, but I think that's been worked out."

Cristina cocked her head quizzically.

The group went around the room, each person telling how they felt.

"My auntie is beginning a new drug for her cancer tomorrow," Carla said. "I'm unsure about how she will react. I would like your prayers."

"Don't know if you've heard, but the city is talking about increasing our property tax," Lem said. "I'd be curious to know how much they're taking about. Folks around here can't pay much more."

"I'm so scared about my grandnephew who is getting into more and more trouble," Precious shared. "I jus' wonder what's going to happen to that boy."

"We've got some new policy changes coming at work. Not sure what all that means," Cristina said.

"I'm jus' excited about being here with all you," Charlie said. "This is going to be nice."

Everyone voiced agreement.

When the exercise ended, the six friends left the dining room for the more comfortable, spacious den.

"Every person needs a family," Trey said, "people who will watch out for them and care for them. People who are in touch with how they are doing, both physically and spiritually. And we all can use help in dealing with the troubles of this world. I really could have used you after my dad died. And who knows what lies ahead for each of us. Plus, have you noticed the folks who live around us and those who are just passing through? There are many people who could use a caring family—people like you. I'd like for each of us to be open to inviting others to be a part of our family. What do you think?"

"We've been in this neighborhood a long time," Carla began, "and we've seen lots of desperate people come through. Many of them still live here. I don't know how this little group could make a difference when there is so much need."

"With God, all things is possible," Precious said. "We's not alone. The Father cares more for his little chickens than we does. I say we jus' do our little part and let him do his."

"Precious is right," Trey said. "I'm asking us to keep our eyes open to opportunities to help. God is at work all around us. Sometimes he just wants us to be there. When we run across a situation that's too big for us, call on one of the others to help. A few willing people can make a world of difference."

"I think when we meet like this, we should let God lead us," Lem added. "I'm not interested in just a party. I like the idea of studying a portion of the Word."

"And having communion. That was special tonight," Cristina said.

"There's a sweet passage in Second Corinthians 14 that focuses the responsibility for the gathering on each person there. The writer says something like, 'When you come together, *each of you* has a hymn, or a word of instruction, a revelation, a tongue or an interpretation.' I suggest we all take responsibility for what goes on during our time together. If there is something special that you need to hear or say, then you carry out what's in your heart," Charlie said.

Everyone agreed to owning the times they are together.

"Precious, would you say a prayer for us?" Trey asked.

"Let's all bow our heads," Precious said. "Heavenly, sweet God, thank you for this evening and these special folks. We don't know what you's up to, but we appreciate you letting us be a part of it. And you knows we need you, Father, so don't you go leavin' us alone. Stay close by. All these things we mentioned, Heavenly Father, we ask you to take care of. Be with Carla's auntie. Don't let the city raise our taxes. Keep my nephew, Douglas, out of trouble. Don't let the changes at sweet Cristina's hospital shake her up. Thank you again for these wonderful people. And thank you for my blessed husband. In Jesus, Amen."

"Amen," the group said in unison.

After a little more conversation, members of the group began to leave for home.

"We're looking forward to next time," Lem said as he and Carla left.

"What you say about coming over to meet Douglas?" Precious asked Trey.

"Perhaps if he meets you, he'll not be shy about coming next time. He's not expecting you, so it will be a surprise," Charlie said.

The walk over to the Smits' took twice as long as it usually took Trey to walk. Precious walked slowly, and Trey wondered if he should offer to pick them up each week in his car.

"Lord, we never knows what we is going to find when we come home to Douglas, no, sir," Precious muttered, as if she were thinking out loud.

When they arrived at the Smits', Charlie and Precious found their seventeen-year-old grandnephew watching football.

"There's some people we wants you to meet," Charlie said, turning on the lights in the dark room.

"Yeah? Who?" he asked, rubbing his eyes. It was obvious to all that he had been dozing.

"Douglas, this is Trey Glass and his friend, Miss Cristina," Charlie said.

As much as he tried to hide his shock, Douglas failed. Charlie thought it was because he was meeting an NBA superstar, but the look on the nephew's face was more than that of an admiring fan.

Trey immediately recognized the young man from the vacant mill a few days earlier. He had locked eyes with the young man when he caught him breaking glass bottles.

Trey stuck out his hand, hiding the fact he knew the teen.

"Great to meet you, Douglas."

The young man quickly shook Trey's hand, then backed away just as quickly.

"Who you watching?" Trey asked, nodding toward the TV.

"Steelers and Giants classic game," he muttered. "I already know who won, so it ain't too interesting."

"Your uncle Charlie tells me you like the Rockers," Trey said, trying to break the ice.

"Yeah, they're all right, I guess." Douglas wouldn't look at Trey.

"Maybe sometime you can come see a game with your aunt and uncle."

"Yeah, maybe," the young man said, looking down at the floor.

"What grade will you be in this fall, Douglas?" Cristina asked.

"I'll be a junior, if I go back. School and me don't get along too well," he said, mainly for shock effect.

"What do you like?" she asked.

"Nothing," he said.

"Nothing? Do you play any sports," she asked persistently.

"No. Just hang out with my friends," he said, plopping back down on the couch.

"Well, we look forward to getting to know you better, Douglas," Cristina said.

"Guess we'll head on back home," Trey said. "We'll make sure you get to a game next season, okay?"

"Whatever," Douglas said as he reached for the Coke can on the TV tray beside the sofa. When he turned his hand over, Trey saw it—the pinkie ring that Trey's niece had given him last Christmas, the one he was wearing the night he was hit in the head with a bottle in a dark alley not far from where they stood.

CHAPTER 17

As night approached, Trey and Cristina walked back toward his house hand in hand.

"There's something about that kid," Cristina said.

There certainly is, Trey thought to himself. He couldn't let Cristina in on his suspicions until he had a chance to talk to Charlie and, eventually, to Douglas; otherwise, he figured the discussion amounted to gossip, something Trey detested.

"Are you going to be able to go with me to pick up Mom next weekend?" he asked.

"I think so. When do you plan on leaving?" she said.

"I'd like to go on Friday so I can visit Lonnie Long before he leaves for state prison."

"I think I can do that. I may have to trade my Friday shift. Let's plan on Friday."

"Hey, why the tears at dinner tonight?" he asked, letting go of her hand and putting his arm around her shoulders.

"Oh, I don't know; I'm just really happy right now…and thankful. I hadn't taken Holy Communion in years, and the whole scene tonight was touching. I'm so glad you love God," she said as she laid her head against him.

"And I'm so glad God loves *me*," he said, kissing the top of her head. "And you," he added, kissing her again.

When they got back to his house, the couple said goodbye in the driveway. He watched her tail lights until they were out of sight, and then he uttered a prayer of thanks for the gift of Cristina in his life.

Trey woke up early the next morning and drove to the Rockers' practice facility at the FedEx Forum, where he spent three hours working on his game. By late morning, he was home again. Tyler had prepared lunch of two chicken salad pita sandwiches, baked potato chips, pickles, and iced tea.

"Is this it?" Trey protested, only partially joking. "How's a growing boy supposed to survive on this?"

"Yeah, well that's what you're *not* supposed to be this summer…a *growing* boy," Tyler said. "I don't want the men in charge on my butt because you gained weight during the off-season. How'd your meeting go last night?"

"It went great, I think. You know you're welcome to join us, don't you?"

Tyler thought for a moment, then said, "You really think your friends would want a gay guy as part of their church?"

"Tyler, the way we look at it is, if God would take any of us, he'd take you too," Trey said laughingly. "I know any of my friends would love to have you be a part. It's a very simple gathering: we eat, share what's going on in our lives, read scripture, and pray. Seriously, we'd love to have you and anyone you want to bring."

"I'll think about it. The church I grew up in gave up on me long ago," Tyler said. "Roger and I have been attending a Universalist church, but the people there are old!"

"Now, Tyler, be kind," Trey said. "We've got some nearly eighty-somethings in our church, though I have to admit they think like much younger people. Think about it."

After lunch, Trey walked up to the Smits' house, only to find both front porch chairs empty and the front door open.

"Hello?" he called from the first step. "Anyone home?"

"We's back here, Trey," called Precious. "Come on in."

Trey walked up the front steps and in the front door.

"Where?" he called.

"Back here," she repeated.

He walked through the dark living area and on toward the back of the house, following her voice, and found them in the back bedroom.

Charlie was lying in bed, holding an ice pack to his head. Precious was sitting beside him with a bowl of soup from which she was trying to coax her husband to eat.

"He finally said the wrong thing, huh, Precious?" Trey said, trying to be funny, quickly realizing this wasn't the time for levity. "What in the world?" he asked more seriously.

"Douglas," she said.

"Douglas did this to you, Charlie?"

"Seems the boy didn't like us bringing you two over last night," Charlie said. "After you left, he exploded. Said we was messing in his business or something like that. Lord, we can't figure out that boy."

"He was high on alcohol, Charlie," Precious said. "He done found some whiskey we keep in the cabinets for colds and the like. Drank half a bottle while we's gone. Put it in his Coke."

"Is he okay?" Trey asked, nodding to Charlie. "Do we need to get him to the hospital? What if I call Cristina?"

"I think he's going to be okay. Douglas hit him in the best place to do the least harm...his head," she said, patting Charlie's hand.

"Yeah, I'm gonna be okay," Charlie said. "My heart hurts more than my head for that boy."

"Well, I've got more bad news, I think," Trey said. "Last night, I noticed that Douglas was wearing a ring on his little finger. I'm pretty sure it's the ring my niece gave me last Christmas, the one I was wearing the night I got jumped at the mill up the street. I'm not saying it was Douglas who jumped me; I'm just saying he was wearing my ring last night."

"Oh my goodness, that boy," Precious said, her heartache evident.

"Charlie, what do you think I should do? I don't want him to go to jail. Is there something we can say to him?" Trey asked.

"We's got to find him first," Precious said. "He ran out of here last night, and my niece ain't seen hide nor hair of him since."

Charlie slowly sat up, still holding the ice bag to his head.

"He's an angry young man, Trey. You don't want to confront him right now, especially if he's with his friends. No telling what they'll do. They'd be like angry dogs backed into a corner."

"You think jail might be the best place for him, so he doesn't hurt anyone else?" Trey asked.

"Or so someone doesn't hurt him," Charlie said. "I fear someone taking a knife or a gun to that young man one day."

"When you're feeling better, Charlie, let's you and me try to find him," Trey said.

The next morning, Trey's phone buzzed.

"Douglas came home late last night," Charlie said. "Said he was sorry for what he done. You wants to go over there with me and try to talk to that boy?" Charlie asked.

"Sure. I can go now."

Trey drove over and picked up Charlie and then drove to Precious's niece's house. The two men walked into the small house and found Douglas sitting on the couch playing a video game. Doreen, Douglas's mother, was nowhere to be found. When he saw them enter, Douglas threw the game controller down and started out the door. Trey blocked the exit with his six-foot-seven-inch frame and a smile.

"What you want with me?" he asked, not venturing to take on the tall man before him.

"Come on over here and sit down," Charlie beckoned the teen.

"I don't want to sit down," Douglas protested, looking for another way out.

"Sit down," Trey ordered in the meanest voice he could muster.

Douglas complied.

"We is worried about you, boy," Charlie said; the angry teenager looked down. "We's worried that you's being taken somewhere you really don't want to go by some of your so-called friends. They don't care what happens to you, but we do. Mr. Trey here thinks you have something that belongs to him."

"What?" the boy asked, trying to look surprised.

"A ring."

"I ain't got no ring," he replied, holding up his ten fingers.

"What happened to the ring you had on last night?" Charlie asked.

"I ain't got your stupid ring, I said!"

"The ring is not important, Douglas," Trey said. "We are much more concerned about you. The only future you have as part of a gang is a future of trouble. It's hard enough to make it when you're trying to do right. You got too much to offer to waste it on trouble. How can I help you?"

"You can't do nothin' for me!" the young man said, his anger exploding. "Don't nobody care for me. My daddy, he took off years ago. Everybody's always telling me what's wrong with me. Ain't nothin' wrong with me. Just leave me alone and let me live my life the way I want to!" Trey watched as Douglas quickly wiped a tear from his eye, and before anyone could react, the teen sprang from his seat and bolted out the front door.

Trey started to chase him, but Charlie called, "Don't bother, Trey. He could lead you to some trouble. He's up and run out before, and he's always come back. At this point, I hope he gets caught doing something he shouldn't. Maybe that'll shake him into changing. Some folks jus' have to learn by doing...can't be told nothin'."

"What's the story about his dad?" Trey asked.

"He left Doreen and the kids when Douglas needed him most," Charlie said. "He was about nine or ten. Kind of strange, he and his daddy always got along pretty good, did everything together. Douglas looked up to him, and his daddy seemed to enjoy being with his boy. Then, all of a sudden, he ups and leaves. No one's heard from him since, that I know of. That's when the trouble started. His momma ain't been able to do nothin' with that boy.

"Those youngins he's been hanging out with is plain trouble. They's part of a gang from his high school—all of 'em dropouts. I worry something bad's gonna happen to him if he keeps on." Charlie began to choke up.

Trey reached over and patted his arm.

"You and Precious are doing all you can do. We just need to entrust him to the Lord and pray that something happens to turn him around. Come on, I'll take you home."

The next morning, Trey picked up Cristina, and the two headed for Wayne County. They talked about Douglas, but mainly about life and love during the two-and-a-half-hour trip.

When they arrived, Trey stopped by his mom's house to say hello and drop Cristina off before going to the Wayne County jail. Averill Jenkins had promised that Trey's name would be on the prisoner's visitors list the next time he visited. Sure enough, Trey was led to a small room off the jail's cafeteria, where he waited until guards brought Lonnie in. The inmate was wearing a white prison jump suit, "WCJ" boldly stenciled in black on the back and on each pant leg. Lonnie did not make eye contact with Trey, even when Trey stood up to shake hands. They both sat down and endured a moment of awkward silence.

"I don't want to make this any harder than it has to be, Lonnie. I'm not here to condemn; I want you to know that we don't hold any grudges against you. I just imagine how difficult it is to be where you are, and I want you to know I'm thinking about you."

After a while, Lonnie cleared his throat.

"I don't know what to say. I knowed you was wantin' to come up here. My lawyer says I should let you."

Lonnie's problem with the law went back more than fifteen years when he and a young friend held up a convenience store, stealing seventy-five dollars and two cases of beer. He spent eight months in juvenile detention and a year on probation. Since then, he had been in and out of trouble—mostly in—for a variety of small offenses, many of which involved alcohol to some degree. Before the crash that killed Travis Glass, Lonnie had been involved in six alcohol-related traffic *accidents*, though none of them were really accidents. The judge, in sentencing Lonnie to twelve years in the state penitentiary for the death of Trey's dad, pointed to Lonnie's long, sad legal history with alcohol as a factor. If he did what he was supposed to in prison, he could be eligible for parole in seven years, perhaps five with good behavior.

"I guess I just want y'all to know that I'm sorry for Mr. Glass," Lonnie said after a while, looking directly at Trey for the first time. "I never wanted that to happen, and if I could I'd take it all back. I knowed it was your daddy who gave my momma groceries years ago. She always thought your family was good folks. I'm getting what I deserve."

"Where you gonna be?" Trey asked.

"Gonna start out at South Central up at Clifton. That'll be good for my momma since it will be easy for her to visit, but they said I could be transferred anywhere they want to send me. I hear they got a good substance abuse program up there in Clifton. I hope I get to stay there. The good Lord knows I need help with my drinkin'."

"Would you mind putting me on your visitors list when you get there? I promise I'll visit when I can. If they'll let me, I'll bring you magazines and books. Is that okay?" Trey asked.

"Why you doing this?" Lonnie said, overtaken by emotion. "You don't owe me nothin'. In fact, I owe you. You're a busy man—a famous man—and you don't need to be chasing after someone who done killed your daddy. I sure don't deserve none of your kindness."

"Lonnie, I look at it this way: the only difference between you and me is that your sins are the kind that's put you behind bars. My sins aren't. But we both have sins; yours aren't any worse than mine. And we both can be forgiven of those sins. I trust that you've already taken this up with God. If you haven't, then you should; it's easy, and he's quick to forgive. If you have, then we are brothers by the grace of God, and I want to help my brother out in his darkest hour. We've been thrown together by circumstances that involved my daddy. I know what he'd want me to do, and I'm trying to do it. I'm not going to be able to get to Clifton every week, but I'll come when I can, and I'll write you too. It's going to be hard keeping your faith where you're going, and if I can help you keep strong while you're there, we will both be better off."

Tears seeped through Lonnie's fingers, his face buried in his hands. Trey moved his chair to beside Lonnie's and put his arms around him.

"What can I do for your mom?" he asked.

"She's about to lose her house," Lonnie said through sobs. "I was her only source of income before I got stupid. She gets some welfare, but it ain't enough to keep her going."

"I'll check on her and do what I can, Lonnie. Don't you worry about your mom," Trey said assuredly.

After a while longer, a burly guard knocked on the door, signaling an end to visitation.

"I sure appreciate you coming to see me, Trey. I'm so sorry for this mess. Your daddy was a good man, and I think he done raised a good man too," Lonnie said, wiping his nose on his sleeve.

"Thanks, Lonnie. Next time I see you guess it'll be in Clifton," Trey said. "Be sure and add me to your visitors list, okay?"

"Yeah, I will. You and them Rockers win a championship, you hear? I'll be watching every game I can, you can bet on that."

After a hug and goodbyes, Trey was led back to the parking lot, where he sat in his car and called Attorney Jenkins's office to ask for an appointment. Five minutes later, he was in the lawyer's office.

"Trey, come in. Great to see you," the rotund lawyer said, shaking Trey's hand. "What can I do for you?"

"I'm here to help Lonnie Long," Trey said and began to unfold the details of his conversation with Lonnie.

By the time he walked out of Jenkins and Jenkins Law Offices, he had written a check for $125,000 to pay off Ruth Long's house, finish paying Lonnie's attorney fees, and set up an account to help with Mrs. Long's day-to-day expenses.

"And I want it done anonymously, Mr. Jenkins," Trey said.

Averill smiled knowingly.

The three Glass boys, Becky, a few of Becky's friends, and Cristina spent all day Saturday packing boxes and giving away items that Becky didn't have room for. At mid-afternoon, the men were finally ready to load her remaining earthly possessions into a seventeen-foot U-Haul truck Lee had rented. By the end of the day, the family was spent. Evie had a special dinner awaiting the tired and hungry movers. The rest of the evening was spent sharing stories about days gone by. Cristina loved every minute of it, especially the stories that embarrassed Trey.

At 9:30, Becky kissed each one of her children, including Cristina, good night before heading upstairs to bed. She and Cristina would stay at Adam's that night while Trey would spend the night at Lee's. Before long, the rest of the tired family said good night to each other and went to bed.

Tomorrow would issue a new chapter for the Glass family. Trey was thankful that Cristina was along for the ride.

CHAPTER 18

The court date rolled around for the men caught gambling in the alley near Trey's house. To Trey's astonishment, all twelve of the men showed up; some even wore new or "almost new" clothes for the occasion. Since none of the men could afford attorneys, Trey showed up without representation. He was prepared to accept whatever punishment the court dished out with the rest of his accomplices.

Judge Gladys Perkins, an older black woman, called the City Attorney and Trey to the bench at the start of the proceedings.

"Mr. Glass, I've heard that you are the one who bailed these men out of jail the night of the arrest. Is that correct?"

"Yes, ma'am."

"Why would you do something like that?"

"Well, I'm not sure," he answered, scratching his head. "It seemed like the right thing to do at the time. I guess it's because I believe there is something of value in each of these men, and I wanted to let them know I was in their corner."

"Were you gambling?" the judge asked.

"No, ma'am, I was watching."

"What amazes me, Mr. Glass, is that all the men who were arrested with you showed up today. I've seen a few of these men before, and if I really wanted to be mean, I could send them to jail for a few months, and yet, here they are." The judge took off her reading glasses. "So it seems your influence among these men is pretty substantial. From what I've heard about you, Mr. Glass, you appear to be an unusually mature young man, one who wants to do the right thing."

"Thank you, ma'am." Trey blushed.

"Something tells me jail would not be as constructive as what I'm about to suggest," Judge Perkins said. "I'm inclined to release them into your care. What do you think about that, Mr. Glass?"

"I object—" the City Attorney said.

"Joel, I'll get to you in a moment," the judge said. "Mr. Glass?"

"With all due respect, Your Honor," Trey said, "I object too. I really don't want to take responsibility for these men. As you said, some of these guys have been at this a long time, and I'm not sure there is anything I can do to change them. What I would be willing to do is offer to meet with those who are willing and discuss the effects of gambling, perhaps try to build a more healthy community among them. I'll even encourage those who aren't working to participate in a life skills program and then monitor their progress. And I'd be willing to break up any games I run across in my neighborhood."

"I think I could live with that," the judge said. "Now, Joel, what do you say to what Mr. Glass is offering? And keep in mind, this is highly unusual, but putting these gentlemen in jail is expensive and would probably not result in anything better than what Mr. Glass could bring about by simply being their friend and directing them to programs that could help them overcome their gambling problem or find a job."

"I see your point, Your Honor," Joel said. "The jails are overcrowded and have a gambling problem nearly as bad as on the outside. I think the city could go along with your suggestion as long as Mr. Glass realizes that next time might not bring the same lenient results."

"Good point," the judge said, conceding. "You do realize, Mr. Glass, that if these men come before me again, or any judge in the system, for that matter, they will most certainly be heading to jail? We won't tolerate illegal gambling on our streets."

"I'll pass on that warning, Your Honor. I truly appreciate your mercy on these men—well, on us all."

"We're trying to do what's best for all the citizens of our fair city," the judge said. "It just seems right to give these men a chance to better themselves. But be assured, my grace may be sufficient, but it's not inexhaustible. And Mr. Glass, go Rockers," she said with a wink.

"Thanks, Your Honor," Trey said, grinning. "May I ask one more thing? Could the court supply me with a list of names, addresses, and phone numbers for these men? I mean, if that's not illegal or too much trouble."

"I'll see what I can do," the judge said before sending the two men back to their seats. After scribbling herself a note, she said, "Will all the accused stand?

"Gentlemen," she said, "the evidence is ample that you were caught engaging in illegal activity. I have before me the police report complete with an itemized list of evidence confiscated from the scene the night you were arrested. Is there anyone here who wishes to contest the evidence and go to trial?"

All of the men immediately turned to look at Trey. He shook his head no, and each man returned his attention to the judge and shook his head no.

"Good," the judge said, "'cause you'd lose. Now, I don't need to remind you that gambling is not only illegal but also a dead-end street. You might win a few bucks here and there, but in the end, you will come up short. And there's a very good chance you will lose friends along the way. I've never seen gambling with your buddies as very beneficial to a friendship."

The judge's sermon went on for another three minutes before she said, "Therefore, I am releasing you with the understanding that those of you who need help with a gambling problem will get it, and those of you who need a job will do whatever is necessary to find employment. But hear me now, if you show up in my courtroom again for this same issue, I will send you to jail. Is that understood?"

The men vigorously nodded their heads in response.

"Now, I have asked Mr. Glass to make whatever arrangements are needed to help you move on from here. He has agreed to do what he can for you, but he will not take responsibility for you. Whatever changes you need to make in your life will be up to you. He will serve as a resource person, but that's all, and the court is grateful for his willingness. Cases dismissed," she said, bringing down the gavel.

Once outside the courtroom, the men gathered around their new hero and heaped praises on the man who delivered them from jail or a stiff fine.

"Back off, guys. I was trying to save my own skin as much as yours," he joked. "But seriously, we can't let this happen again. She will throw you in jail if you get caught, and I promise you will get caught if you keep it up. We have to find an alternative to your game nights. And those of you who need help with a gambling problem or finding a job, we've got to find that help for you. Now, how about some lunch?"

Trey led the men across the street to the Blue Plate, where he bought everyone's lunch. The unlikely group attracted the attention of other diners, and not because of Trey's superstar status. The thirteen seemed to enjoy being together, if the laughter and good-natured kidding were any indication.

"Here's the scoop on LoveWorks," Trey said as the men ate. "It's a thirteen-week job-training program that will help you develop or refine the skills necessary for finding a good-paying job. It's free, and lunch is provided every day. One of the best parts is the mentoring. If you wish, you will be paired up with a successful businessman who will meet with you once a week to encourage you and offer good advice. But you have to show up and be on time. At about week six or seven, you will be assigned an internship based on what kind of work you are best suited for. Sometimes the internship turns into a job, but there are no guarantees. If you need your GED, they can help you with that. All in all, it's a great deal, so think about it."

After the meal, the group dispersed, and Trey headed home to check on his mom.

Just as he got in his car, his cell phone buzzed.

"Hey, Cristina," he said in a cheery voice.

"Trey, can you come down here? Douglas has been shot," she said frantically.

When he reached the hospital, he parked on a side street and sprinted toward the Med, where he found Cristina in the ER.

"He's in pretty bad shape. They took him up to surgery about ten minutes ago. Not sure he'll make it," she said, tears forming in her eyes.

"Do Charlie and Precious know?" he asked.

"Yeah, I called Precious before I called you. They're on their way down here."

"Do you know what happened?" Trey asked, holding her hand.

"From what I could gather," she said, "Douglas and some friends assaulted this guy in South Memphis, were beating him up pretty badly until a witness pulled a gun and opened fire. One other boy was hit, but he's not as bad as Douglas. Douglas took bullets to his upper chest and neck. He lost a lot of blood before help arrived."

I'm beginning to really hate emergency rooms, Trey thought, recalling the time his dad was in an ER across town.

The Smits arrived by taxi, and Cristina filled them in on what she knew. Charlie, Precious, and Trey sat in the waiting room. Around mid-afternoon, Douglas's mom, Doreen, arrived and greeted her aunt and uncle with hugs and tears.

"That boy's going to be the death of me," Doreen said.

"Well, honey-pie, it ain't your death we's worried about right now, is it?" Precious said in her sweet, chastising way.

Charlie introduced Doreen to Trey, who shook her hand and expressed his sadness over what had happened to her son.

"He probably done deserved it," she said with little regret. Doreen was a thin woman, not much more than thirty years old, Trey guessed, and she didn't appear to be healthy herself.

The small party sat waiting for word about the teen. Precious sobbed, Charlie prayed, Doreen slept, and Trey called his mom.

"I'll have supper for everyone. Tell Precious, Charlie, and Cristina it will be ready around 6:00, and it's not anything that can't be reheated if something comes up."

"That's nice, Mom. I'll tell them. We may have Doreen, Precious's niece, with us. Got room for one more?" Trey asked.

"Well, of course. Bring her too. Sounds like she needs someone to love on her."

Late afternoon, Cristina joined the group and sat down beside Precious, taking her hand.

"Doctors said the surgery went as well as could be expected. Douglas is stabilized but not out of the woods. It will probably be tomorrow before they'll know how well he's doing. He's in CCU and won't be allowed any visitors tonight, so I recommend everyone go home and try to get some sleep."

"Mom has dinner ready for all of us at our house if you want to come over. If not, that's okay. I'll give you all a ride home," Trey said.

"We gotta eat," Charlie said. "Might as well be with folks we love."

"Excuse me," Doreen said abruptly, "but I have some business to tend to." And with that, she was gone.

Over dinner of chicken casserole, green beans, and salad, they discussed Douglas and Doreen.

"My niece has AIDS," Precious said. "She's been sick for a couple years now. Not sure if she got it from sleeping around or from a dirty needle. She has good days, and she has bad days. But it seems she has little time for that boy—and them other youngins…well, they just about have to raise themselves."

The thin, blond-haired boy took a seat next to Trey's in Mrs. Yancey's second-grade classroom.

"Boys and girls, this is Artie Walsh, a new student from Virginia," the teacher said. Artie's arrival at Trey's school created more heat than anyone could have predicted. Two days after Artie had entered school and word got around that he was HIV positive, parents of half the class pulled their students out, fearing their Johnny or Suzie would come down with the dreaded disease. By the third day, the only students left were Trey Glass and Jennifer Faring. A reporter from the largest newspaper in the state called Travis to ask how he could risk the health—indeed, the very life—of his son by allowing him to be in the same room with someone who was AIDS infected. After schooling the reporter on the realities of AIDS—that the

virus cannot be transmitted by touch—Travis said that the decision was not his, but Trey's.

"His mother and I laid out the facts concerning AIDS, the risks and such, and then left it up to our son to decide if he wanted to go back," Travis said. "All Trey said was that he couldn't imagine being a little boy that no one wanted to be around, let alone touch. So he went back. From what I heard from his teacher, the first thing Trey did was give his new classmate a big hug," Travis reported, a lump in his throat.

"Where do you think your son learned to treat people that way, Mr. Glass?"

"We think he must have been listening real close to the stories from Sunday school of Jesus touching lepers and the like."

CHAPTER 19

"Uh oh," Tyler said as he thumbed through the stack of daily mail, sorting third-class from Trey's personal mail. "Looks like you're in big trouble."

He handed Trey the letter from the Shelby County Court.

"I hope this is what I think it is," Trey said, slipping his finger underneath the flap of the envelope. "Yep. It's the list of addresses for the men I bailed out of jail. Looks like most of them live close by."

"What are you going to do with those guys?" Tyler asked.

"Not sure, but I told the judge I'd do what I can to help them out."

When his mom walked into the kitchen, Trey rose to give her a kiss and hug.

"Hey, Mrs. G.," Tyler said. "Coffee's ready."

"I need it," she said as she retrieved a cup from the cabinet. "Did you hear the thunder and rain last night? Woke me up several times."

"That should help the boys' garden grow," Trey said as he sat down to reread the list of names before him. "Hey, that gives me an idea. Do you think these guys would help me put in rain barrels? We should have already been harvesting the rain from our roof. Don't know why I hadn't thought of that before now."

"I don't see why not," Tyler said as he slid a ham and cheese omelet onto a plate for Becky. "They'd probably do anything you asked of them after all you've done for 'em."

"Oh, Tyler, I feel so guilty having you fix my breakfast," Becky said when the chef set the steaming plate in front of her.

"No problem, Mrs. G. I need the money, and Trey needs someone to make sure he doesn't gain extra pounds. Besides, we're here to serve you. So relax and enjoy."

"He's right, Mom," Trey said. "Tyler is more than just a chef; he's my nutritionist. The team has strict rules about what we can and can't eat, about our weight. Anyway, I have a special project for you, if you want it."

"Of course I want it. What is it?"

"If I can find these guys," Trey said, holding up the letter, "I want to have them over on Friday nights for a meal and a time to talk or work on a project together. That would mean using your gifts of cooking and hospitality. What do you think?"

"I'd love it," Becky said eagerly.

"And maybe Cristina would help you if you asked her," he said.

"I will. I just love that girl. Trey, have you thought of marrying her?" his mom asked.

"Okay," Tyler said, as he took off his apron and headed for the living room. "I think I'll just find somewhere else to be while you field that one, Trey."

"Mom, we've only known each other a few months. Besides, I'm not sure she'd want to marry me," he said, pretending to be absorbed in the letter.

"Oh, honey, I can tell by the look in her eyes that she'd marry you in a heartbeat. You two would make a great pair. And an old woman can never have too many grandchildren," she said demurely.

"Sheesh, Mom," Trey said with fake irritation. "You get right to the point, don't you? And you're not old."

Just then, Trey's phone buzzed.

"Well, speak of the angel. Hey, Cristina."

"*Buenos días, hombre guapo,*" she responded.

"What did you call me?" he asked.

"Look it up," she said teasingly. "I've got some news on Douglas," she said, her tone suddenly serious.

"Let's have it," he said, not expecting good news.

"He's going to live but may have some long-term disabilities. He woke up this morning and asked for water."

"I'm coming up there in a few minutes. Think that will be okay?" he asked.

"Sure. Why don't you stop by and ask Precious if she wants to come. I don't expect to see Doreen, and Douglas needs someone here who loves him. And hurry, I need someone here who loves me too," she said sweetly.

"When you put it like that, I'll be right there," he said with a shy grin. His mom was watching her son's expressions and gave him a wink. "I'll stop by to see if Precious needs a ride. See you soon."

"Oh, Mom," he said as he kissed her and headed out the door.

In a little less than an hour, Trey and Precious arrived at the hospital and found Cristina. She accompanied the two to ICU, where they found Douglas awake but drowsy.

"The police were here this morning to check on him," she whispered. "They want to interview him as soon as he is able to talk. The attending staff told them it might be a while."

Trey moved a chair over to Douglas's bedside for Precious. She sat down and patted the young man's hand. He was hardly recognizable with tubes running in and out of his body. As she bowed her head to pray, Cristina and Trey stepped out into the hallway.

"Shouldn't there be a police officer outside his door?" Trey asked. "Seems like the people he tried to rob would want to get at him."

"There are security guards all over this hospital. The staff is trained to identify suspicious-looking people, and everyone's aware of the situation. He'll be okay," she assured. "Are you here for a while?"

"Yeah, I think so…at least for as long as Precious wants to stay. I feel kind of responsible. I think our visit the other night set him off, maybe pushed him to do something stupid. I should have never mentioned that ring. It wasn't worth it."

"Oh, sweetie," she said, putting her arms around him. "None of this is anyone's fault except his. And maybe Doreen's. He's a troubled young man." On tiptoes, she kissed him gently on the cheek. "I've got to get back to work. I'll check on you from time to time. Want to grab lunch later?"

"Sure. You buying?" he teased.

"We can use my staff discount—all you can eat for $3.89. Maybe Precious will join us." They kissed, and she went on her way. He watched her all the way down the hall. She turned once to throw him a kiss.

I do love that woman, he thought to himself.

Trey returned to Douglas's room. Precious was still holding Douglas's hand and whispering to him. He sat in a chair by the window and offered a prayer for the troubled young man.

After lunch, the three returned to Douglas's room. A nurse had just finished checking on him.

"Hey, buddy," Trey said, gently placing his hand on the teen's arm. "Can you hear me?"

The young man looked up at Trey through droopy eyes, as though he were listening.

"We're praying for you. I need for you to know that a whole lot of people love you and care for you." Trey felt like he was fumbling for words—cheesy words, at that. "When you get out of here, we'll go do something fun. If you can think of anything you need, you let me know. I'll check on you again soon, okay?"

Douglas diverted his eyes to Precious before looking away. Trey thought he saw a tear in the teen's eyes. While Precious said goodbye for the day, Trey and Cristina walked out into the hall.

"You wonder what's in that young man's future?" Cristina said.

"Unfortunately, his story is played out many, many times in this city," Trey said. "Makes me more thankful for the work your brother does with the Boys and Girls Club. That's something I should put some time and money in to."

Trey and Precious left the hospital after assuring Douglas they would be back soon. Trey dropped Precious off at home and said a quick hello to Charlie.

"How you doing, old-timer?" he asked.

"Who you calling old?" Charlie replied, hugging his young friend.

"How you feeling? Headache go away?" Trey asked.

"Yeah, but I sees you brought her back," he said, tickled at his own joke. "Doing pretty good. Kind of worried about the boy. How's he doing?"

"He's…what would you say, Precious? He's…" Trey said, fumbling.

"He's alive, but Lordy, he's a mess. Jus' praying God will let him live. Hurts me to see him that way," she said.

The next morning, Trey planned to find as many of the men on his list as he could. Tyler had helped him put together a simple flier announcing Friday night meals. It read: *Game on! Friday nights at Trey Glass's house, 5:00. Free food and beer. Spread the word!*

"You sure you want to advertise free beer? Some of these guys might be alcoholics," Tyler said.

"Yeah, I wrestled with that," Trey said. "The plus side is that it might get them here. I guess we can address the potential problems when they come over."

"And you'd better be ready to push them out before midnight. They may decide to set up shop," Tyler said.

"I'm going to Lem's, Tyler. I will be back," he said, opening the back door and stepping outside. The walk to Lem's was short.

"Lem, can you help me?" Trey unfolded his plan to his neighbor; he wanted to find the men and have them over.

"Happy to help, Trey."

Trey and Lem started out on foot trying to find the men who lived nearby. For the next hour they tracked down the addresses on the sheet Judge Perkins sent. At the fourth house, they ran in to Perry Riggs, one of the men on the list. Perry was glad to see Trey and took four of the flyers since he knew where four of the accomplices lived. Trey urged Perry to spread the word to the others. Six of the addresses were too far to walk, so the men went back to retrieve Trey's car. After another hour, the men had distributed all the fliers.

"Trey, why are you doing this?" Lem asked over lunch. "You getting some kind of bonus from heaven?"

"Ha!" Trey laughed. "No. It's just everyone deserves a chance. And everyone deserves a friend—someone who won't turn their back on them when the going gets tough. These are good guys; seems like they just need someone who believes in them."

Friday rolled around, and Becky Glass spent the afternoon in the spacious kitchen cooking a huge pot of chili. When Trey returned from a workout at the gym, he caught the pleasant aroma before he got out of his car.

"Mmm! That smells so good, Mom," he said as he entered the kitchen. He leaned down to kiss her cheek.

"You think chili, crackers, and a veggie platter will be enough?" she asked.

"Sure. Looks like you have enough there to feed an army," he said.

"We can always save it for later if we don't eat it all tonight. Just don't want to run short. I'm going to fix ice cream sundaes for dessert."

"Sounds good, Mom. I'm going to take a shower. Cristina's supposed to come over after she leaves work," he said, heading out the kitchen door and upstairs. As he stood underneath the warm, relaxing stream of water, he prayed over the evening, asking God to bless the time spent with the men and to use him as his instrument.

That night, nine men showed up. Only seven of the original twelve made it, but two of the guys brought friends. Perry reported that some of the original twelve were reluctant to come, believing the meeting might be a ruse to force religion down their throats.

"You guys go back and tell them I don't work that way. I wanted to have you over so we could get to know each other, no strings attached," Trey said. "Here's the thing, the judge said if you ever come before her court again for gambling—or any city court—she will throw the book at you. I believe her. So we have to find an alternative to your street gambling. I'm not naive enough to believe that you will all together stop your gambling, but I promised her I would do what I can to turn your attention elsewhere, plain and simple truth.

"Guys, before we eat, I want you to meet my mom. She's responsible for the food tonight."

The men clapped their appreciation enthusiastically.

"And these are our neighbors Lem and Carla. And this is my girlfriend, Cristina."

Again the men cheered, someone adding flirtatious whistles when Cristina was introduced.

"Oh, one more thing. How many of you came tonight because you saw there was free beer?"

The men laughed out loud, and every last man raised his hand.

"That's what I thought. Let me explain that," Trey said. "Yes, there is free beer in that cooler over there," he said, pointing. "But there is a one-beer-per-person limit. Some of you guys struggle with alcohol, and I don't want this to be a time for you to get your fix. I'm not sure we'll ever serve beer again, but I wanted you to know I don't judge you because of any addictions you might have. I have a few of my own. We'll see how everyone behaves and then decide about future gatherings. Let's thank God. Father, thank you for your mercy, your blessings, and these who have gathered here tonight. Please protect the others who are not here. We love you. In Jesus' name, amen. Enjoy your meal."

For the next hour, the unlikely congregation sat knee-to-knee around the large table in Trey's dining room.

This is what it's all about, he thought several times as he surveyed the beautiful site around him. Once the eating slowed, Trey suggested the group go around the table and introduce themselves and offer one personal fact that might surprise all the others. Becky rose to gather the empty bowls, but Lem gently insisted that Becky stay seated while he collected them. This impressed some of the men, who were used to the women handling such menial tasks.

Some of the information shared around the table shocked, some saddened, some caused the group to wail in laughter.

"Well, I guess I'll go. I'm Trey Glass, and when I was in middle school, I got caught smoking weed and almost burned down a neighbor's barn."

The group sat stunned. Suddenly, the entire room erupted in howls of laughter. His mother's mouth flew open, Cristina sat in disbelief, and the whole bunch applauded its approval of Trey's vulnerability.

"Trey-boy, you tell them the whole story," Becky said, her eyes wide. Trey acquiesced, and the men around the table envisioned the young basketball star in trouble with the law.

"Guys, we've all been given a lot more than we deserve. And it seems to me that we should give back to others some of what we have been given. So may I suggest that we meet here each Friday night to eat a good meal? Mom and Cristina have agreed to cook for us, and after we eat, we will go out and do something nice for someone else. I was talking to Mrs. Sumner the other day over on Chuck Street, and she said she needs help taking down an old fence behind her house. Maybe we could do that next week. What do you say?"

Wide eyes looked around the table, as though silent communication was occurring between the men.

"I think it's a great idea," one man said.

As the rest chimed in with ideas for service projects, Trey felt they were off to a good start.

Over the next several weeks, between nine and fifteen guys met each Friday night to enjoy a wonderful meal prepared by Cristina, Becky, and, occasionally, Tyler. Each meal included time for the men to share how they were doing before heading off to do something meaningful to improve their neighborhoods. They took down Mrs. Sumner's fence and cleaned up her back yard, picked up trash in Getty Park, made sandwiches for the men and women who lived under the bridge over Thomas Parkway, erected a series of rain barrels to catch the run-off from Trey's roof, and played checkers with residents of a nearby nursing home. With paint supplied by the city, the men repainted forty-three fire hydrants. Not one of them mentioned that they missed the weekly dice games. As they began to trust Trey more and drew closer to one another, talk of God's goodness became more common. Each week a different man volunteered to thank God for the Friday-night meal.

But not everyone was happy with the intentional community that formed at Trey's house.

One Wednesday night about 8:30, Trey received another call from Reverend Leonard Gosnell, head of the Downtown Clergy Association.

Oh no, Trey thought, sighing when he recognized the name on the Caller ID.

"Mr. Glass, some of your neighbors are concerned about the rabble-rousers who meet at your house on Friday nights," Reverend Gosnell said. "They say they're afraid of what such people might bring to their neighborhood."

"That's funny, Mr., I mean *Reverend* Gosnell, because I haven't heard one complaint," Trey countered. "In fact, only thing I've heard is how thankful my neighbors are for the work these men have done to improve things around here."

"Do you really think you can reform these men, Mr. Glass? I mean, come on, these guys will eventually take advantage of you. They're just waiting for the right opportunity."

"I don't understand, sir. You asked me to do what I could to get the gamblers off the street. I've done that. I'm pretty sure they aren't gambling…at least not on these streets. And now you have a problem with them being in my home and the good works they are involved with. Why don't you come over next Friday night for a meal and meet the guys? I think you will be pleasantly surprised."

"No, thank you. I have more important things to do than eat with the likes of those men. Mark my words, Mr. Glass; you will rue the day you chose to fraternize with the devil's own. Good night, sir."

CHAPTER 20

As the bonds among the men who gathered at Trey's on Friday nights strengthened, so did the health of the Smits' nephew, Douglas. After two weeks in the hospital and another two weeks of physical therapy, Douglas was again out and about, although at about half the pace of other seventeen-year-old boys.

Trey had visited the young man in the hospital regularly and found Douglas more and more receptive to the prayers he, Charlie, and Precious offered on his behalf and in his presence. The Smits were certain that those prayers and the prayers of the Sunday night faith community were what pulled the teen through.

Trey went to bat for Douglas against assault charges levied on him for his attack of a citizen in South Memphis. Since it was the young man's first charge—and because Trey Glass stood by him—charges were dropped after the judge made a stern warning that such behavior would not be tolerated in the future.

On another front, gang activity in Memphis became more pervasive and violent. Armed robberies of businesses, muggings, and drive-by shootings seemed to increase daily. Police warned citizens to limit their outside activities or to travel in groups until something could be done about the out-of-control youth who roamed the streets in search of drugs, money, and trouble.

Trey's off-season was coming to an end. In another few weeks, he would begin two-a-day practices as the Rockers launched another quest for their first NBA championship. The point guard was about to leave rookie status and become, according to some, the franchise's best hope for winning it all. He resisted all the hype local and national sports reporters spread concerning his value to the Rockers organization. Despite how he saw it, his fame continued to grow, and everywhere he went, adoring fans vied for his attention. Both groups that met in his home—his Sunday night house church and the Friday night men's gathering—knew they were in the presence of greatness but saw Trey Glass more as a good friend than a basketball sensation. They felt at ease around him because he made them feel that way. And they were catching the ways of God simply by observing the unusual young man they called friend.

Ten-year-old Trey sat on the hearth in his parents' small but comfortable living room as his dad read a section of the Gospel of John to the family one evening. The story was of the woman at the well who had come to draw water in the middle of the day because she wasn't welcomed among the respected women of the village who drew their water in the cooler part of the day.

Jesus struck up a conversation with the woman, and in a short time the two had engaged in a hope-filled discussion.

"Wow," Adam said, "you wonder how Jesus could feel comfortable around that prostitute. I'm surprised he even talked to her."

Travis put the book aside and thought for a moment.

"You're right, Adam," he said. "But I find it even more amazing that this woman, who was ignored and looked down on by her village, could feel comfortable in the presence of Rabbi Jesus. He had a way of making even the most forgotten person feel at ease around him. He could make the most insignificant person feel very important."

Trey felt more and more comfortable in his neighborhood as he met more of the folks who lived around him; likewise, the people he met felt comfortable around him. Despite the police warnings, he walked the streets nearly every day, sometimes with his mom, sometimes with Cristina, sometimes both, but most of the time, he walked alone. Those who learned his routine made sure they were outside when he ventured by, knowing he'd stop and chat. Trey enjoyed learning their stories and discovering information about their families. He especially enjoyed hearing the rich history of the neighborhood from old-timers who grew up there or moved in long before Trey was born. It was true that things weren't like they used to be, and he was determined to do what he could to dust off the past so that the glory days of the area could be restored. He prayed daily that God's will be done in South Memphis as it is in heaven.

When neighbors got to know one another, unity and strength merged to deter crime, and Trey was certainly doing his part by bringing the people in his neighborhood together. Folks not only felt safer, but pride in property ownership grew. Neighborhood watches sprung up on nearly every street. Even the mayor took note of improvements to the area and publically commended the residents for their contributions toward a more beautiful and safer Memphis.

Still, there were segments that didn't approve of Trey's presence. Some of the reasons were racial prejudice and envy. But most unhappy were the thieves, thugs, and gangs who thrived on the chaos that allowed their kind to flourish. Contrary to what was happening in other parts of the city, gangs in South Memphis were being pushed further underground, and they blamed Trey Glass. Something had to be done.

Leaders of South Memphis's three largest gangs met to discuss the "problem." It was the first time the three gangs agreed on anything, and the first time the gang leaders had ever met except to fight. Although he didn't know it, Trey was even bringing the criminal element together.

Young Douglas was far from being a gang leader, but he was forced to join in the discussion because of his aunt and uncle's friendship with the subject at hand. If Trey could be lured to one of the area's many rotting and deserted buildings, he could be "taken care of," and it was agreed that Douglas was just the one to do the luring. When he heard their plan, he immediately expressed his hesitancy about being a part. In addition to his fear of getting caught, his heart was slowly being changed; he even felt slight affection and appreciation for the NBA star.

"You ain't got no choice," one of the leaders told the teen before slapping him to the ground. "You's either with us or against us."

"'Cuz if you ain't with us, we's going to do to you what we's going to do to Mr. Glass," another leader threatened. "You understand?"

Douglas understood alright. He'd seen what his out-of-control peers could do. He knew if he didn't cooperate, his time was limited.

"So how am I supposed to get him to trust me?" Douglas asked pleadingly. "He ain't gonna just follow me to a dark warehouse, no questions asked."

"That's for you to figure out," the gang leader said. "I say we get this on this weekend."

The diabolical plan was formed. Four days from now, on Saturday night, Douglas would lure the basketball star to the same abandoned warehouse where he was accosted the year before. How he got him there was the teen's business: "Just have him there," he was warned. Each of the three gang leaders would bring two of their "best" guys to dispense a stern warning to the neighborhood hero, communicating that he was not welcomed in the area. The best way to get their message across, one of them suggested, was to make it so he would never play basketball again. Evil ran wild as the gathering of brutes suggested various forms of torture, from breaking both legs to hacking off a hand or foot with a machete. The gangsters giggled like schoolboys at each evil idea. The aim, the leaders agreed, was to maim, not kill—this time. If the warning didn't work, stronger measures would be necessary.

Knowing that he'd soon be heading into the busy season when he wouldn't get to spend as much time with Cristina, Trey took every opportunity to be in the presence of the woman he considered the most beautiful in the world. Thursday was her day off, so the two traveled ninety miles east to Shiloh Battlefield, site of one of the bloodiest battles of the Civil War. The beauty of the historical park belied the travesty that took place there over two days in April of 1862, when nearly four thousand soldiers lost their lives and thousands more were wounded.

Trey and Cristina walked hand-in-hand among the thousands of gleaming white tombstones that marked the final resting places of mostly Confederate soldiers. They sat on a shaded park bench on a bluff overlooking the Tennessee River, each pondering the futility of war.

"My family spent many weekends up here when I was a kid. My dad knew a lot about the battles fought here and nearby and would tell us stories. There's a tree over there," Trey said, pointing, "where General U.S. Grant had his command tent. There's a little gold plaque nailed to it. Hard to imagine on a day like today what a horrible tragedy took place on this very site."

Cristina snuggled closer and put her arm in his.

Trey leaned over and kissed the top of her head, noting her appealing scent.

"Could you ever see yourself married to a professional basketball player?" he asked after sitting awhile in silence.

"No," she answered, looking down.

"No?" he said, a troubled look on his face.

She smiled and turned so she could see his face.

"I could see myself married to the most wonderful man I have ever met, who also happens to be tall and play basketball. I wouldn't care what he did as long as I could be with him forever."

He took her face in his hands and kissed her lips, long and deep. They sat watching the syrupy water flow quietly north toward the Ohio River.

"What would your family think about you marrying a *gringo*?" he asked.

"Trey! That's not very nice," she said in fake indignation. "Besides, they wouldn't be the ones marrying the *gringo*," she said, mocking him. "I would."

"Do you know what you'd be getting yourself in to?" he asked. "I'll be out of town a lot. People wouldn't let us enjoy a meal out. We couldn't go anywhere without being mobbed—"

"Shhh," she said, putting her fingers to his lips. "I don't care about any of that. All I care about is you. I don't care if you are the biggest celebrity in the world or if you quit playing basketball tomorrow. I'd love you and your lifestyle, no matter what, and I'd be honored to spend the rest of my life with you."

"Could you live in my neighborhood?" he asked.

"Of course. I love the people in your neighborhood," she replied emphatically.

"With my mom?" he asked.

"Yes, yes, a thousand times yes!" she affirmed. "I love your mom to pieces. You might ask her if she could live there with me. She might have other ideas."

"No way. She thinks you're wonderful."

"I do think it's important for you to meet the rest of my family, so you'll know what you're getting yourself in to," Cristina said.

"When could that be?"

"I thought we might invite them up once the season starts so they can see you play. If you have a good game, that might persuade them you're worthy of me," she teased.

"We start exhibition games in a month, so that means it would be about six weeks before they would visit." Trey was calculating in his head when he might propose to Cristina.

"Is that a problem?" she asked.

"No, that's fine," he said. "It just seems so long before I get to meet them. And they probably wouldn't all come up here, would they?"

"Probably just Mom, Dad, and my two youngest sisters. We'd have to go down there for you to meet everyone, unless they all came up to Dallas for a game when you play the Mavs," she said, thinking out loud.

"Are you saying you won't marry me until I meet all your family?" Trey asked.

"No. I'm just saying you *shouldn't* marry me until you meet all my family."

"Why? Are they serial killers?" he asked.

"Just my mom."

The couple laughed out loud, frightening two cardinals that sat on a limb above them. Trey and Cristina sat there awhile longer before slowly walking back toward his car. After lunch at a local catfish restaurant just outside the park, they drove back to Memphis.

Friday night came, and fifteen people gathered to enjoy Becky Glass's spaghetti and meatballs. Cristina brought a salad, and Carla brought dessert. Once the men got a taste of Becky's sweet tea, no one mentioned beer. Cristina brewed a big pot of coffee to go along with Carla's apple crunch cobbler and ice cream.

As usual, the conversation was lively and upbeat. The few complainers were drowned out by the other, generally optimistic men.

"Dear Lord, thank you for this food. Let it nourish our bodies so we can do your service. Thank you for this home, in which resides the Spirit of the Living God. Amen." Perry Rigg's prayer was thoughtful and heartfelt.

The others echoed hearty amens. After everyone had eaten their fill, two of the man took Lem's cue and removed dirty plates from the table.

Before heading out to pick up trash at the park, talk turned toward the gang violence sweeping the city. A few of the men knew people who had been assaulted and robbed by small bands of roving youth armed with sticks and clubs. Some of the men actually knew a few gangbangers.

"They ain't as many as they once was, but there's still some hooligans out there," one man reported. "I'm afraid to go anywhere by myself."

"That's a good idea," Lem said. "And the worst thing we could do is return violence with violence. If you run across trouble, get out of there and call the police. Don't try to handle it yourself. These kids are liable to do something stupid they'll regret for years to come."

The men expressed their agreement, although some seemed less convinced than others that nonviolence was the way.

"I think these young men could be redeemed if we could just separate them from the others," Trey said. "Peer pressure is a powerful incentive to do evil things."

CHAPTER 21

While young Douglas wrestled with the details of his heinous assignment, Trey was in the Rockers gym working out with the strength-and-conditioning coach. He finished the Saturday morning practice by shooting two hundred free throws into a shrunken practice hoop and making 83 percent, according to an assistant coach who kept count. Few players worked as hard as Trey at perfecting their game.

Since Becky had moved in, Tyler took weekends off. When Trey got home, his mom had fixed a deli plate of meats, fruit, veggies, and crackers.

"I thought we'd eat a light lunch and have Cristina over for a nice dinner," she said as she poured two glasses of sweet tea.

"That sounds good," he said, thinking again about how much he loved Dr. Garza. "What are you doing this afternoon?"

"Tony's bringing some of the boys over, and we're going to finish harvesting the gardens and get ready to plant our fall stuff. Those boys are so cute. And they are very courteous. They call me *Ma* Glass. Isn't that sweet?"

"Yeah, they're good boys. I'm glad you hit it off with them. They're the lucky ones," he said, patting his mom's hand.

"I meant to tell you, Douglas came by this morning looking for you. Said he'd be back."

"Did he say what he wanted?" Trey asked.

"Nope. But he looked a little bothered."

"I'll try to find him later. Thanks for the lunch, Ma Glass," he said, winking.

Trey showered, read some, and then headed over to the Smits' house.

Charlie was sitting in his favorite chair on the porch, sipping a cup of something warm.

"What's in the cup, hot toddy?" Trey asked.

"Hot tea," the old man said. "Want some?"

"If you're going to fix it, yes. If Precious has to fix it, no," Trey said.

"Done got it fixed," Precious said as she came out the door carrying a cup of steaming water with a tea bag string dangling over the side. "Seen you comin'."

"Does Charlie ever do anything worthwhile around the house?" Trey asked, taking the hot cup from her hands and kissing her cheek. "Thanks."

"Sho' he does. He gets out of the house so's I can clean it!" she said with a hearty laugh.

"You's forgetting that time I changed a light bulb in the hallway," Charlie said, tolerating the friendly ridicule.

"Let me see," Precious said, rubbing her chin. "That was back in '74, wasn't it?" she said with her contagious giggle. Just then, the water kettle began to whistle. "Oops. Forgot to turn the heat off." She went back inside the house.

"Mom said that Douglas came by this morning looking for me. I was at the gym. You know what he wanted or where he is?" Trey asked.

Charlie turned to make sure Precious was not at the door, then he said in a noticeably hushed tone, "Yeah, the boy needs your help tonight after supper." Trey sensed uneasiness in his friend but didn't think it was worth mentioning.

"I'll be glad to help. Where and what time? And what kind of help?" Trey asked.

"I think he wants you to meet him at the corner of Clower and Boyd around 9:00. Seems he's got a friend who wants to meet you."

"Really? Couldn't he bring his friend over to the house?" Trey wondered aloud.

"Uh, I think the kid's in a wheelchair," Charlie stuttered, obviously making up the story as he went along.

"A wheelchair? What's going on, Charlie?" Trey asked. "He wants me to meet his friend who's in a wheelchair at 9:00 tonight?"

Charlie leaned in toward Trey and nearly whispered, "Trey, I can't tell you more than that. Just show up. Douglas needs you. Trust me."

"Okay, okay," Trey said. "I'll be there."

"Alone."

"Alone," Trey repeated, puzzled by the mystery but trusting his friend. Precious reemerged from the house before Trey could ask for more information. It was clear that Charlie didn't want to discuss the matter in front of his wife.

"What're you two scheming?" she asked, laying a small plate of lemon cookies on the weathered TV tray between the two men.

"Ain't nothin'," Charlie said, leaning back in his seat and looking out toward the front yard. His mood was more serious than Trey had ever seen.

"You know where Douglas is right now?" Trey asked.

"He was here earlier today," Precious said. "Ain't seen him since."

"Think I'll take one of these for the road," Trey said, picking up a cookie. He thought Charlie was acting strange but didn't want to push the issue in front of Precious. "Guess I'll be seeing you all tomorrow night."

"Guess so," Charlie said.

"You have yourself a good afternoon, Trey. Tell your momma hello, you hear?" Precious said, hugging him.

"Will do," Trey said, avoiding eye contact with Charlie.

Trey walked home and went inside to get his car keys. On the way to his car, he stopped by to greet Pastor Tony and the five young men working hard in the garden. They all stopped work to say hello and give high-fives and hugs to their hero.

"Headed out, Mom. Be right back," he said, leaning over to kiss her cheek. She was busy shaking dirt off the radishes and never looked up.

He drove down to Clower Street, turned left, and followed the road until it intersected with Boyd. On each of the four corners were signs of urban decay: a closed-down convenience store, a small coin laundry, a busy check-cashing business, and an empty lot surrounded by a chain-link fence in stages of disrepair. He pulled his car over to the curb and surveyed the area.

Looks safe enough, he said to himself. As he pulled away, he turned right on to Boyd and noticed an alley that ran behind the empty lot. He slowed and looked up the alley. About two blocks up, he could see the backside of the dilapidated fabric mill where he was assaulted the year before.

Hmm, wonder why Douglas wants to meet here?

When Cristina arrived at 6:30, Trey was out back getting the grill ready for steaks his mom had bought. Becky was in the kitchen finishing up a salad she was fixing. Cristina gave her a hug and put a bottle of sangria on the counter and reached for two glasses.

"How was your day?" Becky asked.

"Pretty good, but crazy busy," Cristina answered. "Lots of people with allergies who think they've got the flu. And how was yours?"

"Just wonderful. We got the last of the vegetables from the garden and put in some of our fall and winter seeds. These radishes and tomatoes are from the garden," she boasted, showing off her salad. "We sent most of the vegetables home with the boys."

Cristina admired the bowl of salad, picked out a radish, and popped it in her mouth.

"Umm, good," she said. "You are so sweet to help those guys out. I know they must love you."

"I kind of treat them like grandchildren," she said. "Don't know if they like it or not, but that's how I treat 'em. Did I tell you they call me Ma Glass?"

Cristina smiled and poured two glasses of sangria then walked out back to see what Trey had cooking.

"Let the party begin," Trey said when he saw her. He hugged her and gave her a warm kiss.

"Better not let the steaks burn," she said, finally coming up for air.

"The steaks aren't the only thing on fire," he whispered.

"You do have a way with words, big man." She giggled.

He turned the meat, closed the top of the grill, and gestured toward two lawn chairs nearby. He moved his closer to Cristina's, and the two sat sipping their drinks and holding hands. He asked about her day, and she asked about his.

"Worked out this morning, then went to see Charlie and Precious. Strange," he said after pausing.

"Strange?" she inquired.

"Yeah. Something was up with Charlie, but I couldn't ask him about it in front of Precious. He said something about meeting Douglas tonight at 9:00."

"Hmm. That *is* strange. You going to do it?" she asked.

"Of course. Douglas told Mom he was coming back this afternoon to see me, but I haven't seen him. I guess he doesn't need to, now that his uncle Charlie made the arrangements."

"You don't plan to go alone, do you?"

"I'll be alright. I drove by there today; it's safe enough," he said.

"Trey Glass, that's stupid," she said, as forceful as he had ever seen her. "You ask Lem or someone to go with you. You know what the police say about being out alone."

"Look, I told Charlie I'd go alone. Anyway, I'm afraid I'll scare Douglas off if I bring someone with me. I'll be okay."

When the steaks were near ready, Cristina went inside for a platter to put the charred beef on. When she returned, Trey could tell his girlfriend was bothered by their discussion. The three sat down at the kitchen table.

"Go ahead and butter your potato, then we'll say a prayer," Becky said. "Would you mind thanking God for the food, Cristina?"

The three bowed and held hands while Cristina prayed. After she finished, she crossed herself before remembering.

"Sorry, it's just a habit," she said apologetically.

"Honey, don't you worry," Becky said. "I think that's a beautiful thing. We all have our own little quirks, some good and some not so good, don't we, Trey-boy?" Trey and Cristina looked at each other, and he wondered how Cristina took her mom's use of the word *quirk*. The dinner conversation was light, with Becky doing most of the talking. After supper, Trey and Cristina washed dishes while Becky sat and continued talking over her cup of decaf before they all retired to the den. Trey's mom spent the next forty-five minutes leafing through Glass family photo albums with Cristina.

Trey's cries of disapproval apparently fell on deaf ears. Becky seemed to have a story for each picture of her youngest son. He tried to protest again, but the two ladies were enjoying their trip back in time too much to pay him any attention. Every time Cristina "oohed" or "ahhed" over a photo, Trey cringed. The torture finally ended when Becky closed the last album and went to bed.

When they were alone, Cristina said, "I'm going with you."

"What?"

"I'm going with you to meet Douglas," she repeated.

"No, you're not."

"You're not going alone, Trey Glass! Either you take Tony or Lem or me. Who will it be?"

"None of the above," he said, a bit irritated. "I told you, I can't take anyone with me. I promised Charlie."

"This isn't up for discussion," she said. "We'll take your car, lock all the doors, and won't get out until we're sure it's safe. So who's it going to be?"

Trey stood up and began pacing around the large den, trying to come up with an argument. He had never seen Cristina so assertive and knew it was because she loved him. If things worked out as he hoped, there would be many other moments when their fortunes and misfortunes would be interlinked.

Why keep her out of this one, be it for better or for worse?

CHAPTER 22

At 8:55, Trey backed his car out of the drive and steered toward Clower. As they approached the intersection at Boyd, Cristina observed—to her relief—that the street lights were working, giving an eerie, yellowish glow to the area. Sure enough, Douglas waited on the street corner and paced nervously in his gray hoodie.

"Hey, bud!" Trey called out as he pulled to the curb across the street.

"Why'd you bring her?" Douglas shouted when he saw Cristina.

"I didn't; she brought herself. Long story. So where's your friend?"

"Um, he's around the corner. We have to drive there," the teen said as he tried to open the back door. It was locked until Trey pushed the unlock button, and the young man got in.

"What's this all about, Douglas?" Trey asked.

"You'll see, man," he said.

A chill crawled up Cristina's spine.

"Pull around the corner and head up the alley."

Cristina grabbed Trey's arm.

"Don't do it," she whispered, her tone anxious. "I don't feel good about this. There's no telling what or who is in that alley. Let's go home, Trey. We can meet his friend some other time."

"Trust me," Douglas countered. "I'm trying to do the right thing, man. Just drive on up there, you'll see."

Trey felt trapped. He didn't feel good about the whole scene, but something in the spunky point guard kept him going—the same spunk that propelled him headlong toward some of the biggest inside men in the NBA. He was confident that he could protect Cristina should anything happen. And he knew God was always there to offer protection beforehand, peace during, and comfort after.

"It'll be alright," he said, patting her hand.

The alley was nearly overgrown with bushes on both sides. The screeching sounds of branches against the car gave the whole scene an even eerier tone. As they neared the back of the old warehouse, Trey noticed another car with its headlights reflecting off the large concrete side of the building and lighting up the open space in between. The grassy area looked like a playing field lit by stadium lights.

"Pull up there next to that car," Douglas ordered. "Leave your lights on and get out."

"Cristina's not getting out," Trey said emphatically. "This better not be some kind of trick, Douglas." Trey undid his seatbelt, and before he opened the door, he put his wallet and cell phone in the glove box. "You stay here. Lock the door. If something happens, you get out of here as fast as you can. I can take care of myself."

Douglas led Trey over to the center of the lighted area, and the two stood staring at the headlights of the two cars parked side by side. In a moment, a raucous group of eight young men emerged from the overgrown brush and bushes that surrounded the small open space. Each man carried a bat, chain, or tire iron and formed a circle around the two bewildered captives.

"What is this?" Trey demanded.

"Get the girl," one of the older ones shouted, nodding toward Trey's car.

"Gosnell, you ain't said nothin' about the girl," Douglas said in protest.

Trey turned in disbelief.

"Gosnell?"

"What of it?" the young man said.

"Leave her out of this!" Trey said, his voice a growl from deep inside his chest. He ran frantically toward the car. When he got close, one of the men swung his bat and caught Trey squarely across his back, knocking him to the ground. The assailant raised the bat again to deal a lethal blow to the head.

"Save it!" the leader shouted just in time. "There will be time for that later. Right now, let's just check out the girlfriend."

When Cristina refused to unlock the car door, the man with the bat administered a crashing blow to the driver's-side window and dragged the frightened young doctor out of the car by her hair. He threw her to the ground in the middle of the circle. Trey couldn't move to help her.

"What do we have here?" the leader said, probing her breasts with the end of his bat. "Sweet. Looks like we got us some dessert. Douglas, my man, you done good," he said, his voice sinister. "Real good. You can stay around to watch, or you can get yourself on home. Your job is done here."

In an instant, Douglas was gone, disappearing into the thick brush.

"Drag him over here. I want him to watch what we do to his girlfriend before he gets his."

Two of the hoodlums grabbed Trey under the arms and drug him to the center of the circle, while the bloodthirsty mob moved closer to the impending action, each anticipating his turn at the dazed beauty before them. They whistled and jeered as the leader bent down and began unbuttoning Cristina's top. Trey made an effort to get up but was thrust back to the ground by a sharp kick to his head. In a fog, blood seeping from his ear, he lay semiconscious but aware enough to know that something bad was happening. He turned his head, his eyes met Cristina's, and the two stared helplessly at each other. With one final attempt to save herself from rape and her boyfriend from possible death, she mustered all her strength. A crushing kick to the groin of the man who stood over her was enough to thwart her attacker. He fell backwards, grabbing himself, to the perverted delight of his accomplices, who cheered their buddy's misfortune.

The mob lunged to finish the job he started when a group of twenty or so men, armed with every kind of garden implement, emerged from the same bushes the first group came from. Lem Davis was accompanied by Perry Riggs, others from the Friday night group, and various men from the neighborhood who had developed a fondness for their young friend.

"You boys are clearly outnumbered!" Lem shouted as the larger militia marched toward the young men, now the underdogs. "Drop your weapons!"

"We ain't got no beef with you," the gang leader said, turning to face the larger contingent. "Besides, you don't want this whitey in your 'hood, do you?"

"It's you we don't want in our neighborhood!" Perry called out. "I been wantin' for a good rumble, and this looks like a fine one shaping up."

The army behind him echoed his sentiments and began yelling threats to the frightened teens who still surrounded Trey and Cristina. In the distance, police sirens echoed through the canyons of downtown and got louder as they neared ground zero.

Several of the young men tried to make a run for it but were headed off like calves by men who tackled them and wrestled their weapons away. The main leader, Lenny Gosnell, threw his bat at Lem and took off running. He did not make it far before he was clotheslined by a hoe handle wielded by Perry. The young man fell to the ground clutching his throat and gagging, blood trickling from his mouth.

When it looked like a hopeless case for the teen mob, the other leaders threw their weapons on the ground, and the remaining teens did the same.

From out of nowhere, Charlie appeared and knelt beside Trey and Cristina to check out their injuries.

"Help is on the way. Jus' hang on," he said, tears streaming down his face as he dabbed at the blood that streaked Cristina's arms.

Soon, from the same bushes through which the neighborhood militia emerged only minutes earlier, dozens of Memphis's finest charged, armed and ready to take down anyone who tried to flee.

"Everyone drop your weapons and get down on the ground! Now!" the voice commanded. "I repeat, get down on the ground now, and put your hands out where we can see them. We will not hesitate to shoot you." Two police cars with lights flashing drove up the alley and stopped beside the other cars.

Instantly, Lem, Perry, and their fellow heroes dropped their rakes, hoes, shovels, and machetes and hit the turf. Once it was established who were good guys and who were not, the gang members were handcuffed and led back through the growth toward waiting police vehicles. EMTs appeared and began treating the basketball star and Cristina. Two others attended to Lenny, who would need more medical attention than the EMTs could offer there.

"What in the world? How?" Trey mumbled when he saw Charlie. "Where's Cristina?"

"I'm right here, sweetheart," she said, reaching for his hand.

"They're going to take you both to the Med," Charlie said. "We'll be right up there to tell you all about it. You both gonna be fine, thank God Almighty." Tears continued to roll down his cheeks.

As usual on a Saturday night, the ER at the Med teemed with the injured, sick, young, and elderly from all over the Mid-South. There was not one empty seat in the waiting room, and patients awaiting treatment lined the hallways in and around the ER, some sitting or lying on the floor. Ordinarily, since Trey's and Cristina's injuries were not life threatening, they would have had to wait their turn like everyone else, and tonight's wait would be especially long. But because the two were well known in those very hallways, they were soon ushered into separate examination rooms. Despite Trey's protests that he didn't deserve special treatment, he was treated like a VIP. The doctor assigned to him ordered X-rays and spent more time than usual making sure his injuries were not serious. X-rays confirmed that the blow to the back did not do permanent damage, although it left a clear impression, the beginnings of a colorful bruise. After making sure he suffered no head or neck injuries, the doctor allowed Trey to get up.

Cristina didn't fare as well. Trey found her two rooms down and was alarmed to see a room full of doctors and nurses attending her. She had suffered a few bumps on her head from being pulled through the car window by her hair, but nothing serious. Her biggest injuries were lacerations on her right arm above the elbow from shattered window glass. One cut required six sutures; the others just needed cleaning and bandaging. The crowd she attracted was mainly fellow staff members concerned about their colleague's condition.

When Trey saw her, he pardoned his way through the throng and bent over to hug her. A few of the nurses sighed.

"I was worried about you," he said.

"And I was worried about you," she said. "Looks like you're doing better than me. What'd they say?"

"They examined my head and found nothing," he said with a straight face.

The examination room erupted in laughter and applause. Cristina pulled him close and kissed his lips.

By eleven p.m.—after a short interview with the police—the two were allowed to leave. They walked toward the door of the waiting room before stopping short. Adding to the usual Saturday night chaos was a throng of news cameras and reporters who had heard Trey's name on the police scanners they constantly monitored.

"We can't go out that way," Trey said. "This is not something I want to deal with tonight."

"There's a back entrance we can sneak out," Cristina said. "Follow me." She led Trey through a series of winding hallways. As they rounded the corner, Trey nearly bumped into a man walking briskly through the hospital.

"Excuse me, sir," Trey said.

"Glass. Trey Glass," the man said.

Instantly Trey recognized his voice.

"Reverend Gosnell?"

"I, uh, is everything okay?" the large pastor asked, obviously embarrassed.

"Yes, sir. We had an…incident. All well with you?"

Trey looked at the reverend knowingly; his son was his spitting image.

"Trey, I—"

"You're in my prayers, Reverend. Please excuse us; we're kind of in a hurry here. Cristina, there's Charlie."

She looked over his shoulder to see Charlie in the waiting room, vigorously waving his arms in an effort to get their attention. Charlie worked his way through the crowded room toward the ER door.

"How are you two?" he asked.

"Tell you later, Charlie," Trey said seriously. "And you have some explaining to do. But right now, we have to get out of here. Cristina knows the way."

She led them through the labyrinth of hallways and passages, through a mechanical room, and out a side emergency exit.

"Your car's around the front," Charlie said.

"What? My car?" Trey said. They walked briskly through the cool night air and soon spotted Trey's car backed into a parking space. "How did my car get here, Charlie? Did you drive it?"

"Nah, sir. Had a chauffeur," he said with a grin.

As they neared the parked vehicle, Trey saw the twenty or so men who had come to their rescue. They clapped and cheered when they saw the three coming their way. He noticed the shattered side window; other than that, the car seemed to be in good shape.

"Never in my life was I so glad to see your ugly faces," he said, giving high-fives, handshakes, and hugs to the cheering mob. They pressed around, gingerly patting his back and hugging Cristina until Charlie and Lem got their attention.

"Brothers!" Lem shouted. "Give them a break. They've been through quite a bit tonight. I'm sure they will want to thank you all for your help, but let's let them get on home."

Despite their exuberance, the friends began to back off and give them space to get into their car. Trey noticed a lone figure cowered in the back seat. It was Douglas.

"Now before you react," Charlie said, positioning himself between Trey and the car, "you need to hear me out."

"I'm listening," Trey said, glaring at the frightened young man.

"Let's get on home first," Charlie said. "Your momma's worrying her head off about you two."

The drive home was silent.

Once in the house, Becky ran to greet her son. She threw her arms around both Trey and Cristina, trying to contain deep sobs. They stood in the kitchen hugging while Charlie nudged Douglas toward the den where Precious sat. She rose and grabbed her nephew around the neck and held on while she cried. He returned her hug.

"You needs to hear Douglas out," Charlie said as he took a seat next to his wife.

"I was trapped," Douglas said. "Those guys was aiming to hurt you real bad, and they used me to get to you. They promised they would hurt me real bad, maybe even kill me, if I didn't help them. I didn't know what to do."

"That's when the boy came to me, Trey," Charlie said. "He told me the whole crazy scheme. This morning we decided to set a trap so we could round up them troublemakers and put an end to their craziness. Lem and me got the guys together, and we come up with this plan. We had no intention of letting it go that far. Everyone was so eager to help you two out. Problem was, we jus' got there too late, and I'm so sorry 'bout that. So sorry you two got hurt…" Charlie trailed off as his emotions took over.

"So how did the police get in on this?" Cristina asked, still shaken from the ordeal.

Charlie composed himself and continued the story.

"We knew we shouldn't let the police in on this too soon or they'd ruin the surprise."

"Which surprise was that, Charlie? The one where I got bashed with a baseball bat, or the one where Cristina was nearly raped?" Trey asked with a hint of anger, still trying to understand it all.

"Oh, Trey, none of that was part of the plan," Charlie said. "We knew we couldn't drive up to that old warehouse for fear we'd give ourselves away. So we walked and we jus' got there too late," he said again, shaking his head.

"And the police?" Cristina asked again.

"When they let me go," Douglas said, "I ran to the Laundromat across the street and told a lady there was a fight and some people was hurt. I asked if she would call the police. Guess she dialed 911."

"Well, if there's anything good about the timing, it's that they caught them right after the assault," Cristina said. "Now they have cause—maybe even an attempted murder charge—to put these guys away for a while."

"What made you change your mind, Douglas?" Trey asked. "Why did you decide to turn against your gang?"

"I don't know," the young man said, looking down. "I 'spose it was all the prayers you said for me at the hospital, all the nice things you done for me while I was getting well."

"I think the boy's had a change of heart, that's all," Charlie said, rubbing Douglas's head. "He told me he wants to straighten up his life. I get the feeling he's truly sorry for all his antics lately. That right, boy?"

"Yes, sir," Douglas replied. He looked around at the folks in the room and said, "I really am sorry for all the grief I've caused you, especially you, Auntie. I know I've been a pain."

"You think the others in your gang might want to change?" Trey asked. "With the leaders going to jail, maybe some of the guys will see how futile gang life really is."

"Some of the younger guys, yeah," Douglas said. "But there will always be guys who want to take over. So pretty soon there will be other leaders. Still, there are some pretty good guys I know who might want to stop all the gangbanging, especially if they can meet a basketball star."

"We can arrange that," Trey said, a smile creeping across his face.

"Mr. Trey," Douglas said, "I think this belongs to you." He reached into his jeans and produced the silver-plated pinkie ring. "I hope you won't ask any questions."

"Thanks, Douglas. My niece will be glad to know I got this back. Yeah, no questions," he said. His cell phone buzzed. "Better take this," he said, moving into the kitchen. "Coach, hey."

"Trey, you are about to give us a heart attack down here," Coach Rollins said. "Our phone's been ringing off the hook, everyone wondering how you are. How you doing?"

"I'm fine, Coach. Ran into a little trouble earlier with a street gang, but some good neighbors and the MPD bailed us out...again. I'm a little sore in my back, but doctors said it's nothing that time won't take care of."

"Think you'll be ready for the first day of practice next week?"

"Sure. Can't wait," Trey said. "Bing out of town?"

"No. Why?" Coach Rollins asked.

"He's usually the one to call," Trey said, remembering the run-ins he'd had with the Rockers' Director of Operations.

"Ha! We decided he's probably not the one to keep tabs on Trey Glass," Rollins said. "You miss him?"

"Actually, I'm kind of relieved. I'd rather explain my predicaments to you, Coach."

"Yeah, well, we'd rather there not be any predicaments to explain, Trey," Rollins said semiseriously. "But I suppose you gotta be what you gotta be. Anyway, I'm glad it's nothing serious. I'll see you soon. Good night."

"Good night, Coach. And thanks."

CHAPTER 23

Three reporters and two video crews were waiting when Trey pulled into his driveway after taking the Smits and Douglas home. He waved, opened the garage door, and waited until it closed behind him before walking to the house. Cristina was still awake, sitting in the den with a cup of hot herbal tea, trying to calm down after the near tragedy. He plopped down and put his arm around her. She set the cup on the coffee table and hugged him back. They held their embrace for a long time.

"I am so sorry I let you go with me tonight," he said, kissing her head.

"I wouldn't take no for an answer, remember?" she said. "I should have listened. I'm sorry. I suppose it could have turned out much worse."

Trey shivered at the thought.

"I could never have forgiven myself if something worse had happened to you." Looking at the ceiling, he prayed, "Father, thank you for your protection tonight. Thank you for sparing our lives. I pray for the young men who sit in jail right now, that you would stir their hearts. I especially pray for the Gosnell family. Thank you for this sweet woman here. She is a gift. We love you. Amen."

They sat holding each other and feeling the relief of deliverance.

"Where's Mom?" he finally asked.

"She's getting my room ready. Insisted that I stay here tonight. I told her I could do it, but she said to sit here and wait for you. She sat with me for a long time. I think she sensed how tired and upset I was. I know she was really worried," Cristina said. "After we left to meet Douglas tonight, Lem came by and told her what was about to happen."

"Not sure how helpful that was," Trey said. "Wonder why they would tell her about all of that in advance?

"You know, things like tonight make you see how unimportant basketball is. Someone needs to spend time with kids like we saw tonight; otherwise, they don't stand a chance. That boy would be lost if it weren't for Charlie and Precious."

"And you," Cristina added. "Douglas really looks up to you, Trey. You've had as much influence on him as anyone. And think about the influence your mom is having on those boys with the garden. You two are making a real difference in these kids."

"Then what am I doing spending my time playing a game when I could be hanging out with folks who need some help?" Trey asked. "And what's with all the people in this town who claim to be followers of Jesus? They say they follow him but keep their distance from anyone who doesn't look or think like them. Haven't they noticed the kinds of people Jesus hung out with? Where in the Bible does it say we have a right to safe neighborhoods out of sight from the people who really need us?" He paused. "Am I rambling?"

"Preach on, brother," Cristina said, stroking his face. "Listen to me, you play basketball to earn the status necessary to influence the Douglases of this world. You play basketball to make money to help agencies and people who need a hand up. You play basketball because God gave you the talent to play, and by playing, you honor him and bring him delight. That's why you play basketball."

"Oh yeah, I forgot." He smiled, looking into her dark eyes. "I love you," he said.

They sat in silence, his head in her lap and lost in his thoughts, she stroking his face.

"Hey, are your folks at home?"

"Right now?" she asked, surprised.

"Well, for the next few days?"

"Yeah. I talked to Mom this afternoon, and they are all home. Why?"

"I was just wondering. Maybe we should call them sometime. Do they Skype?" he asked.

"They're not that technologically advanced." She laughed. "But I suppose we could call them. They know all about you, so it's not like they would be talking to a stranger."

"What's their number?" he asked, pulling out his phone.

"You're not going to call them right now, are you? They're all asleep. Dad gets up early and—"

"No, no. I just want to have their number," he said.

"254-555-3974. That's the home phone. Dad's mobile is 254-555-0117."

Trey entered the information into his phone as Becky entered the den.

"Your bed is all made up, dear," she said to Cristina. "I put clean towels, a clean nightgown, and some toiletries on your bed. You just make yourself at home, you hear?"

"Becky, you didn't have to go to such trouble," Cristina said. "You are so sweet."

"I had to work off some of my anxiety," Becky said. "You two gave me such a scare. I'm better now."

Trey rose from the couch and walked over to his mom.

"I am so thankful for you," he said, wrapping his long arms around her. "I don't know what I'd do without you." He kissed her, stepped back, and changed tones. "I have to make a little trip over the next few days before practice starts next week. I'll check in with both of you while I'm gone. Mom, Tyler will be in every day, so he can help you if anything comes up. Cristina, you're welcome to stay over here while I'm gone, if you wish."

"Where you going?" Becky asked.

"Can't tell you right now. I'll be okay," Trey said. Cristina eyed her boyfriend suspiciously but didn't say anything. "I should be back Tuesday sometime."

"Well, I'm going to bed," Becky said. "I'll see you two in the morning."

"Good night, Mom," Trey said. "We're right behind you."

He walked over to Cristina and held her tight.

"I'm glad you're staying here tonight," he whispered. "I'm also very glad Mom's here, because you are very tempting." Their kiss was passionate, and he felt her mold her body to his. He finally pulled his mouth from hers and said, "I'm tempted to invite you to my room tonight around 3:00. No one would know…"

"I'd be tempted to accept." She sighed. "But we both know that's not what we really want. Maybe someday," she said.

The two said good night and went to their rooms, both fully aware of the tempting power of sex.

Early the next morning, Trey threw two days' worth of clothes into a small carry-on, toasted a bagel, downed it and a glass of orange juice, and left the house. He drove toward Memphis International Airport, where he parked in long-term parking.

I hope they don't think this is an abandoned wreck and tow it to the junkyard, he thought to himself as he climbed out of his car. He rode the escalator up to the car rental counters and rented a mid-sized Ford from Enterprise. From there, he drove across the Mississippi River toward Little Rock. About forty miles from the Arkansas capital, he pulled into a rest area and dialed Mr. Garza's cell phone number.

"Hello?"

"Hello, is this Mr. Garza?" Trey asked.

"Yes, this is Luis Garza."

"Mr. Garza, this is Trey Glass from Memphis."

"Well, Trey, how are you? Is everything alright?"

"Yes, sir. Everything is fine."

Now what do I say?

"Uh, Mr. Garza—"

"Trey, call me Luis," Mr. Garza interrupted, trying to put the young man at ease.

"Okay. Luis, I was wondering if I might come visit you and Mrs. Garza soon."

"Well, sure. When do you think you'll be here?" Luis asked.

"My plan is to catch a flight from Little Rock to Austin and drive up to Cerulian this afternoon. Would that work?"

"Uh, yeah, that's soon." He laughed. "Hmm, let me ask Mary."

Trey's heart was beating fast, and he thought the pause in the conversation would never end. After a minute, Luis was back. "Trey, that would be fine. Do you have a place to stay while you're here? Are you alone?"

"Yes, sir, I'm alone, and no, sir, I don't have a place to stay. I'll probably get a hotel nearby."

"The closest hotel fit for mankind would be in Waco, about forty minutes away. We would love for you to stay here. Lots of rooms and fewer kids. But you do what you need to do. That's just an offer."

"Maybe I'll decide that later. I'll probably see you around four or five this afternoon. Tell Mrs. Garza not to make a big fuss. By the way, what's your address?"

"4707 FM 323, Cerulian, Texas. It will be good to finally meet you, Trey. Be careful now."

"Yes, sir, I will. Thanks so much, Mr. Garza," Trey said with much relief.

"Luis," he said.

"Luis. Sorry. I'll see you soon. And Luis, Cristina doesn't know I'm coming down to see you, and I would like to keep it that way until you and I have had a chance to talk. Would that be a problem?"

"No problem, Trey. I think I understand. And I'll make sure the others know this as well. Okay, Trey. Bye."

"Goodbye, sir." Trey hung up and resumed his trek.

He arrived in Little Rock just after eleven a.m., parked, and found the ticket counters. No airline flew from Little Rock directly to Austin, so he booked an American flight to DFW with an open return date. With an hour and a half to wait, he bought a newspaper and sat down in the River Bend Grill for a salad, toast, and sweet tea.

His plane landed in Dallas a little before 2:30. He rented a car and began the final two hours of his trip to meet Cristina's family. With help from his phone's GPS, Trey pulled up in front of the Garzas' home at 5:15. Two young ladies were sitting in the porch swing, a small puppy between them. When they saw Trey's car, the youngest girl ran inside, squealing, "Mom, he's here!"

"Hi, I'm Sara," the other girl said from the swing. Trey could see Cristina in the young girl's face.

"Hi. I'm Trey," he said, walking up to the porch. "And who is this?"

"This is Cooper. We call him Coop. He'll lick you to death if you let him." Trey bent over to pet the ball of fur who sniffed and vigorously licked his hand. "He's just five months old."

"He's cute," Trey said.

In a flurry of commotion, four others suddenly appeared on the porch.

"Trey, I'm Mary, Cristina's mother," she said, hugging his neck. "We're so glad to meet you. This is Maria, and this is Daniela. And I see you've met Sara."

Two of the girls partially hid behind their mom and blushed when Trey reached to shake hands. Her mom was almost at beautiful as Cristina and nearly as young looking.

Guess that's what Cristina will look like later in life. Not bad, he thought to himself.

"And I'm Luis, Trey. We're happy to have you at our house."

"I am very happy to meet you all. And from what I hear, I've got more to meet," Trey said, looking around at all the Garzas staring back at him.

"These are all you'll meet this trip, I think," Mary said. "Ana is away at A&M. Alex and Ricardo are in Houston. And I think you know where Antonio and Cristina are."

"Come in, Trey," Luis said, ushering him into their modest but spacious house.

The aroma of Mexican food cooking reminded him of how hungry he was. His lunch had worn off long ago. The house's open floor plan featured a large sitting area in clear view of the kitchen and dining room. Walk-out doors opened onto a large back deck that overlooked the backyard with a pool and trampoline. Mary and Luis offered Trey a seat on a large sectional sofa and then took a seat on either side of him. The girls went back to work in the kitchen but kept eyes and ears on the adults.

"It's funny, Cristina called around 2:00 and said you were on some mystery trip," Mary said. "It was all I could do not to tell her you were coming here."

"She mentioned some trouble you two had last night," Luis said. "How are you feeling?"

"I feel fine as long as I stay on the Tylenol," Trey said. "Cristina probably told you she didn't fare as well."

Mary looked at Luis with panic in her eyes, as if his words were a surprise.

"No, she didn't say anything about that. What happened?" Luis asked.

"Oh, well, it's nothing serious," Trey said, trying to backpedal from spilling the beans. "She got a few cuts and bruises, but that's all. Really, nothing serious. She doesn't plan to miss any work. My mom is taking good care of her."

"Oh, well, that's good," Luis said. "I'd like to hear more about that later. Do you see Antonio very often?"

"Not as often as I'd like. He and Cristina come to just about every home game, so I see him there as much as anywhere. He stays pretty busy with school and his job."

Mary excused herself and returned to helping her daughters in the kitchen. The two men engaged in small talk—mostly about Luis's contracting business—until Daniela came over to say supper was ready.

Trey washed up and took the seat he was offered in the dining area. Maria and Sara scrambled to sit beside the tall guest, one on the right and one on the left. After Luis offered a prayer of thanks for the food and for Trey's safe arrival, the gathering dug in. There were the familiar foods—enchiladas, tacos, and tamales—but the daughters were quick to explain some of the other dishes with which Trey was unfamiliar. The food was great, and the conversation was light and held moments of laughter, often at Cristina's expense, as her little sisters revealed stories from their family life. It was clear that this was a close-knit, loving family. And it was clear that the four Garza girls gathered around the table were infatuated with the handsome basketball star from Memphis, Tennessee. Occasionally he would catch one of the younger ones staring back at him.

Dessert was hot fudge sundaes featuring Mary's homemade chocolate sauce. Trey couldn't remember when he had eaten as much or as well.

"That's about the best meal I've ever had in my life," he said to the delight of the women as he leaned back in his chair.

"Me too," Luis said. "You need to come down here more often so I can get some good cooking."

"Oh, Luis," Mary said, tossing a colorful cloth napkin his way. "He eats this good every night," she defended. The three daughters cleared the table and started on the dishes. "I'll bring coffee out in a little while. Why don't you two go sit on the porch," she said to the men.

"You know," Trey said, "in my household, my job at the end of the meal was to help with the dishes, so I insist on pitching in and helping these young ladies. If it's okay, I'll be right out when we're finished."

The three girls, almost in unison, registered their agreement. Maria dug a yellow apron out of a drawer and tied it around Trey's waist. Sara pulled a towel off the oven handle and threw it, basketball style, to him.

"Sara will wash, Trey will dry, Maria will help Mom put food away, and I will put the dishes up," fifteen-year-old Daniela ordered. And with that, the team got to work.

CHAPTER 24

When the job was done, Trey hung the wet towel back over the oven handle and found Luis on the back porch while Mary made coffee.

"Get 'em done?" Luis asked as he rose to offer Trey a seat.

"We did. You have sweet daughters, Luis," Trey said.

"We are very proud of all our children," Luis said. "God has blessed our family."

The two men discussed the Dallas Cowboys, the Texans, and the Spurs' upcoming season before Mary came out carrying a tray with coffee and small cinnamon cookies.

"Wow, those look delicious. What are they?" Trey asked.

"They're called *polvorones de canele*," Mary said. "They're like a cinnamon shortcake. My mom used to make these when I was a little girl. I tried to teach Cristina how to bake them, but she didn't have an interest."

"But she sure can put together a mean Tex-Mex meal," Trey said. "Did you teach her that?"

"Heavens no." Mary laughed, shaking her head. "The younger girls have gone the easy route and picked up on what's popular, not what's good."

"Now, be fair, Mary," Luis said. "Cristina is a very busy woman. She doesn't have time to spend all day cooking traditional foods."

"She's busy, that's a fact," Trey said. "She spends fifty to sixty hours a week at the hospital, and then she does lots of nice things for people when she's off."

They sat drinking coffee, enjoying the view from the deck and getting to know each other. For the next hour—with occasional interruptions by the daughters checking to make sure Trey was still there—they talked about Trey's family, what Cristina was like as a little girl, what brought Mary and Luis to the U.S., how they met, and more. Luis and Mary especially wanted to know about the events that led up to the previous evening's encounter with gang members. Once they were assured that Cristina was doing okay and was safe, Trey turned the conversation toward why he had come to see them.

He cleared his throat and sat up straight.

"I have come to ask for your daughter's hand in marriage," he said bluntly, like he had practiced a hundred times on his trip down.

"Alabar a dios. Aleluya!" Mary cried as she grabbed Trey's arm. "I am so happy."

"Which daughter?" Luis joked and stood to shake hands with Trey. "Can you take all of them?"

"Oh, Luis," Mary said, wiping a tear.

"Neither you nor Cristy need our permission, but I am honored that you asked," Luis said. "I know this, Mama, we had better not mention this to the girls until Trey has a chance to propose. Otherwise, it will be no secret. The girls would call her tonight and ruin the surprise."

"Oh, I hope I can keep it to myself," Mary said, crying and laughing at the same time.

"Just for the record, is that a yes or a no?" Trey asked.

"Sí, sí, sí, sí," Mary said, now mostly laughing.

"Trey, we feel like we have known you much longer than we have after all that Cristy has told us about you," Luis said. "I must admit, at times I thought you were too good to be true, that our daughter was making things up about you to sway our opinion, maybe to put us at ease about being so far away from home. But after this evening, we know she was telling us the truth. We would be honored to have you as part of our family. And we look forward to getting to know your family."

"Thank you both," Trey said. "I want you to know that I love Cristina more than I thought a person could love another. I wasn't really looking when God dropped her into my life. She is one of the kindest people I know. And I promise to take care of her and be devoted to her the rest of our lives."

"This calls for a toast," Luis said. "I'll be right back." With that, he disappeared inside.

"Now, I have your bed all made," Mary said, still holding on to Trey's arm. "I hope you will stay the night with us."

"I would be honored, if you promise it's not an inconvenience," Trey said.

"Don't be silly. We want you here. And we will have lots of room for you and Cristina and your children when you come visit… Oh, did I say too much?" Mary said when she saw Trey blush.

"Well, it's just that we'd better take one thing at a time. I haven't even proposed yet. What if she says no?" Trey said. It hit him that there might be the possibility she would decline.

"Oh, I don't think you have anything to worry about," Mary assured. "And if she does, we have other daughters!"

Luis returned carrying a bottle and three brandy snifters.

"A friend of mine gave me this Spanish brandy many years ago, and I've never had an occasion to open it…until tonight," Luis said. He set the glasses down and held the dark bottle up so he could read the label. "*Gran Duque De Alba XO*. Sounds fancy, doesn't it?" He carefully opened the bottle, poured the glasses one-third full, and handed the first to his wife. After setting the bottle down, he picked up the remaining glasses, handing one to Trey. "To a long, healthy, and prosperous life for our sweet Cristina and her future husband, Señor Trey Glass." He toasted.

"And plenty of children," Mary said, giggling.

"*Salud!*"

After the toast, they sat down to enjoy the brandy. Soon, the Garza daughters came to see what was happening. Their parents sensed that the girls knew something was up; it wasn't every day that their mom and dad sat on the back porch drinking brandy.

"Girls, it's about bedtime. School tomorrow," Mary said, met with groans. "Tell Trey good night."

"Are you going to be around tomorrow?" Daniela asked their guest.

"I plan to be. What time do you go to school?"

"I usually take them around 7:45," Mary said.

"What if I take them tomorrow?" Trey asked. "I want to get up and run off some of that wonderful meal, so I plan to be up."

"Well, I suppose that would be fine. You can take my van," Mary said. The girls seemed genuinely excited.

"Okay, then. I'll see you guys in the morning," he said. Each of the girls gave Trey hugs and started inside.

"Hey, what about me and Mama?" Luis asked, faking indignation. The girls returned, giggling, and lavished hugs and kisses on their parents before running to bed.

"What are your plans tomorrow?" Luis asked.

"Don't have any. Now that you've given me your blessing to marry Cristina, my work is done. I thought I might have to stay and beg you to give in, but I suppose I can go home now," Trey said jokingly.

"Well, since you're here, why not join me for lunch? I'd like to show you some of our projects," Luis said.

"Luis, that sounds great, but I'm serious, I don't want to overstay my welcome. I feel like I've barged in with little warning. I was planning to only stay one night and—"

"Please stay," Mary pleaded. "You've come all this way, and the girls would be heartbroken if you left after such a short time. No telling when we might be together again."

"I suppose there's nothing that can't wait back home. I know that Cristina is going to wonder where I am, but I'll deal with that when I must. Okay, I'll stay just one more night," Trey said.

They sat on the back porch another hour, enjoying the brandy and each other's company. Trey could see facets of Cristina in her parents, and certain expressions, especially from her mom, made him wish his sweetheart were here beside him. After meeting most of Cristina's family, Trey was more certain than ever that she was the woman for him, a true gift from God.

Trey was up at 6:00 the next morning. He put on his running clothes and quietly sneaked out the front door. For the next hour, he ran along the nearly deserted country lanes around the Garza home. When he walked back in the front door, he smelled coffee and breakfast.

"Good run?" Mary asked.

"Yes. It's beautiful out here," Trey said.

"Coffee?"

"I think I'd rather have some water right now." He sat down at the dining room kitchen and finished off two bottles of water while chatting with Mary. Soon, the girls began to trickle in for breakfast, none looking all that perky.

"Good morning, sunshines," Trey greeted cheerily. "All ready for another fun day at school?"

The eight-year-old walked over and put her hands on Trey's knee.

"Are you going to marry my sister?" she asked innocently.

"Maria! Where did that come from?" Mary scolded.

"Daniela said you are going to marry Cristina," she said.

"I did not!" Daniela defended. "I said he *might* marry her—not that he *would* marry her."

"You girls need to mind your own business," Maria said, feeling a bit embarrassed by the incident. "And you'd better not say anything to Cristina about Daniela's little theory, you understand?"

"Well, Maria, what if I did marry Cristina? Would that be okay with you?" Trey asked.

"Sure! Then you would be my big brother. And I'd have...how many, Mommy?" she asked.

Daniela high-jacked the conversation and answered, "Four. Alex, Ricky, Antonio, and Trey."

"Girls, you need to sit down and eat your breakfast," Mary said, more embarrassed. "You have to leave for school soon. Trey, what can I get you for breakfast? We have all kinds of cereal, or I could make you eggs and ham."

"Cereal and a piece of toast will do fine."

The three young ladies and Trey sat eating their breakfasts, chatting, making jokes, and giggling.

Wouldn't my mom love these three cuties? he thought.

After breakfast, the girls scurried off to make final preparations. While Mary helped the little ones, Trey cleaned up the kitchen. He figured Luis had long since left for work.

"You'll drop Maria and Sara off at Bonner Elementary. Daniela will show you how to get there, and Dan will go to Wilson High, just down the road. You shouldn't have any trouble finding your way back. Or I could go with you," Mary offered as the four headed out the door for Mary's van.

"No, we'll be fine as long as Daniela knows where to go. And I have my phone if I get really lost. I'll be back soon." Trey enjoyed the brief visit with the girls. He imagined Cristina at their ages, full of confidence, joy, and wonder. Before Maria got out of the van, she stood up and gave Trey a kiss.

"Will you be home when we get there?" she asked.

"I should be," he said.

After dropping Daniela off at the high school and wishing her well, Trey headed back to the Garzas' house. When he got within sight, he pulled the van to the side of the road and called Cristina.

"How's it going?" he asked when she answered.

"Your mom and I are sitting here having coffee," she said. "Where are you?"

"You're off today?" he asked.

"Until tonight. Where are you?" she asked a second time.

"Somewhere far away, and I miss you terribly," he said, avoiding a direct answer.

"Trey Glass, where *are* you?" she asked with more determination.

"Honey, it should be clear that I'm not answering that question. You'll know in time. How's Mom? And how are you feeling? Did you spend last night there?"

"You're impossible, you know that?" she said. "Your mom is fine. I feel good. And yes, I spent the night here. I could get used to this pampering," she said, her tone mellowing. "Your mom is taking really good care of me, not like some people I know who just take off on secret vacations. By the way, an officer Rob Richie called for you. Said he had some questions for you and that he'd call back. I told him what I knew, but he still wants to talk with you."

"I'll call him when I get home," Trey said. "Glad you're doing well. I really miss you. You would absolutely love where I am right now," he teased.

"Is it in the United States?" she asked.

Ironic, he thought. *Some people would swear Texas is a foreign country.*

"That's for me to know and for you to find out," he said. "I'll be back tomorrow afternoon. Hope you have a great day. I love you."

"Love you too," she cooed. "And I miss you. Hurry home and be safe. Take pictures."

Trey spent the morning chatting with Mary and gaining more insight into his wife-to-be. Around mid-morning, Coach Rollins called.

"Hey, Coach," Trey said.

"Hey, bud. Where are you?" his coach asked bluntly.

"Uh, do I have to answer that?" Trey coughed, caught by surprise.

"No, but a sportswriter thinks he saw you at DFW yesterday and is spreading rumors that you are talking to the Mavs about a trade. I just want to clear the air. Is that true?"

"No, sir, that's not. Can you keep a secret, Coach?"

"You know I can, Trey."

"The reporter probably did see me at DFW because I came through there yesterday on my way to Cerulian, Texas, to ask Cristina's folks for her hand in marriage," Trey said.

Silence.

"Coach?"

"That's either the most outlandish story I've ever heard to cover up for your surreptitious little jaunt or it's really good news. And knowing you, Glass, it has to be the latter. Well, I must say I'm relieved. It's not that you could negotiate a trade all by yourself anyway, but I was just a little confused. Congratulations."

"Coach, you're probably going to get some calls on this today. I bet I get a few myself. But please don't give anyone the real reason I'm in Texas. I'd hate for this to get back to Cristina before I could propose.

I don't want to give her time to think up reasons to say no," Trey said, laughing.

Coach Rollins belched out a hearty laugh.

"I think we'll let the sportswriters and reporters stew in their own juices. We'll let 'em keep their theories, and you can address it in your own good time. How would that be?"

"Well, I hate to do that, even to sportswriters, but I suppose that's the best way to keep our little secret a secret."

Meanwhile, back in Memphis, the buzz that Trey Glass had signed a multimillion-dollar deal with the Dallas Mavericks had flooded the city. Every news outlet carried the story, and friends and colleagues of Cristina's called to offer their regrets that her boyfriend would soon be leaving.

While Becky Glass cried, Cristina Garza seethed.

CHAPTER 25

Not long after Trey hung up with Coach Rollins, Luis called to discuss lunch.

"Hey," Luis said. "If you'll find your way over to I-35 and follow that south to Highway 84, I'll pick you up at that BP station right off the interstate. It'll take you about thirty minutes, so why don't we meet at 11:30?"

"Sounds like a plan. See you soon." Trey hung up, showered, made his bed, and prayed, thanking God for his day, his hosts, his mom, and asking God to watch over the earthly love of his life, Cristina.

"What time will you two be back?" Mary asked as Trey headed out the door.

"Not sure, but I suppose in time for supper. Hey, why don't I take all of you out to dinner tonight? Maybe to the girls' favorite place?"

"That would be McDonald's," Mary said, rolling her eyes. "That's nice of you, Trey, but Luis and I already made plans to cook some steaks out back. Would that be alright with you?"

"Sure. I love steak. And just so you know, there's a fierce rumor circulating in Memphis about me signing a deal with the Mavericks. A sports guy saw me at the airport in Dallas yesterday. If Cristina gets wind of that, she might call you. Just be prepared," Trey warned.

"Oh my. Thanks for the warning. I'll be ready." Mary hugged Trey and sent him on his way.

Trey arrived at the meeting spot early and sat in his car until Luis pulled up in his F-150.

"Hop in," Luis said. "There's this little Italian fast food place down the road I like. Okay with you?"

"Sure," Trey said. "I usually eat pretty light at lunch. Any place is fine."

During lunch, Luis explained the projects his company was working on. Their tour would begin at the largest project, a four-story bank building in downtown Waco, and hit a few other smaller projects through the afternoon. Trey insisted on paying for lunch, which, for him, was a salad and grilled cheese.

Back in the truck, Luis reached behind him, pulled out a hard hat, and explained some workplace safety laws that required everyone to wear such head protection at construction sites. At the bank building site, the two hopped on a construction elevator that hung precariously off the side of the unfinished building and rode it to the roof. From there, Luis pointed out various Waco landmarks. Trey was especially impressed with the sprawling Baylor University campus off in the distance.

Luis called over several of the workers who sported Dallas Mavericks t-shirts and introduced them to their pro team's favorite Rockers nemesis, point guard Trey Glass. Despite the good-natured ribbing and mild trash talking from the ardent Mavs fans, Trey signed more autographs that afternoon than he would ordinarily sign in a week back in Memphis. The men who met him were genuinely impressed that their boss knew the NBA star personally.

Luis and Trey also visited other construction sites—a restaurant, another smaller bank, a car wash—where other workers got the privilege of meeting a genuine professional athlete. Trey took it all in stride, not wanting to complain about all the attention in front of his future father-in-law. The two ended up at Luis's small office next to their large construction yard and warehouse. There Trey found out that Luis was also part owner of a swimming pool company with his cousin. Large blue-green fiberglass pools lined the parking lot.

Once inside, Luis introduced Trey to their office manager, Lilly Rogers, and labor supervisor, Tomas Enriquez, who happened to be in the office. After the pleasantries, Luis and Trey sat and visited in Luis's small, cluttered private office. Framed photos of his children and wife filled the credenza behind Luis's desk. Trey enjoyed looking at each one, finding Cristina at various ages.

"Which reminds me, Luis," Trey said, turning to face him. "I told Mary there is a rumor circulating in Memphis that I'm coming to play for the Mavericks. A sports writer saw me at DFW yesterday and leapt to that conclusion. My coach called this morning, and we agreed to let the thing ride until I get back and address it myself."

"Whoa! What if Cristina hears that?" Luis asked.

"I'm waiting for that shoe to fall," Trey said, sitting down. "She will either call one of you or call me...or all the above. I've been thinking about what I'm going to tell her."

"And that would be...?" Luis asked.

"I think I'm going to admit to being in Texas but claim my right not to say anything else. If she wants to assume I've been with you guys, she has that right. I really hope I can get away with not admitting to being here. But that means I'm going to have to propose sooner than later before she learns on her own that I came down to see you."

"That's okay, isn't it?" Luis asked.

"Sure. It's just that I don't have ring yet, and I'd like to have one before I propose. I suppose she and I could pick one out together. How are those things usually done, Luis?"

"You got me, *amigo*. We'll ask Mary when we get back. She knows how all that stuff works. Trey," Luis said, his tone changing to a more serious one. "I've wanted to ask you about something that has been on my mind."

"Okay. Shoot," Trey said, settling back in his chair.

"Our children have been raised Catholic all their lives," Luis said. "Now, I realize that only the youngest still go to Mass, and maybe Ricardo, but I'm not sure. And the only reason the three little ones go is because we take them." Luis stopped and swallowed hard. "Would you like some water? I would."

"Sure," Trey said. Luis left and got two bottles of water from a small refrigerator in their kitchenette. He said a couple of things to Lilly before returning to his office and shutting the door.

"So, as I was saying, I am really glad that Cristy seems to have a new interest in spiritual things. She says she has learned a lot from you.

She says you act more like Jesus than anyone she has ever known. I believe that. But her mom and I have some questions, coming out of our Catholic backgrounds."

"Luis, I will do my best to answer your questions," Trey said. "I have nothing to hide and no agenda to force on anyone. So, please, feel free to ask anything."

"First, do you have something against going to Mass?" Luis asked in all sincerity. "Cristy says you meet at your house with people from the neighborhood on Sundays. Call me old fashioned, but that just doesn't seem to be enough."

"It's ironic that I should be explaining this to you, because my thinking was influenced by the parish priest model from your church," Trey began. "I've thought about what God wants from me as a believer, and it seems, judging from what I see in Jesus and what I hear him teach, that he wants me to care for those right around me, especially the ones who have difficulty caring for themselves. I love how your church does this; it divides a city up into parishes and puts a priest over each parish to offer pastoral care and to make sure the most basic needs are met. It seems that's how household churches functioned in the New Testament.

"So I have all these men and women in my neighborhood, good people, who struggle sometimes. Actually, I struggle myself in different ways, and what they provide me is invaluable; it's a two-way street. But I have some resources and gifts that can be of help to the people in my neighborhood. Why would I want to walk away from that a couple of times a week so that I can be part of another, less personal group outside my neighborhood? Why would I take resources that can be used for the folks right under my nose and give them to an institution that will use some to add a wing to their church building or pay someone to do what we all should be doing. You get what I'm saying?"

"Go on," Luis said, not admitting to understanding.

"Our church is made up of anyone who wishes to become more like Jesus. We're teaching each other what that looks like. And the more we do that, the more it reflects on God, the Father; the more he receives praise and honor, the more he is worshipped. Luis, think about what an influence we could have on the world through the centuries if every Christian saw their neighborhood—or their workplace or community center—as their parish? By now we could have had a vibrant community of God within easy reach of every person on earth."

"So, are you ordained as a priest?" Luis asked.

"As ordained as anyone. The way I read scripture, I think God calls every person to priesthood. That's probably where you and I would most disagree, and we don't have to hammer that out now or ever, but I feel a calling from God to care for and nurture the folks I live around. There are definitely men and women who know more Bible than I do and can preach better than I can, but none of those things qualifies or disqualifies a person from loving and serving the people around them."

Trey paused to take a drink of water.

"Here's another thing, Luis; more and more people my age are dropping out of church for various reasons. You said yourself that your kids moved away from your idea of faith when they moved out of your house. That's the trend, for sure. One poll I read said that only 4 percent of people in my age group are associated with a mainline religious group. And another poll said that those who have no religious affiliation outnumber those who do, for the first time ever in our country.

"Simply put, fewer people than ever are going to church. But people in my age group are very spiritual, meaning many of them care for the same things that God cares about—the poor, the planet, those who suffer injustice, those in third-world countries without food and water, sex trafficking, the rights of minorities, racism. So how can we who know God encourage these young people when they won't go to church? I think we have to meet them where they are. We have to listen, get to know, encourage, live like Jesus around them, and pray that they will get a vision of how God is working in their lives."

"I've heard some good things about your mom and dad, Trey," Luis said. "How much influence have they had on how you practice your faith?"

"More than even I can fully understand," Trey said. "My parents were the kindest, most accepting, most humble people I've ever known. They were no respecters of persons, I'll tell you that. They believed that no sin, no mistake defined you as a person. They took in the poor, prisoners, gay people, educated, and uneducated, and they treated them all the same. They were probably the only people in town who were best friends with both the mayor and the town drunk," Trey said, smiling while wiping a tear from his cheek.

"So why do you think more Christians don't live the way your folks lived...and the way you live, for that matter?"

"Well, for one thing, it's hard. There seems to be little challenge in living life according to a ritualistic pattern; you know, church one or two times a week, give your tithes, contribute to the annual church campaign, act decently. But it's very hard to give all that up and begin to intentionally look for the folks who have deep and serious needs, loving them, sharing your resources, treating all people as equals, withholding judgment, loving the good folks and the bad.

"Despite the fact that Jesus lived that way and taught his disciples to live that way, few Christians seem to have caught on. None of this happens accidentally. A person has to want it and make deliberate effort to live as a disciple. It truly has to be intentional. And it comes at a cost. People won't understand why you do the things you do, why you would want to love the unlovable, why you're willing to forgive someone who was responsible for your father's death, why you would befriend someone who wants to do you harm. None of those things come naturally. And sometimes they even lead to great personal harm or loss. But that's what Jesus has called every person to."

"Oh, man, Trey, this is indicting," Luis said as he rubbed his forehead.

"Look, Luis, I'm not meaning to sound judgmental. Only you know what God's call has been for you. I'd say you've done very well at raising decent children. No one can judge another person. I must focus only on what God has called me to be and do.

"On the other hand, I think it's fair to make observations about the way things are. And even the casual observer today sees a Christendom that is divided, belligerent, and virtually impotent in its influence. That's why the church has not made more of an impact on our culture. Thank God for his infinite mercy. Most people my age just need encouragement that we are doing the right thing rather than condemnation for not going to church."

"Well," Luis said, "Cristina seems like a different girl when we talk to her—happier and more at peace. She talks about God as she never has before. And we couldn't be happier for her."

"That's one of many reasons I love her so much. And all our new friends love her. She has the heart of Jesus in the way she gives so much of herself. You and Mary have done a great job of molding her into who she is today. And I think the same is true of Antonio, although I don't know him as well."

"As I said before, God is good. He must have overcome our failings as parents to create what my children have become. You will be an additional blessing to our family, Trey," Luis said, offering his hand to Trey.

"I've got one more stop for us to make before I take you back to your car. Let me wrap up a few things here and we'll go. Okay?"

"Sure. My time is your time today," Trey said, knowing that the investment he made by spending time with his future wife's parents would pay handsome dividends.

He took his cell phone out and checked for messages.

"Uh oh. There are one, two, three, seven calls from Cristina. Guess I'd better call her back."

"Then I'm getting out of here. I don't want to hear this," Luis said as he chuckled and closed the door behind him.

"Hey, babe," he said when she answered her phone.

Silence.

"Want to try to explain what I've been hearing all day?" she finally asked.

"What have you been hearing all day?" he asked, trying to sound innocent.

"You know what. That you are moving to Dallas. Don't you dare deny being there. Someone saw you at the Dallas-Fort Worth airport. What's going on, Trey? When were you going to tell me?"

"Okay," he said, taking a deep breath. "There are some things I can tell you and some things I can't. Yes, I was at DFW, but my being in Texas has absolutely nothing to do with basketball. I am not moving to Dallas. I am not going to play for the Mavericks. I'm not going anywhere. Now, that's about all I can tell you right now. I hope you will trust me, sweetheart."

More silence.

"Sweetheart?" he finally said.

"Do you know how worried your mom is right now?" she asked. "The least you can do is call and tell her what you just told me."

"I can do that. I'll do that right now. And I'll see you tomorrow. Want to have dinner tomorrow night?" he asked, testing the waters.

"Maybe," she replied coldly.

"Just know I love you, and all this will be clear to you very soon," he said, trying to move on.

"I love you too, Trey. I just don't want there to be any secrets between us."

"I can't promise that there won't be any secrets, but I promise I'll be honest with you, and that in time you'll understand any secrets there might be. I expect there will be times you will not tell me everything I want to know. That's just the way marriage is...so I'm told."

"Call your mom," she said. "I'll see you tomorrow, and yes, I'll have dinner with you. Can't wait to see you. Love you."

Trey breathed a sigh of relief.

"Love you too. Bye."

He punched in his mom's cell number.

"Mom—"

"Trey-boy, where are you?" she asked.

"I'm in Texas, Mom. And no, I'm not moving down here. I still play for the Rockers," he said, anticipating her questions.

"Then what's all this fuss about? There are more reporters in our front yard, and the news stations haven't stopped talking about this all day. And Cristina is so upset; you've got some explaining to do to her."

"Mom, I'm going to tell you a secret. You must not tell Cristina. Will you promise me that?"

"Well, I suppose—"

"Mom, you have to promise me you won't breathe a word of this to Cristina. Promise?"

"Yes, I promise. What is it?"

"I am down here in Texas visiting Cristina's folks. I asked them what they thought about me marrying their daughter."

"Oh my! What did they say?" Becky asked seriously.

"They said absolutely not. There's no way they would let their daughter marry a basketball player," he teased.

"They did not!"

"You're right. They said they would welcome me into their family. And they said they can't wait to meet you. So, that's what all of this is about. I plan to propose to Cristina as soon as I get back. But I want it to be a surprise. Okay, Mom?"

"I hope I can keep it to myself. But I will, Trey-boy, I will." She giggled.

"Thanks, Mom. I'll see you tomorrow afternoon. I love you."

"I love you too, honey. Gotta go. There's another reporter at the front door. Can I tell him our little secret?"

"No!"

CHAPTER 26

"How'd it go?" Luis asked when he came back in the room.

"As well as can be expected," Trey said. "Talked to my mom too. She said the reporters and their rumors are out in force. Guess I'm going to walk back into a firestorm tomorrow."

"I've got just the medicine to ease your mind. Let's ride."

On the way back to Trey's car, Luis went a little out of the way to stop at *La Cantina*, a small watering hole on the northwest side of town. The parking lot was filled with pick-up trucks, giving the first indication that this was a working man's bar. Once Trey's eyes adjusted to the subdued lighting inside, he noticed that he was about the only non-Hispanic customer there.

"Come on, Trey!" Luis yelled above the music. "You can meet some of my *amigos*."

For the next hour, Trey was thoroughly entertained by the seven other men sitting at a large, round table, all friends of Luis's who usually gathered on Friday afternoons to drink beer and swap lies. Luis made some calls the night before and got his friends to agree to come today to meet his future first son-in-law. He promised it would be worth their trouble.

Trey nursed his *Dos Equis* Amber and listened to the men tell their stories, sometimes all at once, and in Spanish. And though he didn't understand very much, he felt drawn into the fellowship, feeling that they were impressed by the presence of a professional basketball player and just as impressed that he was Luis's friend and future husband to Cristina.

When they tried to ask Trey questions and failed to communicate, Luis translated. The group made Trey feel welcomed, and he was glad to sign autographs and pose for pictures with anyone who asked. The bartender agreed to take a photo of his celebrity visitor and everyone in the bar in exchange for the privilege of displaying the photo on the wall.

This is a true intentional community, Trey thought. *Every man is made to feel important.*

When it was finally time to leave, each of the seven, as well as most of the bar's patrons who recognized the NBA star, gave Trey a warm farewell hug and invited him to return next time he was in the area.

Back at the Garzas', Trey was met by a bevy of young girls, each vying for his attention. And he was glad to give it. They sat on the back porch and talked about their days. Sara had drawn a picture of a basketball player slam-dunking the ball. The name on the back of the jersey was "Glas."

Close enough, he thought. Maria sat as close to Trey as she could get. Daniela sat across from him, trying to act less interested than she really was. The warmth of the home reminded him of earlier days when he grew up in a much different setting but just as nurturing.

During dinner of New York strip steaks, salad, and baked potatoes, the Garza family and Trey told stories and laughed. Mary nearly let the cat out of the bag when she accidentally mentioned her ideas for food at the wedding reception. None of the young girls seemed to have noticed, and the adults breathed a sigh of relief.

After the meal, as he did the night before, Trey donned an apron and helped the girls clean up the kitchen. Then, for the next hour, he sat on the floor in the living room and played games with them until their mom announced it was bedtime. Once faces were washed, teeth were brushed, and PJs were on, the young ladies came and said good night to all.

"Will you be here when we get up?" Sara asked Trey.

"Yes, but I will have to leave before you go to school. So, I'll see you tomorrow morning. Sleep tight."

"You sleep tight too," Maria said, giving him a big hug.

"Do you think you could take Tony Parker in a one-on-one?" Daniela asked, stalling.

"Probably, if he was on crutches."

"Good night, girls," Mary said sternly, putting an end to the stall tactics.

Once the girls were gone, Mary, Luis, and Trey returned to the porch.

"Beer or wine?" Luis asked.

"I've had all the beer I need today," Trey said. "But I could take another small glass of that brandy, if that's an option."

"Me too," Mary said.

"Brandy it is," Luis said as he went back inside. When he returned, he poured three glasses and raised a toast to Trey and Cristina's future, Trey's family, and his good health.

After a while of watching darkness descend on Central Texas, Luis broke the silence.

"Trey's got a problem, Mama."

"He does?"

"I do?" Trey asked.

"Circumstances apparently will force Trey to propose sooner than he had planned. Right, Trey?" Luis asked. "And he doesn't have a ring yet. Do you think he could propose without a ring?"

"No," Mary said emphatically. "But I just thought of something. Wait here." She sat her drink down and ran back in the house.

"As if we'd wander off somewhere," Luis said dryly.

"I've had this for years, and for years I've planned to give it to the sweetheart of the first daughter to get married," Mary said as she sat back down. "That would be you, Trey." She pulled a small box from an old velvet bag that showed evidence of slight moth damage. "It belonged to my great-grandmother Angelina, who wore it for sixty-seven years while married to my great-grandfather. She died many years ago at age ninety-six." Mary carefully opened the box to reveal another ring box, which she handed to Trey. "See what you think."

Trey slowly opened the yellowed box to reveal a thin gold band topped by a small diamond.

"You know, I don't know anything about engagement rings. I suppose the value is in the sentiment. If so, this should be equal to a million-dollar ring. It's amazing, Mary. Are you suggesting that I can give this to Cristina?"

"Of course," Mary said. "I showed this to Cristy and Ana when they were teenagers, and they both loved it. I think she will be so surprised."

"I'm flattered," Trey said. "I bet I can find a matching wedding band when the time comes, or have one made. But I can only take this if I can pay you for it. What do you say it's worth?"

"More than you got," Luis said. "The payback will be the joy in our daughter's heart receiving this ring from the man she loves."

"Thank you both so much. Tell you what I'll do, I will make a donation to the local Habitat for Humanity in honor of the Luis and Mary Garza family. Would that be alright?"

"Oh, Trey," Mary said, hugging her future son-in-law. "That's so sweet. Of course that will be alright."

"When do you think you might give it to her?" Luis asked.

"Maybe tomorrow night," Trey said. "Not sure I can hold off the suspense much longer. Once the press knows why I was down in Texas, they'll back off. Practice starts soon, and I don't need any distractions once things kick off. Which reminds me, we'd like for you all to come up for a game sometime before Christmas. We've got room for everyone, between my place and Cristina's. Think about it and let us know."

"Maybe we could catch a Rockers-Spurs game," Luis said. "Mind if we cheer on the Spurs?"

"No problem. I'll just make sure I get you tickets in the rafters," Trey teased.

"What are your plans for tomorrow morning? Will you have time for breakfast before you leave?" Mary asked.

"American has a flight to Little Rock at 11:40, so I'll need to leave here by seven or so. I think I'll say goodbye to the girls and then head out. Don't worry about breakfast for me. What time you leaving tomorrow, Luis?"

"Probably around seven. I'll see you in the morning," Luis said. "It's been good having you here, Trey. Glad we got to spend some time with the man who means so much to our daughter. We couldn't be happier for you two. Good luck in fielding the questions when you get back. I don't envy you that."

Trey bade his hosts good night and headed for bed. He decided not to call Cristina since he would see her soon.

The next morning, after saying goodbye to the Garza family, Trey set out to reverse his travels of two days before. He drove to Dallas and had time for an egg-and-cheese bagel and coffee before boarding his plane for Little Rock.

The *USA Today* he picked up carried a small mention of Trey's trade to the Mavericks. The story made him laugh out loud.

Someone's going to lose their job over that one, he thought, chuckling.

Once in Little Rock, he found his rental car and drove to Memphis International Airport, two hours east, where he traded in the Ford for his aging and recently battered Camry. He arrived back at his house a little after 4:00 and warmly greeted his mom. They sat in the kitchen while Trey told her all about his trip.

"Mom, I'm going to propose to Cristina tonight," he said. Becky burst into tears and hugged her son. "And this is what I'm going to give her." Trey pulled the ring box out of his jacket and opened it. "It belonged to her great-grandmother Angelina Perez. Think she'll like it?"

"She will love it. It's beautiful! What's the plan, Trey? Where are you going to propose?"

"The Rockers have a private dining room at Top of the Clark out east. I've made arrangements for a special meal. I'm trying to figure out a clever way to give her the ring, like having the waiter hide it in her salad," he said, teasing.

"Oh, don't you dare," she scolded. "There's no substitute for just getting down on one knee and asking her. I think she'd like that better than anything. Do you think she suspects anything?"

"She probably suspects a lot after the events of the past few days, but I'm hoping this will be a surprise. Guess I'd better get cleaned up. Great to see you, Mom. We'll come by here after dinner so she can share her news with you."

When Cristina opened the door to her condo, Trey stepped inside and, without a word, pulled her close and kissed her hotly. She pushed the door shut with her foot as she returned his embrace.

"I missed you," he finally said. "I don't like being away from you. How would you like to be the new Rockers ball girl so you can go on out-of-town trips with the team?"

"I'll take it," she whispered. "But right now, I'm hungry," she said, laughing and deflecting the natural sexual tensions the two increasingly felt when alone together. "Where we going?"

"It's a surprise," he announced.

From downtown, Trey drove Cristina's SUV out Poplar Avenue toward East Memphis and the thirty-four-story Clark Tower. On the thirty-third floor, the Rockers owned and managed the Tower Room, an exclusive club for the organization's management, players, VIPs, and guests. He had called ahead and requested Cristina's favorite: shrimp with crabmeat stuffing, rice pilaf, and asparagus tips. He also asked for one of the few private booths where he could make his case for marriage away from the prying eyes of fellow diners.

On their way to their table, Trey acknowledged those he knew scattered at tables around the elegant club—three fellow players and their wives or girlfriends, the team's executive vice president, and two assistant coaches. The few who knew asked how he was feeling after their close encounter with the gang members, but no one asked him about the trade rumor.

Once at their table, Trey ordered a bottle of Chardonnay.

"This will be my last alcoholic beverage, maybe until the end of the season," he said. "To the future," he toasted and touched Cristina's wine glass.

The table candle cast a flickering glow on Cristina's face, and as she reached for his hand, she asked, "Well, you going to tell me where you've been, Mr. Mystery Man?"

"You will know by the end of the evening," he assured her. The combination of wine, close quarters, and the imminent proposal caused Trey to feel warm. He loosened his tie and took a sip of ice water.

While they waited for their food, the two discussed a variety of topics: the incident at the abandoned warehouse, Cristina's work, the new basketball season. Not a mention was made about Trey's mystery trip. Dinner arrived, and Trey refilled their wine glasses.

"Thank you, Father, for this food and this evening. Amen."

"This shrimp, it is so good," Cristina said, savoring each bite.

"I wonder if Tyler could fix something like this? I could eat it every day," Trey said. "Speaking of cooking, did your mom cook a lot when you were growing up? Did she teach you to cook?"

"Yes and yes," Cristina answered. "She cooked all the time. You can imagine, with ten mouths to feed. And it wasn't just easy stuff. Mom cooked real Mexican food from scratch. We kids didn't have the patience to learn what she tried to teach us, so we settled for recipes that didn't take a lot of time. All the recipes I know are fairly easy and can be made in a hurry. So, I'm a whiz at breakfast, most anything on the grill, and Tex-Mex. If you ever eat my mom's food, you'll know the difference right away. She's awesome!"

Trey wiped his mouth with his napkin to hide his smile.

"Want dessert?" he asked. "Tell you what, let's share a piece of Italian wedding cake with our coffee."

When the waiter came again, Trey ordered one piece of cake, two forks, and two cups of decaf coffee. He felt in his pocket just to make sure the ring box was there. He was surprised at how nervous he felt. He took another sip of water, then a longer sip of wine.

"You feel okay?" she asked when she saw him loosen his tie some more.

"Sure. Why?"

"You just seem a little nervous," she said. "And you're a little pale."

"I'm okay. What do your two brothers do in Houston?" he asked, moving the focus off himself.

"They own a small wholesale import business. It's actually nearer Galveston. We are praying they make it. They've had a tough few years."

"What's been the problem?"

"Economy. Strength of the dollar overseas. Stuff I don't understand. They are such good men; they deserve a break. They worked with Dad for a while but felt they needed to make it on their own. Why?"

"Just curious. I saw their photos recently and remembered that I don't know much about them." The moment he said it, he wished he hadn't. "Alex and Ricardo, right?"

"Where did you see their photos?" Cristina asked with a wondering look.

"Uh, I suppose it was at your condo," he said. "There's a photo of them there, right?"

"Yeah. I mean, where else would it be?"

The waiter came back with their coffee and cake at just the right time.

"Oh look, our coffee," Trey said with relief.

Once dessert was gone, Trey thought, *This is it. It's now or never.*

As he reached into his coat pocket for the small ring box, a wave of nausea swept over him, and he quickly excused himself. He got to the restroom just in the nick of time to lose his dinner.

CHAPTER 27

Trey splashed water on his face and returned to the private booth, feeling much better than when he abruptly left.

Let's get this done, he thought.

He stood beside the booth where Cristina sat while fishing for the ring box in his pocket.

"You are acting very strange, Trey. Are you sure you're okay?" Her concern melted as he knelt beside her and began his speech.

"Cristina, I love you with all my heart. In fact, I never thought I could love anyone as much as I love you. You have brought me joy in ways you will never know. As surely as I sit here…uh, kneel here…I believe God brought us together that night at the Med. With the full consent and blessings of five of nine members of your family, I ask you—no, I beg you—to be my wife. I pledge my undying love and devotion to you in the presence of God. Will you marry me?"

He opened the ring box and held it out for her to see just as the waiter came through the curtain.

"Oops," the waiter said, embarrassed. "I'll be back."

Cristina clasped her hands to her mouth and sat speechless. Tears poured down her face. After a moment of stunned silence, she began to nod her head. Trey pulled the ring out of the box and reached for her hand—the wrong hand. She took her right hand back and extended the left for him to place the ring on her finger. It fit perfectly.

"Oh, Trey, yes, yes, a million times yes! Oh, I can't believe this. What an unusual ring," she said, turning it on her finger.

"Do you recognize it?" he asked.

"Yes, but I recognized the box first," she said, laughing through her tears. "This is my great-grandmother's ring. How in the world did you get it? Wait. Did you go to see my parents?"

"That was my mystery trip," he admitted, scooting beside her. "It nearly cost me the element of surprise when the guy saw me in the airport. Your folks said to tell you hello, by the way. Well, here—let's let them tell you." He fished his cell phone out of his pocket and punched Luis's name from his contacts list.

"Hello?" Luis said after two rings.

"Daddy!"

"And Mama," Luis said, turning on his speaker phone.

"*Hola, niña*," her mother said.

"Mom, speak English. Trey is here. And guess what? He just proposed! But I suppose you already know that."

"How did you answer?" her father asked.

"She said she'd think about it," Trey joked.

"So, Mom and Dad, Trey just admitted that he came down to see you," Cristina said. "You all are a bunch of sneaky-sneaks."

"Cristy honey, we had the best visit," Mary said. "Trey is a very special young man. Your little sisters just love him. And we do too. We wish you two all the happiness."

"Mom," Cristina said, "you gave him *Tartarabuela* Angelina's ring. It's more beautiful than I remember. And it fits perfectly."

"I'm so glad," Mary said. "Have you set a date yet?"

"Mom! It just happened! We haven't even told Trey's mom."

"Which reminds me," Trey said, "we'd better go do that before it gets any later."

"Okay, kids," Luis said, "we are very happy for you. Tell us what you need from us. Can't wait to see you both."

"We love you. Bye!" Mary shouted.

Trey left a hefty tip on the table for their young waiter; the dinner tab would be charged to his account. The young couple walked back through the main dining room, greeting some of the patrons as they went. Cristina made it a point to grasp her purse at chest level so as to display her newly acquired jewelry.

When they arrived home, Becky was waiting at the kitchen table in her bathrobe. When she saw Cristina walk in, she jumped up, squealed, and grabbed her soon-to-be daughter-in-law. They stood hugging and jumping and squealing. Trey sat down and watched the show. He thought about turning on the TV but decided what was happening in his kitchen was more entertaining. As the initial celebration wound down, the two ladies sat, and Cristina began describing the events of the past few hours to Becky.

Trey watched and sometimes listened. But mostly, he sat in awe of God.

The past eighteen months were the most significant of his young life. He finished college and got a job—not just any job. He lost his dad because of a tragic lack of judgment by one man who chose to drive a car after having too much alcohol. He faced physical and emotional assaults from people who were victims themselves—victims of a culture of greed and fear and lack of concern for fellow man. He found a community of people who loved and gave and delighted in the awareness of a loving Father, giving Son, and comforting Spirit.

Trey thought about the occasions when he had to choose between the way most people handle trials and the way he saw his dad, Travis Glass, handle trials. Trey followed his father's examples of forgiveness and kindness, discovering that route really worked and led to peace. He tasted the bitter rebuke of well-meaning but deluded Christians who misjudged his mercy as leniency and his compassion as weakness. Trey thought about the beggars he met and the integrity he noticed in each one once he got beyond the shabby clothing, acrid body odor, and slurred speech.

These are real, made-in-the-image-of-God people, he thought.

He remembered the fuss put up about where he chose to live and the arguments fellow believers made against his choice.

"Christians have the freedom to live anywhere they wish, associate with anyone they wish, spend their money as they wish," some said.

"The rich need God too, so live in the wealthy neighborhood where you belong," said others.

Trey knew that was not correct, that following Jesus meant there are no such liberties, that following Jesus means sacrificing personal liberties for Kingdom mandates to literally feed the hungry, hydrate the thirsty, entertain the stranger, clothe the naked, look after the sick and feeble, and visit prisoners. And if such people don't live in close proximity, then God's mandate prompts us to move to where those folks are.

Trey thought about how God uses circumstances to bring about good things—things like meeting Cristina, the Smits, Douglas, Tyler, the twelve street gamblers, and the five young gardeners.

Watching the two most important women in his life reminded him of how very blessed he was. He had all the essentials: family, friends, mission.

Fame and fortune just happened to be two unfortunate byproducts.